Lee Duigon

VALLECITO, CALIFORNIA

Published by Storehouse Press

P.O. Box 158, Vallecito, CA 95251

Storehouse Press is the registered trademark of Chalcedon, Inc.

Copyright © 2015 by Lee Duigon

This book is a work of fiction. Names, characters, businesses, organizations, places, events, and incidents either are the product of the author's imagination or used fictitiously. Any resemblance to actual persons, living or dead, events, or locales is entirely coincidental.

All rights reserved, including the right of reproduction in whole or in part in any form.

Book design by Kirk DouPonce (www.DogEaredDesign.com)

Printed in the United States of America

First Edition

Library of Congress Catalog Card Number: 2015952271

ISBN-13: 978-1-891375-69-9

Winterlands
River Winter
Heathen Lands
Northern Wilds
Pass
Bell Mountain
North Obann
Chariot River
Nevereen
Ruins
Hills
Abnaks
Wallekki
King
Oziah's
Woods
Trywath
Cardigal
North
Mires
City of Obann
Ninneburky
Imperial River
Hills
Caristun
Pass
Durmurot
Maze
Wusk
Ruins of
Old Obann
Lintum Forest
South
Mires
Silvertown
Caryllick
South Obann
Ruins
Ruins
Obann, West of the Mountains

CHAPTER 1

How Helki Changed His Mind

There were no more wagons to be loaded. The drivers waited only for their lord's command to begin the slow trek down from the Golden Pass. It would have to be slow because the wagons, dozens of them—no one had bothered to count how many—were loaded with gold: hundreds of sheets of beaten gold. If any more if it were piled on, axles would break and wheels would sink into the ground.

This was the gold that had covered the Thunder King's great hall, top to bottom, until an avalanche had smashed the hall to pieces and buried it. When the snow had melted, it had left the gold there for the taking.

And Lord Chutt took it.

Now the work was finished, but Lord Chutt, mounted on his horse, hesitated.

"What's the delay, my lord?" asked Captain Born, commanding Chutt's Obannese spearmen.

"It's all ready to be moved," said Ilfil, chief of two thousand renegade Wallekki who rode with Chutt. They'd sworn themselves to Chutt's service because they had nowhere else to go and Chutt had promised them great things.

Chutt didn't answer right away. He contemplated the vast heap of shattered timbers that used to be the hall. Some of his men had been injured, and one crushed to death, pulling out the gold.

Chutt sat on his horse comfortably, having finally learned to ride. His old colleagues on the High Council of the Oligarchy wouldn't have recognized him. Months in the saddle had transformed him from a pot-bellied, pasty-faced man into a hard, tanned, compact one. But they were all dead, perished in the Thunder King's assault on the great city of Obann. Only Chutt, who'd fled into the north before the siege was laid, remained.

"I can't help thinking that there's more gold lying under all that wreckage," he said at last. "Maybe we ought to round up some more wagons and come back for the rest of it."

"Are you mad?" Ilfil said. "We already have enough gold to buy all of Obann for you several times over."

"We'd need a thousand more men and a thousand good, strong oxen to move those timbers," Born said. "The work would take us into the winter. It would not be wise to take the time."

A fourth man, standing beside the captain, spoke.

"All the same," he said, "if you don't take whatever gold is left, my lord, someone else will."

Ilfil, mounted on a fidgeting black gelding, glared down at the speaker. "You weren't here to see how hard we had to work to fill these wagons. My men won't do any more! We are warriors, not laborers."

Chutt couldn't take his eyes off the ruin, and didn't answer.

"Maybe you'd like to stay here and guard it for us," Born

said. But the other man just shrugged, giving up easily.

"Lord Chutt, it's time for us to go!" said Ilfil. "Heavy-laden as these wagons are, it won't be easy to bring them down the mountain."

"We've been up here long enough, my lord," Born added. "The men are tired. They shouldn't be pushed any harder."

Chutt blinked like a man waking from a dream.

"You're right, of course, my friends," he said. "All Obann is ours, if we do wisely. Give the order to move out."

"About time!" Ilfil snarled under his breath. He raised his voice and cried out the order in Wallekki, "Yalaah, yalaah!" Born echoed it in Obannese.

The drivers flicked their whips. The wagons creaked and groaned. Horses, mules, and oxen tugged mightily to get them started.

Slowly, very slowly, on the road hewn out of the forest by the Thunder King's slaves, they started down the mountain.

You wouldn't think a man as big as Helki the Rod could find concealment easily. But Helki could. His garment, a crazy quilt of multicolored patches, no two alike, blended into the underbrush so that even the scolding blue jays and the busybody scarlet cappies didn't notice him.

He'd ventured as close as he dared, close enough to see and hear Chutt and his lieutenants arguing, hiding in a stand of birches ringed around with wild raspberries.

For a long time after the last wagon rolled out of sight, he stayed in hiding, motionless. He'd recognized one of the men with Chutt and wondered what his presence meant.

"That's Gallgoid, or I'm a muskrat," he thought. Gallgoid was the chief spy, supposedly a servant of King Ryons. A year ago and more, Gallgoid came up the pass with Lord Reesh and came down again alone, just before the avalanche, and Helki saved his life.

Gallgoid had joined Lord Chutt two days ago. He must have offered Chutt his services, Helki thought. "I reckon he's turned against the king." That would be news to deliver to the chiefs in Lintum Forest. Helki intended to deliver it. But first he had a little more work to do up here.

The king had marched into the East with half his army to confront the Thunder King. With him had gone Helki's friends—the army's chiefs, his brothers in battle; old Obst, their teacher; Ryons' little hawk, Angel, and his hound, Cavall; and Gurun the queen. "I reckon the only way I'll ever see them again is if I go down there after them and find them—if they're still alive," he thought.

He missed them. He'd never missed anyone before. He felt a sense of loss that was a new thing for him, who'd lived all his life alone in Lintum Forest.

But here he was, separated from them by no one knew how many days' hard marches, and here he had to stay. Ryons' kingdom needed defending here at home, and that was Helki's duty now. He loved the boy king, and nothing would have pleased him more than to see him again and take him into the woods for a fine, long spell of hunting, just the two of them; but it couldn't be. All he could do was to offer up a silent prayer, as Obst had taught him, for the safety of King Ryons and his little army.

Midway through the afternoon, when Chutt's caravan was two hours down the road to the lowlands, Helki the

Rod came out of hiding.

Helki wasn't the only one waiting for Lord Chutt and his men to depart.

On the opposite side of the ruins, three men crept closer and closer to the site. They never came close enough to overhear Chutt's discussion with his officers because their leader feared they might be spotted. Even now he feared that some of Chutt's riders might come back. And now they saw Helki striding toward the ruins with his staff in his hand.

"Who in the world is that?" wondered the man called Hrapp, who owned a cobbler's shop in Ninneburky and would have given anything to be back in it, mending shoes.

"He's after the gold, curse him!" muttered the man who crouched behind a fallen log next to him: Gwawl, another Ninneburky townsman, a drifter who had no steady livelihood. "Hadn't we ought to run down there and stop him?"

Their leader bared his teeth at them, and they shrank back. This man had a fearsome face, marred by an ugly scar on one cheek.

"Quiet!" he hissed. "I'd need ten men better than you'll ever be to deal with him."

Ysbott the Snake, whom Helki had chased out of Lintum Forest, had been waiting to pick up whatever Lord Chutt had left behind. He and his followers had gotten to the site first, but had only been able to remove and cache seven sheets of gold before the arrival of first the baron and his men from Ninneburky, and then Chutt's army. They'd been in hiding ever since, living on short rations and resentment. Ysbott had some lethal mushrooms in his scrip, to be fed to his two underlings as soon as he needed them no more.

He ground his teeth. What was Helki doing, and how long had he been here?

"Who is that, Tobb?" whispered Hrapp. He and Gwawl didn't know their leader's real name.

"An interloper," Ysbott said, "and a thief." It was among his dearest wishes to wear Helki's scalp on his belt someday, but he knew well that no one could sneak up on Helki and kill him, even in his sleep. Too many Lintum Forest outlaws had died trying. "If he finds out we're here, none of us will leave this place alive."

"Is he a murderer?" Gwawl asked.

"Many times over," said Ysbott. "Now be quiet, and let's see what he's up to."

If he'd even suspected Ysbott's presence, Helki would have hunted him down and slain him on the spot. A breeze might have carried Ysbott's scent to him, but Ysbott was on the north side of the pass and the prevailing wind was east to west.

Even so, Helki proceeded cautiously. His eyes told him the site was now deserted, but his other senses weren't so sure.

Here was where the Thunder King had reveled in his golden hall. Some would have said that some evil still clung to the place, even after its destruction by the avalanche. It was Gallgoid who'd discovered that there was no ever-living, deathless Thunder King, but only a succession of mortal men behind the golden mask—the ruse by which King Thunder's mardars duped the nations of the East.

Somewhere in the depths of that heaped ruin lay the golden mask. Chutt hadn't found it. It was Helki's plan to find it, so that all those peoples could be shown that the tyrant they feared was only mortal.

Helki had spent many days here, watching Lord Chutt to see what he would do. Several times he'd stolen into Chutt's camp by night and listened to his talk.

Now the departure of Lord Chutt and his men had left a void that the hours hadn't filled. Maybe it was a void that couldn't be filled. Maybe the noise of the men and the wagons had only masked it.

Helki paused, motionless. He was not a superstitious man, to believe in ghosts or gnomes or witches, but even his skin was telling him there was something wrong about this place. Nothing he could see or hear or even smell—but something raised prickles on the back of his neck. Helki stayed alive by listening to such warnings.

"Hah!"

He spun around so quickly, a human eye could not have followed him. His rod swished through the air, swifter than a stroke of lightning. Whoever or whatever might have been behind him would have been destroyed. His cry, intended to startle and freeze an enemy, silenced all the birds and echoed in the pass.

But there was no one there.

"Now why did I do that?" he wondered. Anyone else would have put it down to nerves, but Helki had learned to trust his nerves.

There was a danger here that he didn't understand and couldn't name. Maybe it was something Obst could have explained to him, if Obst were there.

The caution that he'd learned from animals and birds whispered urgently to him to leave this place and find some other way to serve his king. Maybe it was time for him to return to Lintum Forest, where God had placed King Ryons' throne. Maybe the golden mask of the Thunder King was something not meant for his hands to touch.

Obeying his instincts, Helki strode back into the woods.

"He's leaving!" Hrapp whispered. "Why do you suppose he's leaving?"

"Quiet!" Ysbott answered. "It may be a trap."

If he had to, Ysbott would wait another year, maybe more. He had instincts, too, and his told him there was yet something hidden in that piled ruin that Baron Bault and the other army hadn't found. It was all he could do not to run out and dive into that mass of timbers and wriggle to the bottom like a worm, in search of one last treasure. Fear of Helki, who might be lurking out of sight, was all that held him back.

He couldn't imagine what had made Helki turn around and leave the site. He knew that Helki the Rod wouldn't hesitate to attack a dozen men by himself and slay every one who couldn't get away. He feared no man. And yet he hadn't set foot upon the ruin.

"What are we doing this for, anyhow?" Gwawl said. "There's no more gold. That army got it all."

Ysbott glared him into silence. Tonight, he thought, the mushrooms: he'd been lumbered with these two long enough.

Whatever remained inside the ruin, he had no thought of sharing it.

CHAPTER 2

How Others Missed King Ryons

Roshay Bault, Baron of the Eastern Marches by appointment of the king, had sent out scouts to watch the road that led down from the Golden Pass. With his daughter, Ellayne, and his adopted son, Jack, safe at home in Ninneburky, the baron had placed Martis, the children's sworn protector, in command of the scouts.

Originally the plan had been to send Martis up the pass with Gallgoid, to win Chutt's confidence and try to recover the golden mask. Martis used to be Lord Reesh's chief assassin, and Gallgoid the late First Prester's right-hand man. Between them they ought to be able to outwit Chutt and lure him into difficulties. But in the end they decided Gallgoid ought to go alone. Chutt might remember him as Reesh's trusted servant and be convinced to see in him someone who, like Chutt himself, wished to restore the old order in Obann.

"I know what he'll try to do," said the baron, who had known Lord Chutt by reputation and had met him face-to-face at the Golden Pass. "He'll buy loyalties that ought to go to the king. He'll buy the armies of Obann and their commanders. All he has to do is promise to rebuild the Temple and he'll have the College of Presters eating out of his hand and the lesser clergy, too. And the people are fickle. He might win them over.

"And who will stand against him? God only knows where King Ryons is—somewhere way out East, if he hasn't yet been killed or captured by the enemy. And the First Prester, Lord Orth—we'll miss him, too! The Abnaks have him on the wrong side of the mountains, and I doubt they'll let him go."

Here his wife spoke up, the baroness, Vannett.

"Our king has you, Roshay, and me," she said. "He has his chiefs in Lintum Forest and Prester Jod in the city. He has you, Martis, and that clever fellow, Gallgoid. He has the love of all decent, grateful men and women who remember how he saved the city, and their lives, by a miracle. And most of all, he has God's blessing on him."

Not long ago—before her daughter and Jack rang the bell on Bell Mountain, King Ozias' bell, before her husband and the men of Ninneburky fought off a Heathen host and were saved by an out-of-season storm of snow and ice and freezing rain—such a speech would have been unthinkable, coming from Vannett. Outwardly she was the same delicate, birdy-looking, exquisitely mannered woman who used to fret and fuss over very little things indeed. But that woman was long gone.

The baron grinned at his wife, his mustache bristling.

"Yes, that ought to be enough!" he said. "Provided that we all keep our heads and make use of what wits God has given us."

Jack and Ellayne overheard that conversation in the baron's parlor. They'd been with him at the Golden Pass and had come down with Martis when it seemed the baron would fight to keep the gold. They were glad he chose not to, in the end: Lord Chutt's army would have swallowed him up.

But it troubled them that as great events loomed, it seemed they would have no part to play in them.

Ellayne took Jack's elbow and led him out to their private place between the hedge and the back of the baron's stables. They'd both grown several inches since the day they'd set out for Bell Mountain, and it wasn't easy anymore to disguise Ellayne as a boy.

"Are we supposed to just sit still and watch, while that Chutt person buys King Ryons' kingdom out from under him?" she said.

"I don't see what we can do," Jack said. "The baron will do everything that can be done."

"If only he hadn't had to give up all that gold! That man just came up there with an army and took it. He's no better than a robber. Martis should have stabbed him in his bed."

"Don't let Martis hear you say that!" Jack was shocked. Sometimes Ellayne said things he never expected to hear. "You know he doesn't do that anymore."

"Well, all right, of course not—but the man's a traitor. Someone ought to stop him. Mother thinks he's going to start a civil war before he's done. Doing the Thunder King's work for him!"

Jack had thought of that. Not long ago, King Thunder invaded Obann, pouring armies out of the East. They besieged the great city, broke the gates, and burned down the Temple. But the great beast, whose like no man had ever seen, rose up from the river and, with King Ryons clinging to its back, demoralized, scattered, and destroyed the Heathen horde. Now the Thunder King's dominions in the East were torn by revolts among the captive nations. But everyone in Obann believed the Thunder King would come again. It would be too bad if he found the Obannese fighting among themselves.

"Unless King Ryons stops him, somehow," Jack muttered, unaware that he had spoken.

"And that's it, isn't it?" Ellayne said. "No one knows what's happened to him. If only we could get some news of him! But it'd be awful if he came back at last and found he didn't have a kingdom anymore."

"I wonder how far away he is," Jack said. "I wonder what he's doing. And Obst and Gurun, too. I wonder if they'll ever come back."

"I wish we'd gone with them," Ellayne said. But as far as her father was concerned, her adventuring days were over, and he let her know it. "I wish I could've gone with Ryons, too," he had admitted to her when he'd come home from the pass. "But I'll have more than enough to do right here. It won't be easy to keep his kingdom for him—if it can be done at all."

"I can't imagine them ever coming home again," said Jack, shaking his head.

Many miles to the south, on the other side of the mountains, Abnak warriors and their families gathered to celebrate their victory over the Thunder King. The last of his forces had been driven out of their country. In obedience to Obann's First Prester, who had told them it would please God, they'd spared all the enemy warriors who'd surrendered and sent them home—hopefully to revolt against the tyrant in their own lands. The Wallekki and the Fazzan, and even the Zeph, seemed primed for it, but King Thunder's Zamzu fought to the last man.

The First Prester, Lord Orth, was to lead the Abnaks in a great festival of thanksgiving, the first ever held in their country. "It was God who strengthened your arms and gave you victory," he told the Abnak chiefs. And they believed him.

"We'll never go back to our puny little gods," said Foxblood, the war chief. By the consent of all the other chiefs, he'd directed the campaign. "We never accomplished anything until you came and preached and prayed and the True God fought for us. Thanks to Him, we are free."

At the site of their last battle with the Zamzu, the Abnaks heaped an earthen mound. Here Orth would preach to them. Here they would feast and celebrate and honor God, and here Orth planned to build the first chamber house ever seen in Abnak country. Here he hoped to render the Scriptures into the Abnaks' language. Here, God willing, the great work of teaching would begin.

But that was not the only thing on Orth's mind.

Morning and evening he prayed for the safety of King Ryons. Following Foxblood's example, many of the Abnaks joined in these prayers.

"Abnaks praying to Obann's God, for Obann's king—who would have ever thought it!" Foxblood said. "But there are many of us here whose wives and children had a refuge in King Ryons' country, while we stayed here and fought. That's not something we'll forget."

News from the north trickled down but slowly. The last word to reach them was that Ryons still lived, but had yet to cross the Great Lakes. Few Abnaks had ever seen those lakes, and they had only a vague notion of the lands and peoples of those regions. But they all knew that on the far shore of the greatest lake stood Kara Karram, the Thunder King's fortress, where he imprisoned the gods of all the nations that he'd conquered and where the mardars offered human sacrifices to their lord. That Ryons should ever arrive there was a thing the Abnaks found hard to imagine.

"Trust in God," said Orth, "who chose this boy to be king of Obann."

"There will be an army waiting for the king ten times the size of his own," said Foxblood. "And we're too far away to help!"

"God is never too far away to help," Orth said.

But privately he feared. He couldn't help it. With his own eyes he'd seen the multitude with which the Thunder King had surrounded the great city of Obann. The nations that the Great Man had conquered and enslaved could not be numbered. It was said his realm extended eastward all the way out to a great sea that no man living in the West had ever seen. It was said that the host he'd sent to Obann was only a single finger of his mighty hand. And if Ryons fell, King Thunder's hordes would come west again, innumerable as the grass; and this time the Abnaks would not be able to defeat him.

"Trust, trust, trust!" Orth repeated to himself, a hundred times a day. "Trust and believe."

And he prayed, every time, with a lump in his throat, most fervently.

CHAPTER 3

The Burned Island

Ryons' army—bigger now, with the addition of some thousand Griffs and Zeph who'd joined it—crossed the westernmost of the lakes, which the Griffs called the Door of the Sun, on ships and boats that had once ferried the Thunder King's troops in the opposite direction.

Two persons in the army were divinely happy: Gurun, because she was on the water again, which was the birthright of every Fogo Islander, and the old Abnak sub-chief, Uduqu, who rejoiced not to be walking anymore. For the Zephites and the Dahai and the Griffs who manned the vessels, it was work they'd done before. For the black Hosa, none of whom had ever been aboard a boat in all his life, and never imagined such vast bodies of water existed anywhere, to sail out of sight of land was a trial of their courage. They sang to keep up their spirits. For the king's Wallekki riders and his bodyguard of Ghols, it was a poor substitute for traveling on horseback. And for the horses it was an ordeal.

For King Ryons himself it was a novelty, not unmixed with fear. He rather liked the motion of the boat beneath him. He sailed with Gurun, and her delight did much to abate his uneasiness.

"I wish I could take you sailing on the sea, my king!" she said. "To feel the cold spray on our faces and to see the great whales playing in the waves and spouting—then you'd really see something! There is nothing quite as exciting as riding out a blow in a good, sound ship." She didn't add that riding out a mighty storm that went on and on for days and nights, in a little skiff that could barely stay afloat—that was how she came to Obann in the first place—was a bit more excitement than anyone needed.

"What's a whale?" asked Ryons.

"A great fish, much bigger than any of these boats of ours. We hunt whales for their flesh, and for their bones, and their fat, which we use for fuel in the winter. Without our whales, we would find it hard to live."

They crossed the Door of the Sun in under a day and marched overland to the Lake of Islands, which the Griffs and Dahai said was a much bigger lake. "But we can go from island to island," they said, "and never have to spend a night on the water." Gurun wondered if they would have to devise some way to transport their boats, but the Zephite chiefs said they'd find all the boats they needed at the Lake of Islands.

Ryons' hound, Cavall, ran all around the army, barking and stretching his legs. There was another passenger from Gurun's boat even happier to be on land again, although he didn't show it—Baby, the gigantic bird as tall as a horse. His handler, Perkin the wanderer, who'd raised him from a chick that could fit in the palm of his hand, walked him for the exercise. They could all tell Baby was happy because he'd stopped snapping at people. The bird's snaps were only bluffs, not meant to kill: his beak could crush a human skull. He never snapped at Perkin, or at Ryons, and he seemed soothed by the Fogo Island lullabies Gurun sang to him. But aboard a small, crowded vessel on the water, his moods made him a difficult companion.

Standing tall and silent, Obst startled when Uduqu jogged his elbow.

"What're you thinking, old man?" said the chief. "You look like you're already studying the next lake and peering across it to the next—and all the way out to Kara Karram. Do you see something that the rest of us can't see?"

"I don't know." Obst shrugged. "Ozias was the last king of Obann to come this way, and he came alone.

"Do you know, Uduqu—I can almost see Kara Karram, perched on a cliff above the last lake like a bird of prey. Who would have dreamed we'd ever go there?"

"Not me—and I must be the most widely traveled Abnak who ever lived. And my legs know it, too," Uduqu said. At the moment he didn't share Obst's forebodings, whatever they were.

He turned aside and suddenly scooped up Ryons from behind and set him on his shoulders as a rider. The boy king yelped, then laughed.

"Someday soon you'll be too big for this, Your Majesty, and I'll be too old," Uduqu said.

"Don't drop our king," said Shaffur, chief of the Wallekki. "What's gotten into you?"

"Just feeling good, after my boat ride. Shaffur, have you ever come this way before?"

"Once, with a trading caravan, when I was young. This land among the lakes is Dahai country now. They've settled on some of the islands, too. We may have fighting, if they're in the mood."

Ryons' own Dahai, Chief Tughrul Lomak's men, had been left behind to help guard Lintum Forest. But the army had taken many Dahai prisoners at the Battle of Looth's Hill, and most of these now volunteered their service.

"Let us go on ahead, my lords," said their spokesman, "and see if we can persuade our people to be friendly. Some of our islands are very rich in crops, boats, and fighting men." The chiefs considered the offer and decided to accept it.

"But no tricks!" Shaffur said. "Remember that Looth and his Attakotts will be scouting the way for us—and they have poisoned arrows."

The Dahai spokesman made a face. "King Ryons spared our lives when he could have easily taken them," he said. "Do you think the Thunder King would do that? Never! Having surrendered to you, we are already dead men in his eyes. No, we will not betray King Ryons."

It was not a long march to the Lake of Islands, and along the way, a hundred Dahai warriors joined them. These warriors hated the Thunder King, and hated even more the Zamzu man-eaters, his favorites. Ryons' army had wiped out the Zamzu at the Door of the Sun, and news of that feat had traveled swiftly, converting many Dahai to his cause. When the army reached the lakeshore, friendly Dahai villagers already had a great flotilla of large and small boats waiting for them.

"King Thunder's empire is withering away," said Shaffur.

"Only this small portion of it," Obst said.

Summer was moving on. Before long it would be fall. Here, in this hilly country nestled among the lakes, the grass was still as green as emeralds, the weather mild and balmy.

"This is a lovely land," said Perkin, as he clung to the

stout leather strap around the base of Baby's neck. The Dahai villagers were curious about the giant bird, pressing in to get a closer look at him, and Perkin didn't want anything to happen that they'd all be sorry for. "I think it would be nice to settle down here when the war is over."

The Dahai feasted their guests on fish and roasted corn: plenty for all, because their country was a fertile one. Beyond the Lake of Islands, they said, lay the greatest lake of all, Lake Urmio, whose waters washed the base of the cliffs of Kara Karram.

"I wonder if we'll get there without a battle," Uduqu said. "Maybe the Thunder King is only waiting for us. It must look like we're determined to thrust our necks between his jaws."

That sobered the chiefs. They'd all seen the invading host that blanketed the plain around the city of Obann. They all knew there were many more armies where that came from.

Ryons confided his deepest fear to Gurun. "One of the Thunder King's chiefs told me the Thunder King wants to take me alive and put out my eyes and keep me in a dungeon till I die," he said. "And I'm making it easier for him to do it! I'd give anything to be back in Lintum Forest. King Ozias would be ashamed of me."

They were sitting with the other chiefs around a great bonfire on the shore. Night fell quietly upon them, like a coverlet of dark silk. A short distance away, the Hosa were practicing maneuvers, rhythmically clashing their short spears against their tall cowhide shields. It seemed to Ryons an evil thing to bring them all to such a place as this, so far from their homes, to fight and die on King Thunder's doorstep. He was ashamed of that.

"Be of good cheer, my king," Gurun said. "I have come from farther away than even those Hosa. But it is by God's will. He would never send us here for any but His own good purpose.

"Someday, of course, I would like to go back home to Fogo Island. What a tale I would have to tell! But not now, not yet. Not when God has chosen us to be His servants."

Early the next morning, they boarded the boats and set off for the nearest island—a place called Hadra, a big island of farms and fisher-folk.

"There was some trouble there, a while ago," a Dahai headman said, "and since then, no one has come here from Hadra. Nor do we go there."

"What kind of trouble?" Shaffur asked, but the Dahai only shrugged.

In the afternoon the island came into view, a series of dark humps on the water—"like a family of whales sleeping on the waves," said Gurun.

Ryons' hawk, Angel, had flown on ahead, circling over the island. Now she came down with a cry and landed on his forearm.

"She doesn't like what she's seen," he said. The hawk was fidgety; he couldn't calm her.

The chiefs had planned for trouble. The boats carrying the Attakotts would go in first. If need be, their arrows would clear the way for the five hundred Hosa to land, and then the Griffs and Zephites. They would fight to make it possible to land the Wallekki, the Ghols, and their horses.

"It seems strange," said Chagadai the Ghol, chief of

Ryons' bodyguard, "that these islanders have not come out in boats to meet us. The last time we were here, these waters were full of fishing boats. Where are they now?"

Ryons and Gurun watched as the Attakotts' boats went in and landed. The Hosa followed quickly. There was no sign of a fight. Indeed, the shore seemed to be deserted.

"Maybe they've all gone into hiding," Chagadai said.

Cavall raised his head and let out a long, deep howl.

At first Ryons didn't understand what he was seeing. Boat after boat landed on the shore. The men got out and then just stood there, or milled around a little. Certainly none of the Hadra Islanders had come out, neither to greet them nor to fight them.

Gurun touched the tiller, captured a little more wind in the triangular sail, and brought the king's boat closer in. Ryons stood up in the bow, and soon he could see what his people on the shore had already seen.

Except for where the lapping waves had washed it clean, the whole land, all that you could see of it, anywhere you looked, was all black, burned clear of any sign of life. No blade of grass, no charred tree trunk, no trace of human habitation—as far as eye could see, nothing remained alive on Hadra Island.

Obst, who'd been standing amidships, sat down with a gasp. A shudder shook him head to toe.

"What?" said Uduqu. When Obst didn't answer, Uduqu gripped his shoulder and shook him, but gently. "What's the matter, Obst? Are you ill?"

The old man shook his head.

"This is what we feared the most, Martis and I," he said. "Martis especially—he was afraid of this."

"But what was it that he feared?" said Gurun.

"The powers of the ancient world, from before the Day of Fire. The Thunder King has acquired them." Obst looked up at her. "We'll find nothing living on this island, Gurun—neither man nor beast."

CHAPTER 4

How Ysbott Found What He Sought

Ysbott had decided to remain in hiding the rest of the day and all night long, in case Helki were waiting in ambush. Ysbott had murdered more men than he could remember, but he knew Helki's rod would end his career before he drew two breaths, if he ever came in reach of it.

But even as he impressed this danger on his two followers, every passing minute sharpened his desire to climb into the ruins and see what he could find. It was as strong as his fear of Helki, and growing stronger by the moment. Sweat poured from his body.

"There's something there!" he thought—something that everyone else had overlooked. Something as good as gold, or better: more desirable, maybe, than all that gold that was now being carted down the mountain. He was sure of it. Something waited for him deep inside the ruin, calling to him, tempting him.

Hrapp and Gwawl spoke not a word. They'd never seen their leader in such a mood before, and they feared it.

Ysbott ignored them. Except for the occasional chirp or twitter from birds in the trees, all of the Golden Pass lay still and silent, like an empty room.

By mid-afternoon he could resist the urge no more. He rose on stiff legs.

"Tobb?" whispered Hrapp.

"Helki's gone. Let's get busy," Ysbott said.

He led them out to the hill of broken timbers that was once a tyrant's hall. Chutt's army had wrested many of them off the heap, at great cost in labor. Now that Ysbott had surrendered to the desire to crawl into the belly of the ruin, it had completely mastered him. Not even Helki could have stopped him now.

"You two keep watch," he said. "Don't touch anything."

"We won't!" Gwawl promised.

Leaving them behind, Ysbott climbed onto the timbers, looking for a way down. Once or twice the splintered beams stirred perilously underfoot. He didn't care. A great treasure would come into his hands, if he didn't lose his nerve.

A black hole beckoned to him. On hands and knees, Ysbott thrust his head and shoulders into it. His body blocked out what little light there was.

He crawled into the dark passage, creeping on his belly. His fellow outlaws had nicknamed him the Snake for his gift for striking his victims suddenly, giving them no chance to save themselves. Now he was earning the name another way, he thought, slithering into the darkness like a snake. Not a fanciful man, he nevertheless suddenly imagined himself turning into a snake, supple and smooth, effortlessly flowing along the twists and turns in the dark. The notion brought a twisted smile to his lips.

Unable to see, he crawled deeper and deeper into the pile, always seeking a way down. It already felt like he'd crawled for a mile. A sane man would have worried about finding his way back up, but at the moment Ysbott was not quite sane. He imagined, indeed, that some invisible power was showing him the way because it wanted him to come down, so it was guiding him. Sometimes a timber creaked or shifted overhead or under him. But he took no notice of it.

Ysbott the Snake crept and slithered on, groping with his hands. He would know the feel of gold when he encountered it.

And, by and by, he did.

His fingers slid over human bones, ribs and skull, and then met a surface cool and smooth. This was it. He clutched at a curved edge, met resistance, tugged. The whole ruin, disturbed, might have suddenly crushed him in the dark, but that thought never entered his head. The gold scraped noisily as he pulled it free, but now he had it.

There was no room for him to turn. He had to find his way out backward. Splinters tore his clothing, clawed his flesh. He didn't care. Something wanted to be brought back into the light. He was doing it. Writhing, pushing with his elbows, he battled his way back to the outside world.

And suddenly he was out, back out into the light, out through the very same passage that had let him in.

Gwawl and Hrapp had hardly said a word the whole time they were waiting. And it was a long time, too: they saw the sun march down toward the horizon in the west. All either of them wanted was to go home with their gold and live like kings, but without Ysbott, they knew they'd never find it where he'd cached it. Seven sheets of gold they'd plundered for themselves—enough to make them rich men many times over.

The sun was low and red by the time they saw a ragged, filthy figure emerge slowly from the heap of timbers. It could only be Ysbott: otherwise they never would have known him. His whole face was black with grime.

He struggled for a moment before he found his footing, like an old, sick man forced out of bed. In his hands he held a golden object that caught the red rays of the setting sun—gold dipped in blood, thought Hrapp. It gave him a shiver.

Ysbott showed his teeth and raised his prize over his head. He tiptoed cautiously among the fallen timbers.

The moment he set foot on solid ground again, the whole heap groaned and suddenly the middle of it collapsed on itself in a chaos of loud, sharp cracks.

Ysbott was mildly surprised the day was almost done—had he truly been down there for that long?—but he was far more interested in the heavy object in his hands. He held it at arm's length, blinked away some dirt and sweat, and took his first good look at it.

It was a face—the face of a man, with empty holes for eyes, a golden beard that was a mass of stylized curls, a long, commanding nose, high forehead, and gold lips pursed as if it were about to speak. It took him a moment to understand it was a mask: a golden mask.

"Ha-hah!" he cried, his voice breaking. His feet broke into a jig. "Mine, mine, mine!"

"What did you find, Tobb? What is it?" Hrapp and Gwawl ran up to join him. "You were gone ever so long!"

"Do you know what this is, you fools?" Ysbott shrieked at them. "The Thunder King—the face of the Thunder King—and now it's mine!" He brandished it at them, and it shone as if it were on fire. They both stepped back.

"Is it safe?" Gwawl muttered. But Ysbott didn't answer him.

"All that work," cried Ysbott, "and they missed this! Didn't even try for it! But I did—I did, and now I have it. Mine!" He panted, out of breath, and trembled all over. Hrapp thought he was going to fall, but he didn't.

"It's too late in the day to start traveling," Ysbott said. "We'll camp here for one more night and then be off tomorrow.

"But at least we'll all dine well tonight, my lads! This calls for a celebration. I've saved some particularly delectable mushrooms for this very night. I know I've been hard on you, but this will make it all up to you. Come on, let's see if we can make ourselves comfortable."

That night he fed his men the poison mushrooms, and neither Hrapp nor Gwawl returned to Ninneburky.

CHAPTER 5

What Happened on Hadra

By the time Ysbott came out from under the ruins, the chiefs of King Ryons' army had all come ashore on Hadra. The horses had not been landed because there was no forage for them there. As far as anyone could see, the island was burned bare. The Attakotts scouted around for a mile or two, but found nothing different.

When Cavall came ashore, he stuck close to Ryons. His ears went flat; the hair stood up stiffly along his neck and back. When Ryons touched him, he felt the dog's every muscle tense.

The chiefs gathered in a semicircle around their king and had the Dahai guides brought before them.

"What has happened here," Obst asked them, "and why have you brought us to this place?"

"I am Ghur Manyan," their spokesman said, "an elder of the He-goat Society." Dahai warriors grouped themselves into fraternities, each with its own distinctive tartan. "As for what happened here—well, the Thunder King has done this, and we brought you here to see it for yourselves—and so we could see what you would do after you saw it.

"Hadra revolted against the Thunder King. The mardars exacted too much from them, and children were going hungry. The people couldn't stand any more.

"And then one night, those of us who happened to be awake saw a terrible red flash over the waters of the lake. It was only for an instant, and no one knew what it could be. Some of our boats went out the next day and found this island as you see it now."

"Why didn't you tell us about it sooner?" Obst said.

"What was there to tell?" Ghur Manyan's wispy beard trembled. "Some of us have wives who were born on Hadra. Some had sons and daughters living here. The islanders were kin to us. Now they're gone, every last one. No one escaped to tell us what was done to them.

"Now you have seen it with your own eyes, O King of Obann. And we must ask you now: What will you do?"

Ryons could think of nothing to say. For a long time no one spoke. It was Shaffur who finally broke the silence.

"Do?" he said. "We've come a very long way to see this! Few of us ever expect to see our homes again. King Thunder plucked us up like grass and sent us into Obann to conquer it. But we serve the God of Obann now, who is our God, and we have come this far in obedience to Him. We will continue to obey. We will go to Kara Karram and see God's vengeance on the Thunder King."

Ryons was surprised. The army did hardly anything without Shaffur objecting to it.

Jiharr the Zephite spoke.

"I only live because the God of Obann gave me life when I should have died," he said. "The man who struck me down is here beside me now, as a brother. I will go wherever the king of Obann goes."

Uduqu, who had cut down Jiharr in single combat, nodded.

"When I first laid eyes on King Ryons," he said, "he was only a slave, without even a name to call his own. But God made him king, and God has rescued us, His people, from more and worse dangers than this. I don't think there's a man among us who will turn back now."

Those who heard him cheered and clashed their weapons. The Hosa raised their deep voices in the army's anthem, "His mercy endureth forever." The rest of the army, even the men still on the boats, joined in. The Dahai were amazed. And after the anthem, the chieftains, one by one, swore to carry out their mission in obedience to God.

But Obst said, "The decision must rest with King Ryons himself. Your Majesty, what is your pleasure?"

"Pleasure? It's not a pleasure!" Ryons blurted out. "I'd give anything to go back home to Lintum Forest. But then you'd all be ashamed of me, and it'd serve me right. And I think God would be ashamed of me, too. After all we've been through, we can't stop now.

"So we'll go, right on to the end. God has protected us so far. If we don't fail Him, He won't fail us."

The chieftains rumbled their assent. They were proud of him. Ryons knew it, but found no comfort in it. He still felt like a fool. He used to think the sight of that vast Heathen host swarming into Obann City, with the night lit horribly by the fire that consumed the Temple, was the worst thing he had ever seen. But what had been done to this island was worse.

Ghur Manyan bowed to him. His forehead almost swept the ground.

"King Ryons, and you chieftains, there are many islands in this lake, islands full of people. Let some of us go on ahead and prepare the way for you. For too long, far too long, the

Thunder King has chewed our flesh! I think the people of the lake will go on to Kara Karram with you and fight for you. Let us go on ahead to rally them."

"First we need to find a grassy isle where we can graze our horses," said Chagadai.

"There is a suitable place not far from here," the Dahai said. "If you leave now, you can be there before the night is old. Rest there for a day or two, while we bring tidings to the other islands."

Shaffur feared some treachery, but the other chieftains voted him down.

"An hour or two of nighttime sailing won't hurt us," Gurun said. "I will steer us by the stars. It will be good to leave this place behind."

Wytt lived under the baron's back porch, dining sumptuously on table scraps Vannett saved for him. The sight of him still made her uneasy, but she was happy to feed him. The scraps he shared with an old rat who was of a peaceful and companionable disposition. Vannett would not have liked to know she had a rat living under her kitchen.

Wytt had accompanied Jack and Ellayne on all of their adventures, protecting them. You might wonder how much protection could be provided by a little, hairy, tailless, man-like thing about the size of a squirrel, armed only with a sharpened stick. But it was Wytt who'd given Ysbott the Snake the ugly scar on his cheek, and he'd once killed a man who was going to sell the children into slavery.

It puzzled him that these Big People should take so long to grow into maturity. ("Some of them never get there!"

Roshay Bault would have said.) His kind, the Omah, come into the world pink and hairless, as tiny as newborn mice; and yet in just under two years they are fully grown and able to fend for themselves. But Wytt didn't waste time trying to work out puzzles. If it took forever for Jack and Ellayne to reach their full growth, he would be content to protect them forever.

So he never went so far from them that he couldn't come back quickly. But there was a little patch of woods just outside the main gate of Ninneburky, and since they'd all come down from the Golden Pass, Wytt had been spending most of his daylight hours there.

He did this because there were birds in that little wood that had migrated down from the Golden Pass months ahead of season, and he wanted to know why.

It was not that Wytt could have a conversation with a bird: not even an Omah could do that. But their calls and their behavior spoke to him in a way that no human being—except maybe Helki—could understand. If their communication could be rendered into human speech, it would sound something like this:

"There's something wrong with the place. It was always such a nice place to live, but it's no good anymore. It's gone bad, like it was when that great flock of human beings had that huge nest up there—the one that was wrecked and buried when all the snow and ice fell down on it.

"After the big nest was destroyed, the place was fine again, as good as ever. But then another flock of humans came and pulled it all apart, and it's all gone bad again. The bees left first, and we should have had the good sense to go when they went."

Wytt had been at the Golden Pass with the children and the baron, Ellayne's father. Even then, the more wholesome sorts of animals were giving it a wide berth. Skunks, wood mice, turtles, stoats, and deer—they all kept well clear of it. When Wytt himself crept some little distance into the belly of the ruin, he understood why so many wild creatures shunned it. Even snakes stayed away. Wytt clambered out of it as quickly as he could, and never went back in.

He understood from Ellayne that her father, too, was worried about the Golden Pass—not the place itself, but about the man who'd come there and forced him to leave. Wytt approved of Roshay Bault: the big man loved his daughter and had a streak in his character that would make him ferocious in a good cause. Omah fathers cuddled their babies and protected them.

Meanwhile, the birds were flying down from the Golden Pass, looking for new homes. It was because men had let something out of the ruins that should have been kept in.

It didn't occur to Wytt to discuss this with Ellayne and Jack—although, since their visit to the summit of Bell Mountain, they understood perfectly every thought he communicated to them in chirps and whistles, purrs and chatterings, just as if they shared a common human language. Omah can understand humans much better than humans can understand the Omah, but these children and Wytt could speak with one another. Still, Wytt seldom spoke of anything unless it was time to act on it.

That time, he thought, would be here soon.

CHAPTER 6

Tidings from Lord Orth

Far away in the city of Obann, in the seminary, scholars and students toiled away to produce faithful copies of the Scriptures—the Old Books, not the new—to be read in every chamber house between the mountains and the sea. Farther away yet, in Durmurot, Prester Jod's people copied the Lost Book, the Book of King Ozias, rescued from the cellar beneath the ruins of the First and Second Temples. For twice a thousand years those scrolls lay where King Ozias himself had hidden them. It was Ellayne and Jack and Martis who'd recovered them, but that was a well-kept secret. Not even the First Prester knew it.

Rather than rebuild the Temple that the Heathen had destroyed, it was Lord Orth's policy that all the Temple's resources should be spent in making God's word available to every man, woman, and child in Obann. "Preaching and teaching, from the Scriptures themselves—that is now the function of the chamber houses and all the clergy in Obann," he said. "Our new Temple will be a temple made without hands, which no men's hands will be able to destroy. Let the Temple consist, from now on, of God's word and God's people, its only floor the earth itself, its only roof the sky." To this the College of Presters had agreed.

But now Lord Orth himself was out of reach in Abnak

country, and the wreckage of the Temple in Obann remained in the heart of the city, too massive to be cleared away. People shook their heads when they walked past. The work of removing the rubble went on daily, but never seemed to make a dent in it. For centuries the building was the heart of Obann. Despite Lord Orth and the presters, most of the people couldn't accept the loss and yearned for the Temple to be rebuilt.

Preceptor Constan, at the seminary, had charge of all the work of copying and distributing the Scriptures. He would have struck you as a man entirely absorbed by his duty and oblivious to all else. The few who knew him well, knew better.

Prester Jod was still in Obann, serving as vicar for the First Prester until Lord Orth's return—for which Jod prayed every day. But today Constan had news that suggested Jod's prayer would not be granted. They met at Jod's townhouse to discuss it.

Constan had a letter from Lord Orth, carried all the way from Abnak-land by a pair of runners who would carry back the answer. How Orth had come by such a nice piece of parchment in that country was anyone's guess. For ink he'd made do with berry juice that had already begun to fade.

Constan read the letter to Jod, slowly, giving every word its proper weight.

"To my dear colleagues and fellow servants of the living God, in God's name, peace.

"I regret that I am unable to return from this faraway country. With God's help the people have driven out the armies of the Thunder King, and they are well aware that it was God who gave them victory.

"There is a great hunger, among this nation, to know the Lord and to become His people. I have seen this for myself, and heard it from their greatest chiefs, who every day entreat me to pray for them and to teach them. Their supreme war chief, Foxblood, has become my friend and brother and disciple, and fellow laborer in the Lord's vineyard.

"In light of this great need, I must stay and do everything I can. Furthermore, I must ask for as many copies of the Scriptures as you can send me, along with brave men who will join me in my labors.

"For the way is open for God's word to go forth and to be preached to all the nations of the East. And I very much fear lest the Thunder King's New Temple prove a snare to them. What the enemy may not hold by force of arms and terror, he may yet hold by false teaching: for how are these Heathen to know the difference, unless they hear the Lord's word for themselves?

"And so, as I must remain here to minister to this Abnak nation, and to others, I ask you to give me all the help you can, whatever seems good to you and whatever you can spare from your own labors in Obann.

"And again I offer to lay down my office, and bid you choose a new First Prester to serve in Obann City.

"Orth, First Prester by the grace of God, and Foxblood, the Lord's disciple, salute you."

Jod sighed. "This is a good and godly man," he said, "and a man wise enough to know that when God opens a door for you, you'd best go through it. How can we replace him as First Prester, when he's doing the Lord's work? Abnaks as God's people! It staggers the imagination."

"The two messengers are both disciples," said Constan.

"Orth has taught them well. They're staying at my house."

"My fear is that this will be too much for the people to take in," Jod said. "They'll say the First Prester has deserted them in favor of the Heathen."

"He's only being faithful to his calling."

"I know! And I agree. We must send him all the help he needs. This is a moment in history, a time to be remembered forever. We mustn't fail to rise to it." Jod shook his head. "But the people are slow to understand that we don't need a stone-and-mortar Temple anymore. They don't yet share Orth's vision."

"We must teach them to share it," Constan said.

"Many nations came together to form Obann in ancient days—the Tribes of the Law," said Jod. "Why should there not be more tribes added? But will the people understand?"

"One other thing I've thought of," Constan said. "If Lord Chutt takes possession of the gold at the Golden Pass, he'll have more than enough to rebuild the Temple and make himself overlord of all Obann. He will try to take King Ryons' kingdom."

"If only we could hear from Gallgoid!" Jod said.

"No word from him as yet," said Constan.

It was a long way down the mountain with such heavily laden wagons as Chutt had. They had to spend three nights encamped on the Thunder King's road. Ilfil fretted over the slow progress.

"At this rate it'll take us all year to get back to Obann City!" he said, the third night. It was Chutt's custom to dine with his officers in his tent—Ilfil, Captain Born, and, because he'd once been Lord Reesh's servant and had won Chutt's confidence, Gallgoid.

"We can't go any faster without damaging the carts," Born said. "Once we get back to settled country, we can get more carts, and the roads will be better. We'll travel faster then."

Chutt had already sent out messengers to many of the great men of Obann, to tell them that he had the gold and bid them to join him in restoring the old order of Obann—to bypass the king, if indeed the king still lived, and restore the Oligarchy. It would be some time before he got any answers.

"We must be patient, Chieftain," he said to Ilfil. "We have a great enterprise in hand, and for the life of me, I don't see how anyone can stop us. We'll have only ourselves to blame, if we fail. I'm sure that's what Lord Reesh would say if he were here to counsel us. Eh, Gallgoid?"

"Even so, my lord," Gallgoid agreed. Chutt had promised to make him a prester when the Temple was rebuilt—maybe even First Prester, "if I find you indispensable."

Born and Ilfil didn't like him and didn't like him coming aboard as one of their lord's advisers. Ilfil had dreams of living like a prince, the general of Obann's armies. Born had similar ambitions.

"When we're well away from these infernal mountains," Chutt said, "maybe even before we get all the way back to the city, we'll meet with the great men face-to-face and enlist them to our cause. This war has left many vacancies among the ruling oligarchy—vacancies that these men will want to fill. As long as we do everything under color of the law, the old law, I can't imagine anyone daring to resist us."

"There's that baron you forced to surrender the gold,"

said Ilfil. "He'll resist us."

"Leave Roshay Bault to me," Chutt said. "If he stands, he'll find himself standing alone against families much greater than his own. He won't be slow to see the folly in that."

"How will you deal with him, my lord?" Gallgoid asked.

"Peacefully and lawfully," said Chutt, "and irresistibly."

CHAPTER 7

How Helki Returned to Ninneburky

In Lintum Forest, the boy who was King Ryons' double, with the little girl who was his prophetess, built a fort of twigs for soldiers made from acorns. The prophetess giggled with delight as the boy named Fnaa finished an acorn-headed doll and told her, "This one's Helki. See? He's bigger than the others."

"Daddy Helki!" cried the girl, Jandra. "We give him this when he comes home—a nice present!" The toothed bird that followed her everywhere hissed, but otherwise ignored them.

"I'm sure he'll like it," said Fnaa. Except for the one red streak in Ryons' dark hair, you could hardly tell Fnaa from the king. Once upon a time, that close resemblance saved Ryons' kingdom for him. It might do so again, someday, Obst said: "You never can tell." It was one of the reasons Fnaa was left behind when the king marched forth from Lintum Forest.

Half his army had been left behind, too, to guard the throne. The chieftains didn't like being separated from their king, but they did their duty.

No one knew how old Jandra was, because she was an

orphan and couldn't remember what had happened to her family. Helki found her wandering, alone, on the plain below the mountains and brought her back to Lintum Forest. No one believed she could be any older than five, if that. But God spoke through her to proclaim Ryons king—the descendant of Ozias.

"Make one for Obst, too, Fnaa," she said. "And one for Ryons, and one for you—and a little teeny one for me."

The settlers around the ruined castle of Carbonek were working hard to raise the crops that they and the Hosa men had planted. It looked like it was going to be a good harvest. But the people missed their king and Obst, their teacher. A young clerk from the city, Dyllyd, read to them from Obst's big book of Scripture, but they would rather have had it from Obst. And they missed Helki even more, who'd founded the settlement and driven out the outlaws. Chief Buzzard's Abnaks fulfilled that duty in his absence, but they had more faith in Helki.

"It's too quiet," Fnaa thought. "That always means something's going to happen." But the Abnak scout, Trout, now married to Fnaa's mother, said the whole forest was at peace.

"The trouble won't start until all that gold comes down from the mountain," he said.

Jandra placed the acorn-men inside the fort, humming contentedly as she played. It had been a long time, Fnaa thought, since she'd spoken any prophecies. The Fazzan chieftain, Zekelesh, was anxious to hear more.

"She can't do it just because you want her to," said Abgayle, Jandra's foster mother. "In fact, she doesn't do it at all! The Lord does it when He pleases. I'd rather you never talked to her about it."

"I won't," the chieftain promised. He was uneasy about the girl's long silence, but from then on, he kept it to himself.

Chutt wasn't the only man in his army who coveted the gold. Gallgoid kept his ears open. There wasn't a man in all that host, Obannese or Wallekki, who didn't think he was entitled to a share. The gold sheets hadn't even been counted yet. He would take an inventory, Chutt said, after they reached the city and chose a safe place to store the gold. Then, he promised, every man would be paid a bonus.

They were impatient, Gallgoid thought. They wanted what they thought was rightfully theirs. How much of the treasure would be doled out in bribes to men who were already rich and powerful? And how much would be left for those who'd done the hard work of collecting and transporting it?

Half of Chutt's following were Obannese spearmen under Captain Born, the other half Ilfil's Wallekki. Between the two divisions of the army, Gallgoid noted, was less than perfect trust and hardly any comradeship. How easy it would be to play on this, he thought—not to mention their desire for their rightful share of gold. But it was not yet time to foment a mutiny, Gallgoid judged.

"My lord," he said to Chutt, when they'd at last reached the plains between the Chariot River and the Imperial, "there will be many men in Obann who will be tempted to try to wrest the gold from you."

"Oh, I know it!" Chutt said. "I won't be easy in my mind until it's all safely under guard in the city. In the meantime, though, I trust I have the strength to keep it against any attempts to take it by force. Who else in Obann can call up two thousand men to fight for it?"

"There are those who might combine their forces," Gallgoid said. And lowering his voice, he added, "And there are those who will never trust a lord whose strength is in Wallekki renegades."

"Soon I'll have more strength than that," Chutt said.

They rode along in a companionable silence, at the head of the army, wheels and cart-frames creaking, oxen lowing, mules and horses snorting, behind them. Ilfil and Born were busy with their duties. Scouts had been sent out to fetch more wagons.

"I know what you're thinking, you villain," thought Gallgoid. "Lord Reesh used to read you like a book. Ambition has made you wiser, my lord, but it hasn't changed your character. Reesh would have had you stuffed and mounted in his study by now. But I'll take more time about it."

He would have been surprised to learn that Helki had shadowed the army all the way down the mountain, and had been watching him particularly for any overt signs of treason to King Ryons.

When Lord Chutt emerged from the wooded foothills of the mountains, Helki turned aside for Lintum Forest. Two of Chutt's Wallekki riders caught him in the plain. They wouldn't be returning to their master. The incident persuaded Helki to make for King Oziah's Wood and come out near Ninneburky. There he would stop to confer with Roshay Bault, and then head home.

He would have liked to detour through the foothills of Bell Mountain and visit Hlah, who might have news of the king. Hlah's settlement of Obannese—slaves who'd escaped the Thunder King and fugitives from Silvertown—and Abnak warriors who'd rebelled against King Thunder and found refuge in the hills, was growing. Old Chief Spider's son had an Obannese wife, a child of his own, and many scouts and hunters to bring news to him.

"But it's time I was back to Carbonek," Helki said to himself. "There's going to be trouble, I reckon, and we'll want to get ready for it." He supposed Baron Bault could tell him much that the chiefs in Lintum Forest would need to know.

He made good time through King Oziah's Wood. Lumbermen and trappers lived there. War had swirled all around the wood but never got inside, like wild waters washing around a massive rock. Tradition had it that King Ozias found refuge here from all his enemies, on his way to exile in the East, and that God's blessing had remained on the wood ever since. Helki met a number of the woodsmen on the way and warned them to have nothing to do with Lord Chutt.

"He's got a horde of Wallekki at his back and wagons full of gold—more gold than you ever dreamed of," he told them. "It's all for mischief against the king."

"We've never seen King Ryons," said a grizzled trapper who'd lived there all his life. "But if he ever comes to King Oziah's Wood, he'll find a welcome. We're all king's men here." And Helki believed him.

It took him only two days to pass through the wood and come out by Ninneburky, just across the Imperial River.

Ellayne and Jack were overjoyed when he turned up at the baron's front door, although disappointed that he brought no word of Ryons.

"I left him when he went down into Heathen lands because I reckoned I ought to keep an eye on the Golden Pass," he said. "I was there when your father marched away and left the gold to the Wallekki."

"He had to do that," Ellayne said. "He didn't have the men to fight for it."

Vannett sent for the baron and ordered dinner to be made for Helki. When Roshay Bault came home, he ordered the children out of the parlor so he could speak with Helki.

"Oh, let us stay!" said Ellayne. "We've already got so many secrets that we have to keep, a few more won't make any difference."

"Let them stay, Roshay," Vannett said. "They've always been a part of this. Indeed, they started it!"

"You've picked up a knack for surprising me," the baron said. He looked sternly at Ellayne and Jack, seated side by side. "I hope you can continue to keep secrets, the pair of you."

"Who would we tell?" said Jack.

"Just don't tell anyone," Vannett said.

So Helki learned that the man with the gold was Chutt, last of the old ruling oligarchs, and that Gallgoid was with him by the baron's counsel, acting as the king's chief spy.

"But what about the golden mask of the Thunder King?" Roshay asked. "Gallgoid was going to get it for us, if he could. Does Chutt have it?"

Helki shrugged. "It's still there, for all I know, buried in the ruin. I was going to dig it up after Chutt left, but something told me I'd better let it be."

"But why?"

"I don't know," Helki said. "Just a feeling that I had. But I don't think Chutt found it. I would've seen the excitement in his camp, if he had."

"I think we'd better have it," Roshay said, after a long pause. "Maybe Martis can go up for it. We can use it as proof that King Thunder is only a man and not a god. It'll shake his hold on the East."

"I think so, too," said Helki, "but it's not for me to put my hand on anything like that. I've got to get back to Lintum Forest and get ready for a war."

CHAPTER 8

How Ysbott Planned a New Career

Finally alone at the Golden Pass, having hidden the bodies of Hrapp and Gwawl in the wreckage of the hall, Ysbott found that the golden mask fit him perfectly.

He'd half-expected to see things differently through the mask's eyeholes. Ysbott never believed in witchcraft, until the baron's daughter nearly blinded him with some infernal spell. If a mere girl could do that to him, what power must King Thunder have? Surely some of it would be inherent in his mask. But when Ysbott peered through the holes, he saw only his campfire and the night around him.

One thing the mask would have, he assured himself, would be the power to command—a power that would make him like the Thunder King. He closed his eyes and imagined himself standing over a throng of Heathen warriors that stretched as far as eye could see, all of them roaring, saluting him with weapons whose blades flashed like the biggest forest fire ever: worshipping him, vowing their flesh and blood to him, as he prepared to launch them into battle. His heart raced. He gasped for breath.

"No!" he panted to himself. "I'm not as big a fool as

that!" Maybe it was the mask inflaming his imagination. He would have to be careful.

How would he command the Heathen? He had a smattering of the Abnak language—but they were rebels, King Thunder's enemies—and a mere few words of Tribe-talk. The moment he appeared among them, they'd cut him down and take the mask.

"And what good is the mask," he mused, "if I don't have the clothes to match it?" He was dressed in rags; you could hardly call them clothes at all.

Ysbott was wise enough to realize that his knowledge of the Thunder King had limits. Outlaws living in the depths of Lintum Forest got little news of the wider world outside. Once upon a time the greatest of the outlaw chiefs, Latt Squint-eye, aspired to be king of Lintum Forest in alliance with the Heathen armies. Helki's rod put an end to that.

"Oh, yes," thought Ysbott, "caution is the game for me. Don't want to wind up with my head on a pole, do I?"

The first thing to do, he reasoned, was to come down from the Golden Pass with the mask wrapped up so no one would see it. Hrapp's clothes would suffice for that. The next thing would be to obtain some fancy garments for himself. Somewhere he would find some he could steal.

Ysbott didn't know who Chutt was and had no inkling of what Chutt might intend to do. All he knew was that that man had the gold, and a horde of Wallekki riders in his following.

"What if he didn't have those Wallekki?" Ysbott thought. "What if I had them, instead? The Wallekki are superstitious dogs: everyone knows that. What if they thought their master has come back for them—back from the dead because he cannot die?"

He rubbed his palms together. With the mask, and suitably impressive robes, he might easily win over those Wallekki. And there were still outlaws in Lintum Forest who would follow him, if he led them against Helki. And what if all that gold, in all those wagons, fell into his hands?

And surely, before he was through, he would hang Roshay Bault from the highest gallows in Obann and devise a fitting death for his daughter, the witch.

Hlah received a visitor from Abnak country, who brought him word from his old friend, Sunfish—now known to the world as Lord Orth, First Prester of the Temple of Obann.

"He wishes you would come down and learn how to be a prester," said the visitor, a warrior named Sparrow. "We're going to be the Obann God's people from now on, but we need teachers. Et-taa-naa-qiqu wants very much to see you again, but he will understand if you'd rather stay here. Even a short visit, though, would please him very much. That's what he asked me to tell you."

Hlah's settlement had grown. Abnak hunters provided it with meat and taught their skills to the Obannese who lived with them. A few Abnak women, with their children, whose men had fallen in the war against the Thunder King, had joined them. All looked to Hlah as their chief, and every five days they assembled to hear him read the Scriptures to them. He read from one of the new copies that Orth had sent him all the way from Obann City. Hlah spoke perfect Obannese, but reading it was still hard for him.

"A prester—me?" Hlah laughed out loud. Sparrow said, "If your father, old Chief Spider, could hear about this, he'd laugh even louder." Spider had died in the city and had a tomb there, and an honored name.

"He'd do more than laugh," said Hlah. "He'd think poor Sunfish had lost his mind again."

"You mustn't say that!" Sparrow answered. "Your old friend is a great man among our people. His prayers moved God to grant us victory. He's taught many of our chiefs to pray. He would like to teach the whole nation, but he'll need some help with that."

Hlah's Obannese wife, May, picked up their little son, Wulf, who was about to overturn a basket of freshly gathered berries.

"It would be good to see him again," she said, "and he is Wulf's godfather. A child should see his godfather now and then."

"But if I go, who would read the book to all the others?"

"Reciter Uwain could do it more easily than you do," May said. "He taught you to read. He can teach others."

"You want to go," said Hlah.

"Of course I do. I love Sunfish, and I've missed him. You love him, too—don't say you don't. Besides, he needs you. It'll be good for him to have us there with him."

"But he's the First Prester of Obann! Sooner or later he'll have to return to the city."

"He says he can't go back until his work is done," said Sparrow.

In the end, Hlah decided to go.

"When my father let me leave the king's army," he said, "it was because I longed to bring God's word back to our own people. I never expected to settle here with you."

"Well, then," May said, "you'll only be doing what God called you to do in the first place."

CHAPTER 9

A Feast on the Isle of Shurk

Slowly, although they'd commandeered more wagons, Lord Chutt's army crept past King Oziah's Wood, following the south bank of the Chariot River. Near the point where the Chariot flowed into the Imperial, Chutt received his first emissaries from some of the great families of Obann.

They came to see the gold, to assure themselves he really had it, and Chutt proudly showed it to them.

"With this," he said, "we can rebuild the Temple, raise great armies to defend ourselves, and restore the old order in Obann—everything the way it was, and even better. The old Oligarchy will be restored, the ravages of war repaired. We can rebuild the Palace, too, as a fitting place for the oligarchs to sit in government. All this we can do, and more, if all the great families work together. And all shall be done according to law."

These were the sons and servants of great houses. The magnates themselves would come, once they were assured Chutt's great treasure of gold was no idle rumor. He'd expected them to be cautious.

"My first messages must have struck them as fantastic,"

he confided to Gallgoid, "but now they'll know they weren't. By the time we reach the city, they'll all be on our side."

"All except Roshay Bault," said Gallgoid. "Have you decided how to handle him? As long as one man holds out for the king, he'll be a rallying-point for others."

"Baron Bault must learn to know good sense when he sees it," Chutt said. "Otherwise, I fear he'll end his days as a prisoner in the city, convicted of treason by the Oligarchy, all according to law."

"He'll have to have a fair trial."

"And he'll get one!" Chutt said.

"But what of the king himself?" asked Gallgoid. "What will you do about the king, my lord, when he returns?"

"He's never coming back," said Chutt.

Ringall, an uninhabited island, wore a coat of sweet green grass, enough for all the army's animals to graze to their hearts' content. It was a nice place to rest, although Gurun was impatient to move on.

"Men will brood over what they saw on Hadra, if they are not kept busy," she confided to the king.

"How do you know that, Gurun?" Ryons asked. He understood she was much younger than the rest of his advisers, but she was wise.

She broke into a smile and suddenly bent to kiss him on the head. "You will grow up to be a very shrewd man, my king! I know it is unwise to stay here for long because I've heard some muttering, even among the chieftains. And besides, I can hardly stop thinking about Hadra myself." Her smile faded. "Who has ever seen anything like that? A few of the prophets, speaking of God's wrath to come, hinted that such things might someday come to pass. Your New Books, which we in the North have never had, speak of the Day of Fire. Obst has told me this: how in a single day the great cities of Obann's empire were all destroyed, along with all the cities of the East. It's much on Obst's mind, just now."

Elsewhere on the grassy isle, it was Uduqu who soothed Obst and the other chiefs.

"If King Thunder could do every day what he did to Hadra," Uduqu said, "he'd have done it to the Abnaks by now, and we'd have heard about it. Let's not yelp before we're bitten."

"But you and Gurun were in Obann when the Palace was destroyed by fire. You saw it with your own eyes. That fire came out of a box that the Thunder King gave Goryk Gillow. You saw the power that was in it!" Obst shook his head. "Who knows what else he has at Kara Karram, recovered from the ancient time? That was Martis' greatest fear."

"Well, it's not mine," said Uduqu. "Goryk Gillow let that power out of the box, and it devoured him instead of us. Something like that would be a fitting end to King Thunder and his fortress, don't you think?"

"Now you sound like Helki," said Tiliqua the Griff.

They spent a full day on Ringall, and the next morning Ghur Manyan returned to them in a boat.

"All's well, my lords!" he said. "Our people on the isle of Shurk will welcome you, and many of the warriors are eager to join you. Our poets have composed a song in honor of King Ryons. You'll hear it as you feast."

Uduqu grinned at Ryons, and the king blushed. There was a song about Uduqu, too, and you could embarrass him by singing it.

"If you set sail today," Ghur said, "you can arrive at Shurk tomorrow morning at the latest. It looks like good sailing weather all afternoon and all night long."

"What about King Thunder's mardars?" Shaffur said.

"You'll find none of them alive on Shurk."

Shurk was a big island with a mountain in the middle and villages all along the coast. Intermixed with the Dahai on Shurk were smaller, darker folk who resembled the Attakotts and spoke a language similar to theirs: the original inhabitants of several of the islands in the lake. They'd lost the art of making poisoned arrows, but learned how to raise cattle, grazing them around the mountain. "Very fine cattle!" said Xhama, chief of the Red Regiment of the Hosa, after he'd seen some. Looth didn't think much of Attakotts who tended cattle instead of making war, but no untactful words escaped his lips. The islanders that night feasted their guests on roast beef, and it was much appreciated.

A pair of Dahai bards sang the song to King Ryons, plucking musical notes on strings stretched over empty tortoise shells, accompanied by a player on bagpipes. The bards sang in a high-pitched, nasal style that Ryons found oddly unsettling, although it seemed to go well with the twanging of their strings and the droning of the pipes. Ryons didn't understand a word of it; Obst gave him a rough translation, after the singers took their bows. It was a long song, and the part Ryons liked best went something like this.

Wind upon the waters:
Whose the hand that stirs it?

Wind upon the waters:
The old gods sleep, they wake no more.
A king comes,
A mighty God has sent him,
And there is wind upon the waters.

"Many times have the peoples of the lake risen up against the Thunder King," said Ghur Manyan. "His mardars have depopulated several islands. You saw what was done to Hadra: that was the worst. There have been no uprisings since then. But now I think there will be the greatest uprising of them all."

All along the shore the feast went on, till far into the night. The islanders had thousands of guests to entertain. But Ryons' chieftains, while they ate, conferred with the chief men of Shurk, with the king and Gurun listening intently.

"How far is it from here to Kara Karram?" Obst asked. "How long would it take us to go there?"

"You could be there in three or four days, depending on the weather and how fast you wished to go," said Ghur. "But I think you would be wiser to visit more of our islanders first. You will add good warriors to your host, and the people have a great desire to see the king of Obann." He nodded to Ryons. "A boy king, Your Majesty—our people see it as a marvel, a sign that could have only come from heaven. You are much in people's hearts. If you could know how we've suffered from the Thunder King, you would understand."

"Sir," said Ryons, "I'm only here because God sent me. Look at me! I was just a slave, not long ago. A mardar was going to cut me open so he could read the future in my innards. Don't think too much of me! Worship God, and trust only Him to save you. Only God could make a king out of the likes of me." Truly, it made him squirm when grown-up men and women waited on his words. He was the descendant of King Ozias—God Himself had said so, speaking through the little girl who was His prophetess—but Ryons very seldom felt like the heir of King Ozias. Most of the time he felt like just a boy who was doing something very dangerous, and someday he'd be punished for it.

Three days from Kara Karram! They could be there in three days, if they sailed straight for the eastern shore of this lake and straight across the next. The thought of it squeezed Ryons' stomach.

"Has anybody here ever been to Kara Karram?" he couldn't help asking.

"Father," said Chagadai, "we Ghols came in sight of Kara Karram when we first came out of our own country, to join the host that would invade Obann. But we were not invited in."

"No one goes to Kara Karram of his own free will," Ghur said. "Our gods went there and have not come back. At Kara Karram the mardars dine on human flesh." Ryons saw this stout man shudder, and thought, "If that place scares him so badly, what will it do to me?"

Angel the hawk was with Perkin and Baby and Cavall, set apart from the crowd of feasters. "No sense in having Baby mix with a lot of strangers. We don't want him getting spooked," Perkin said. He took the animals aside and fed them on roast beef, brought continually by small children who then sat at a safe distance and watched, fascinated, as the giant bird gulped down steak after steak in single swallows. Even these islanders knew the saying, "I could eat a horse." With Baby it was no mere figure of speech.

Twice now had Angel flown ahead, and many times circled King Thunder's fortress on its cliff looking down on the lake. She could not have said, even if she could talk, what drew her there. Some little notion of it she was able to communicate to Cavall, who was very intelligent for a dog—enough to make him mildly uneasy. But the human beings, and Baby, were too dull to understand.

Kara Karram was a huge structure, much bigger than the Golden Hall. Once it had been the seat of a mighty king, the King of the Lakes. The Thunder King captured it many years ago, slew the king and all his people, and took it for his own. He'd added to it ever since. All Angel knew was that she'd never before seen anything like it. The size of it alone was dreadful. She felt it could be no natural thing.

On a nearby cliff sprawled another great nest of humans—the Thunder King's New Temple, which he had made to replace the Temple in Obann.

Both were evil places, Angel's senses told her, good places to avoid. They reminded her of enormous wasps' nests, filled with unimaginably big swarms of wasps that would swoop out of it in black clouds and sting to death anyone who dared come close. Not for a plate of fresh liver would Angel have landed on the least of the towers.

Somehow the hawk understood that Ryons and his humans meant to go there, and she couldn't make them stay away. She loved the king, and Gurun and Chagadai, who understood hawks. She was fond of Cavall and even Baby, and felt protective of them: they needed a wise hawk to protect them. Angel didn't want to lose them. A lesser hawk would have simply deserted them all, but Angel had been trained by Helki. Wherever her human beings went, she would go, too. Even to Kara Karram, which was great folly.

CHAPTER 10

A Man Who Saw a Fiend

As Baron of the Eastern Marches, Roshay Bault was charged with the safety of King Ryons' realm from Ninneburky all the way up to the mountains. His successful defense of Ninneburky, when the Zephite host attacked it, had made him famous.

So he wasn't surprised when people came to see him, from the towns and villages and logging camps along the great river, asking his help against bandits and the few stragglers from the Thunder King's shattered host who'd wandered this far eastward. The expanse of territory that had to be covered, and the need for speed, had inspired him to convert much of the militia into cavalry.

But he was surprised by a story told by a lone hunter who came all the way down from the hills.

"My lord baron," said the hunter, "I've seen a thing unnatural." Inger, his name was, a stocky, grizzled man of middle age who'd spent most of his life in the wooded hills and occasionally came down to Ninneburky to trade pelts for ale and supplies. Captain Kadmel knew him, and vouched for him as an honest, ordinary man. The day being fine, Roshay received him on the front porch of his house.

"Tell me what you saw," said the baron.

"My lord, it was a fiend! It walked upright like a man, striding down King Thunder's road—but it made me think of—well, a spider, of all things!—when I saw it. Something about the way it moved. Spiderish!

"And more marvelous, it had a head of solid gold! Oh, it burned when the sun's rays struck it! You would've thought it was a fire marching down the mountain. But otherwise it was dressed in the filthiest rags I ever did see. My lord, it was like a dead man walking—like something out of a tale from long ago. I've hardly slept a wink since I saw it. When I close my eyes, there it is. Ugh!"

This was indeed a tale, thought Roshay. He turned to Kadmel. "Send out a man to find Martis," he said. "I want him." The militia captain saluted and went off to see to it.

"My lord, do you believe me?" Inger asked.

"I do!" said the baron. "But what you saw was only a man. If you see him again, watch carefully to see where he goes and what he does, and come back and tell me all about it. Don't try to meddle with him. Don't let him see you."

Inger made a ghastly laugh and showed his teeth. "My lord, I thought I might stay here in Ninneburky for a while! And get good and proper drunk, too, while I'm at it. Then maybe I'll get some sleep."

Roshay found a silver coin for the man. "Enjoy your ale with my compliments, Inger, and stay as long as you please."

So someone had found the Thunder King's golden mask! That could be the only meaning of Inger's story, Roshay thought. It hadn't turned up in Chutt's diggings. Helki probably would have found it, if he'd dug for it: too bad he hadn't, thought the baron. "Now some fool has it, and God only knows what mischief will come of this." He hoped Martis and the scouts would track the fool down and take the mask from him before much harm was done.

Having heard their father tell their mother about his conversation with Inger, Jack and Ellayne went looking for Wytt. When they couldn't find him under the back porch, they went to search for him in the little wood outside the gate.

They knew about the golden mask, having been the first to hear Gallgoid's story when he came down from the Golden Pass. And Ellayne knew some of those old tales that had frightened Inger.

"Sometimes," she told Jack, "when a really evil person died, he'd come out of his grave and go up on people's rooftops and scare them out of their wits with clumping around up there and shrieking. Then they'd have to dig him up, during the day, and pin him down with a wooden stake through his heart."

"Oh, that's bunk!" Jack answered. He certainly wanted it to be bunk. "If that thing ever really happened, then why doesn't it happen anymore? I think those old-time people told stories like that just to scare themselves."

"I didn't say the stories were true. It's just what people used to say, a long time ago."

"There's enough trouble in the world without dead men climbing onto rooftops." Jack would have said more, but at that moment Wytt jumped out from behind a tree, provoking a startled yelp from Ellayne.

"How many times have I told you not to do that!" she cried. "Sit down with us, Wytt, we want to tell you something."

Since their descent from the summit of Bell Mountain, the children had the gift of understanding Wytt as if he spoke their language. He understood them, too—but not to the extent of understanding why human beings behaved so strangely. Human wars and politics and customs made no sense to him, and no Omah would even try to make sense of it. For all that he'd shared in the children's travels and adventures, and all that he'd seen, Wytt didn't understand or care why great masses of big people tried so hard to kill as many of each other as they could.

But he knew what evil was, and shunned it. He'd burrowed into the ruins of the Thunder King's hall and knew that evil lurked there.

"It's out now," he told the children. "Birds fear it. They won't stay there anymore. They come here instead—then go farther away still."

"It's the Thunder King's golden mask, Wytt," said Ellayne. "Someone came there after we left, and dug it up."

Wytt knew nothing of masks or gold, but he chattered angrily. Jack heard it as, "No good! Very dangerous." Jack remembered it was Wytt who'd warned them of the potent menace that was inside the special box that Goryk Gillow brought with him to Obann. Back in Silvertown, Goryk had used it to strike a man blind. When it was let loose in Obann, it destroyed the Palace.

Martis had taught the children that there were certain ancient items left over from the Day of Fire. Lord Reesh collected them, he'd said, but nothing in Lord Reesh's collection had any power left in it. But Jack and Ellayne used to have one, a little one, stolen from one of the agents of the Thunder King, that gave off light, showed a picture, and played strange, tinny music—until it blew up in Ysbott's face.

"The mask must be a thing like that," Ellayne said. "Who knows what power it gave the Thunder King, when he wore it? Who knows what it can do now, with someone else?" She turned to Wytt, now sitting in her lap. "Could you help Martis find it, and take it to my father?"

"Not a good thing for a man to have," he answered.

"We don't want to keep it! Will you help us?"

"I help," Wytt chirped. He wore a lock of Ellayne's golden hair around his neck, and he would always help them.

Ysbott soon found that wearing the mask made him feel strong and full of energy, and fearless, too. Besides, wearing it was easier than carrying it: after a mile or so, it felt like it would tear your arm off. Ysbott got down the mountain rather faster than he thought he could—thanks to the mask, he believed.

Because so much war had swept over it, no one lived on the plain between the foothills and King Oziah's Wood, no one from whom to steal fine clothes. Ysbott never used to care about such things, but now he was sure the rags that clung to his body were beneath his dignity. How could he appear before Lord Chutt's Wallekki and win their obedience without fine clothes? He was tempted to shuck off his rags and walk naked.

His life in Lintum Forest had taught him how to find

food in places where a townsman would never think to look for it, so he didn't go hungry. Once a gigantic bird, looking for easy prey, spotted him out in the open, no hope of escape. It trotted a few steps toward him, but when he raised his arms and shrieked curses at it, it turned and ran away. Helki would have said the predator was only reacting to the strange appearance and bizarre behavior of the prey, but Ysbott knew better. The mask gave him the power of command, even over wild animals.

"Golden robes—that's what I want," he thought. "I'll bet the Thunder King wore golden robes. And sat on a gold throne, too!"

He followed the trail of Chutt's wagons along the south bank of the Chariot. It did seem to him that whoever this man was that commanded the Wallekki, he would send out riders to scout for the approach of enemies. So Ysbott traveled by night, making much better time than Chutt could with his laden carts. The condition of the ruts and horse-droppings satisfied him that he was steadily closing the gap between the hunter and his quarry.

Ysbott made it his practice to rest during the day, after foraging for food. This he did at dawn, when he could see.

One damp morning he was on his knees, digging up edible roots with his knife, when he heard the neigh of a horse, practically on top of him. He threw himself flat on his belly, hidden by the tall grass. Removing the mask because it limited his field of vision, he raised himself on his hands and peered cautiously over the grass.

Not fifty yards away was a Wallekki rider, a lone scout, who'd reined in and was looking all around to see what had made his horse neigh.

What would happen, Ysbott wondered, if he put on the mask and suddenly stood up? Would the rider obey him—or just gallop off in a panic, to bring a wild story back to his comrades? Ysbott would have liked to try his luck. Temptation gnawed at him like a biting insect.

"But no—," he thought, "not in these rags! Not unless he comes too close, and then I'll have to."

After a long moment, horse and rider trotted off in another direction. Ysbott felt slightly disappointed. Still, he reminded himself, no outlaw survives for very long in Lintum Forest without a deep reserve of cunning. It would be foolish now to abandon the guile that had made him Ysbott the Snake, and a chief among sly and ruthless men. He let the scout go on his way and then went back to finding breakfast.

CHAPTER 11

How Cardigal Got a New Oligarch

Because some of Chutt's messages went to houses in Obann, and because servants hear their masters talking and then talk to other servants on the streets and in the shops, before long the whole city knew Lord Chutt—whom many had thought dead—had the Thunder King's gold. Prester Jod's servants and Constan's students lost no time passing the news on to their masters.

"So Chutt has got the gold!" said Jod, when he went to see Constan at the seminary and the preceptor had shut his office door. "And still we have no word from Gallgoid. I wonder if he's still true to us."

Constan sat behind his desk, as motionless as a moss-covered boulder. Finally he answered, "I think he is. He will have attached himself to Chutt by now and be waiting to see what might be done."

"You trust him?"

"He saved the First Prester when there was a plot against him. He protected Gurun and the king."

"Chutt has gold to buy men's allegiance," Jod said.

"Could he buy yours, Prester?"

Jod raised his eyebrows. "God forbid!"

"He's coming here to Obann with that gold," said Constan, "and with an evil purpose."

The Abnak messengers had been sent back to Lord Orth with Jod's reply, encouraging him to continue his work in the East, pledging the loyalty of the clergy in Obann, but refusing to accept his offer to resign his office. Constan sent two young scholars with the messengers and several new copies of the Scriptures.

"I'm not so sure anymore," said Jod, "that I can promise any cleric's loyalty except my own—and yours, Preceptor. If Chutt has gold enough to rebuild the Temple, and promises to do it, the people—and the clergy!—will embrace him. Especially with King Ryons far away somewhere, off in Heathen-land, and who can say if we'll ever see him again?" He sighed. "You and I are in for a very difficult time."

Lord Chutt crossed to the north bank of the Chariot and made camp near the town of Cardigal. His draft animals badly needed rest, and his men needed the good food that could be bought in Cardigal. The Thunder King's invading army had handled the town roughly, but rebuilding and repairs were well advanced, and the crops thrived in the countryside.

All Cardigal turned out to see the carts full of gold and the savage Wallekki who guarded it. "Let them see," Chutt ordered his captains. "I want all Obann to know the gold is ours." He was careful to say "ours," not "mine." But Gallgoid knew what he was thinking—and he wouldn't be surprised if Ilfil knew it, too.

Although the king's ministers had proclaimed the Oligarchy to be no more, Cardigal still had an oligarch: a new one, whose only claim to the title was that his father was an oligarch. This was not according to law, for the rank was not hereditary. Oligarchs were appointed by the High Council, of which Chutt was the sole surviving representative.

The young oligarch came eagerly seeking audience, and Chutt received him.

"I believe you knew my father, sir. He died in the war."

Chutt had bathed and shaved, although cold water from the river for those purposes was something he would not have to put up with for much longer. He received the young man in his tent, which had been kept as clean as the rigors of the journey would allow—a blue and white-striped pavilion, the white stripes beginning to show grey.

"I knew your father for a strong and able man," Chutt said. "Yes—Gilvaith, Oligarch of Cardigal. You do resemble him."

"My name is Gilvaithwy, my lord." Tall and lean and fair, he looked nothing like his father, a dark, blocky man with a bald head. Chutt did remember the name, but not the man's appearance.

"Is there something I can do for you, Gilvaithwy, son of Gilvaith?"

"My lord, there is." The young man bowed slightly. "I have come to ask you to confirm me in my office. I took it on myself because war has disrupted the order of things."

Nothing could have pleased Chutt more. But he said, "Surely you know the new king has done away with our ancient Oligarchy."

"I don't understand how he could do that lawfully, my

lord," said Gilvaithwy. Oh, yes, thought Chutt: he wanted his father's post and all its privileges. Why should a king take it away from him? "Whatever else this king may be, sir, he has yet to be crowned. What law of Obann established him as king? They say he's been elected by God Himself—but anyone can say that, can't they?

"My lord, you are the High Council of the Oligarchy, until new colleagues are elected for you by the surviving oligarchs of Obann's towns and cities. Until then, the law gives only you the authority to appoint or to dismiss an oligarch."

Chutt's eyes twinkled. "You have made a study of the law?"

"Sir, my father was a stickler for it."

"And so am I," said Chutt. "Well, it is my position that all the old laws of Obann are still in force, never mind what the king's followers may say. War and tumult do not erase a nation's laws.

"Gilvaithwy, return to your town and summon its chief men to serve as witnesses. Come back to me as soon as you can, and by the lawful power vested in me, I will confirm you in your office. Obann needs men like you."

Gilvaithwy bowed at the waist and hurried off to fetch his witnesses.

"He never even mentioned the gold!" Chutt marveled to himself.

Gallgoid kept a careful eye on all the day's proceedings.

Those townsfolk who weren't already at the camp to see the gold came out to see their oligarch confirmed. Gilvaithwy now wore a snow-white cape over the finest clothes he had, all in shiny blue and scarlet, with his father's golden chain of office on his breast. The half-dozen witnesses, older men, had also taken time to decorate themselves. They were not the only ones.

Ysbott the Snake had caught up to Chutt at last, and during the night stole into the town and possessed himself of some decent garments that someone had left hanging on a clothesline. They were just ordinary clothes, trousers and a homespun tunic, and he certainly had no intention of appearing in them with the mask. But they would allow him to mingle with the crowd and see what he could see; and the mask he carried in a burlap sack he'd found. Lest the garments' rightful owner should discover him, he disguised the clothes by rubbing them with dirt and grass.

No one gave him a second glance. They were all too busy watching Chutt swear in their oligarch. The sight of the young man's rich clothing gave Ysbott hope that he would find what he needed here.

And what did Gallgoid observe that interested him?

For one thing, it struck him that the folk of Cardigal weren't altogether pleased that the last of the High Council had a mob of renegade Wallekki in his train. The Thunder King had given Cardigal a stiff dose of fire and sword, and fear. For all the townspeople knew, some of these same Wallekki had slain their friends and kinfolk. Gallgoid watched Chutt closely, and decided the man was not so big a fool as to fail to notice this. It would be interesting to discuss it with him later—out of Ilfil's hearing. It would be good for Ilfil to suspect his lord was having conversations behind Ilfil's back.

For another, Gallgoid was not convinced the people of Cardigal wanted another oligarch. As had already been done in Obann City, Silvertown, and elsewhere, the king's regime had restored to the people their right to elect mayors and councilors of their own choosing—as had always been done in Ninneburky and other towns deemed not important enough to have an oligarch. What ought to have been an occasion for rejoicing, the people received in relative silence.

The one thing Obann didn't miss about the Temple, Gallgoid mused, was the Temple tax. Lord Orth had done away with it, preferring to rely on free-will offerings and a small head-tax for the upkeep of the clergy. Despite the wealth of gold that Chutt brought with him, Gallgoid, as he moved among the crowd, heard mutterings.

"You'll see—they'll keep the gold for themselves, and we'll have all the old taxes back again."

"Old Gilvaith taxed us every time he threw a party!"

"Why don't they lay out some of that gold right here and now and help us to pay for our new walls?"

"You'll be a long time waiting," Gallgoid thought, "for Lord Chutt to part with any of his gold. He himself will be surprised by how firmly it sticks to his fingers."

CHAPTER 12

How King Thunder Offered Peace

There was some excitement in Shurk, early in the morning after the feast. Two fishermen came ashore with a big, flat-headed fish of a kind no one had ever seen before.

"Look at those jaws!" they said, after they'd laid it out for everyone to see. "It might've bit our boat in half, had we been less ready with our clubs. And look at the scales on it—a regular suit of armor plate! No use trying to spear this fellow."

The fish was almost as long as the fishing boat itself. Gurun, Ryons, and Obst stood over it, marveling at it on the beach.

"It's another one of those strange creatures that God has put into the world in our time," said Obst, "like the giant birds, and the knuckle-bears on the fringe of Lintum Forest." Cavall came up and sniffed the fish, and backed off with a growl.

"We catch other strange fish from time to time," said a fisherman. "No telling what you'll pull out of the water, these days. This spring I hauled up a worm as thick as my forearm. It stunk like the devil and smeared black slime all over my boat."

"It's a sign the world is changing," Obst said.

Toward noon there was something else that made everyone lose interest in the armored fish. A single boat approached the shore, under a white sail and a flag of truce. Its curving prow displayed a round shield trimmed with horsetails.

"That's from the Thunder King!" said Ghur Manyan. "But whoever heard of him wanting a parley or coming under a banner of peace?"

"Get the council tent set up," Shaffur said, "and have Looth's men ready with their poisoned arrows."

Around the big black tent stood Hosa warriors in formation, ready with their spears and shields. Behind it, out of view from the water, waited Wallekki horsemen and some of the Ghols. Looth's archers hid themselves behind cottages and boats, poised to let fly their arrows at any moment. Village elders herded all the women and children out of sight.

"It seems a lot of preparation for just a single boat with four or five men in it," Uduqu said. "I wouldn't want them to think we are afraid of them."

"Remember the Burned Island," answered Tiliqua the Griff.

The boat landed three sailors and two other men, who waited until it was all secured before they stepped on land. Ryons didn't see this. With Obst and Gurun standing on either side of him, and himself hurriedly dressed in the Wallekki chieftain's finery that served him as a king's robes of office, black-feathered headdress and all, Ryons sat on his ivory chieftain's stool amid his chiefs. Shaffur remained outside to direct the fighting, if there was any, and to usher the newcomers into the presence of his king.

He brought them in—a burly man with close-cropped hair and beard, Dahai by the look of him, and another man who wore the insignia of Obann's Temple. Obst gulped back a cry of astonishment.

"Greetings from the great king, the king of all the East, the Thunder King, to our royal kinsman, Ryons, King of Obann!" said the man in Temple livery. He spoke in Tribe-talk for the benefit of the chiefs, but with an accent. This man was Obannese, Obst thought: "And born and bred in the city itself, by the sound of it!"

Ryons was amazed. Royal kinsman? The last emissary from the Thunder King threatened to put out his eyes and keep him in a dungeon till he died.

"Who are you, sir," said Obst, "and what's your errand here?"

"My name is Greyr, a prester of the Temple of God at Kara Karram. I am a graduate of the seminary of Obann, ordained a prester by Lord Reesh himself—half a lifetime ago, it seems. The late First Prester sent me here on a diplomatic mission before the war broke out. I was for a time a prisoner, but His Grace the Thunder King raised up my head and honored me. I serve him in the New Temple now, but I am still a diplomat.

"And this is Mardar Hian Koral, who was born on this very island of Shurk.

"We come on behalf of our lord the Thunder King to make peace with you."

Greyr was not as young as he looked at first glance; there was more silver than gold in his hair and beard. But he stood as straight as a spear and had a pleasing voice.

Ryons' chiefs looked around at one another. This was the last thing they'd expected.

Greyr took another step forward and bowed deeply to Ryons on his stool.

"I am honored to see you, Your Majesty," he said. "All men in all lands know your name, and your brave chieftains are famous in their own right. My lord King Thunder welcomes you."

"You'll understand that we're amazed to hear it!" said Obst. His voice sounded harsh.

"When King Ryons himself chased my master's army from the walls of Obann," Greyr said, "my master understood it as a sign from God. He might have easily raised another army, and another, as many as required, and sent it to Obann. Instead, he bent his efforts to building a New Temple to the God of Obann, to replace the Temple he'd destroyed. It is his dearest hope that now there will be peace on earth and that the New Temple will be a house of worship for all nations, to the glory of God."

And Uduqu thought, but didn't say, "Things must have gone very badly indeed for him of late."

"This is wrong!" thought Ryons. But how could it be? Wouldn't God want all the nations to honor Him? And how could it be bad to turn around and go in peace, back to Lintum Forest? What could be better than that?

"It's a trick," he told himself. "These men are full of lies."

Ghur Manyan, who had been given a seat among the chiefs, spoke up.

"I know a place where the Thunder King's peace can be seen for what it is—Hadra Island!"

"Let me answer," said the mardar, Hian Koral. "Hadra rose up in rebellion. Its people murdered King Thunder's mardars. Even so, it was not our master's doing, and the men who burned Hadra have all been punished with death. I saw them die.

"Do you chieftains of King Ryons not know that our master could, at any time he pleased, send ten or twenty times your number against you and destroy you? But he hasn't! He has made you a present of your lives. What more proof of his intentions would you have?"

"Mardar Hian speaks roughly," Greyr added quickly, "but he speaks the truth. Which is better—to swear peace before God at His Temple and to part as friends, or to force my master, much against his will, to deal with you as enemies? The New Temple stands for peace and holiness and healing. Will you not let it do its work? But what say you, King Ryons?"

"It's not right to ask such a question of a boy, king though he be!" snapped Shaffur. His hand strayed to the hilt of his sword.

"Shall he not speak?" said Greyr.

Ryons shrank inside his robes. They were all looking at him now, as if he were the only person in the tent. Hawk and Xhama, the Hosa; Chagadai the Ghol, chief of his bodyguard; Ghur Manyan and the elders of Shurk; Tiliqua the Griff, Helki's man; Jiharr the Zephite—all of them, and Obst and Gurun and Uduqu most keenly of all—they all waited on his word.

And he had no word for them. He couldn't think of a single thing to say. He'd give his right hand for some good advice!

But then the words came—from where, he didn't know.

"We will go to Kara Karram," he spoke, "and God shall judge between us. For all the burned islands and the poisoned wells, and for all oppression, God will demand an accounting. For the enslavement of nations, for the countless dead, and for the hate and dread and terror, God shall make a reckoning. So says the Lord, the Living God who made the heavens and the earth."

The boy ran out of breath and clutched at the handles of his stool, unaware that he'd said anything at all. But Chagadai drew his knife and clashed its pommel on his shield, and then all the other chieftains did the same—a clamor of weapons.

"You have your answer," Obst said, his voice rising above the tumult in the tent. "Your answer comes from God, through the speaking of a child. Now go, and don't return."

Mardar Hian peered nervously around the tent, fearful of what his own people might do to him. Greyr's eloquence deserted him. He took Hian by the elbow and led him out of the tent, straight back to the boat. The sailors needed no command from him. As soon as the envoys were back on board, they launched.

Some time passed before the chieftains were quiet again.

"Well, that settles that," Uduqu said.

"My lords—I don't know what I said!" Ryons piped up.

Obst reached down and touched his hair. Ryons stopped trembling.

"The spirit of God, which once spoke through King Ozias, has spoken through you, Ozias' seed," he said. "Those words will be remembered."

"Even so," said Gurun, smiling gently at the king, "I think the time has come to change our plans."

CHAPTER 13

An Unforeseen Difficulty

Martis and the scouts did not catch the man with the mask, but they followed Chutt's caravan all the way to Cardigal. Today Martis was back in Ninneburky, reporting to the baron.

"Whoever it is who has the mask, his woodcraft is better than mine," Martis said. "We could never keep on his track for long—just long enough to say we think he was following after Chutt."

"Now why would he do that?" Roshay Bault wondered. "One glimpse, and Chutt would seize that mask."

"Sir, we lost the mask's trail at Cardigal. Chutt has made his camp outside the town. He's appointed a new oligarch for Cardigal, which is an act against the king."

Roshay frowned. Something would have to be done about this. He wrestled with it all afternoon, and announced his decision over dinner.

"We can't have Chutt going around appointing oligarchs," he said. "I see where this is going. When the king returns, he'll find himself an outlaw in his own kingdom."

"Just like King Ozias!" the baroness said. Now that she read from the Scriptures every day with the children, she was quick to see such things. Jack and Ellayne saw it, too. Traitors drove Ozias from his kingdom. Would they do the same to Ryons?

"He'll be creating oligarchs all along the river," said Roshay, "and renaming old ones to their office. They'll follow him to the city, I suppose, and there elect a new High Council with Chutt as governor-general. And that'll be the end of King Ryons' kingdom."

"I think he'll stay at Cardigal a while," Martis said. "His men and animals need rest, and people are coming from miles around to see the gold."

"That's why I've decided to go there myself," the baron said. "Someone has to speak against this and stand up for the king."

"Father, he won't let you!" Ellayne said. "He'll have you put in irons."

"That's exactly what he'll do," said Martis. "Don't go, my lord. Leave things up to Gallgoid. He'll find a way." He did not suggest that, if worst came to worst, Gallgoid could put a stop to Chutt with a well-placed dose of poison. You couldn't be sure of that anymore. "He's like me," Martis thought, "touched by the finger of God. He won't resort to poison." Still, he might think of something.

"Martis is right," Vannett said. "Ryons is king by God's election. That's what we believe. If his kingship is of God, then Chutt's schemes to overthrow it will come to nothing."

"I serve the Lord as best I can," said Roshay, "and I'll do my duty by the king. But I'll need help! Dash off a letter to Prester Jod, informing him of all we know, and send it by our swiftest rider. He and I together, maybe, can find a way to put an end to this—or at least slow it down."

"That man would put Prester Jod in irons, too," Jack said.

"He wouldn't dare," said the baron.

In Cardigal Lord Chutt faced a difficulty he might have foreseen, had his mind not been so narrowly concentrated on his own prospects.

The town was in an uproar. A young married woman, on her way to visit her parents on their farm, had been attacked and abused by one of the Wallekki. A couple of drovers who heard her cries for help caught him in the act. They overpowered the Wallekki and brought him back to Cardigal, and it was all Chutt could do to persuade the new oligarch to turn the man over to him for judgment. In this he had no choice, thanks to Ilfil.

"My lord," said the Wallekki chief—and Chutt didn't altogether like the way he said it—"my men will not stand by and see one of our fellows hanged by a lot of cowardly townspeople."

"Be reasonable, Chieftain!" Chutt said. "The man has committed a terrible offense. With all Obann ready to fall into our hands, it'd be folly to throw it away for the sake of one cuss't fool who was caught red-handed. We've set ourselves up as those who would restore law and order. I thought you understood that."

Ilfil glared at him. "It's always been our custom, when at war in a foreign country, to take whatever we please," he said. "It's not easy for us to change our ways."

"You'll have to change them," said Chutt, "for the sake of our great enterprise."

"I am not demanding that the man be spared—only that we ourselves should punish him, and that for disobeying orders. My people will stand for nothing else."

So Chutt had to go to Gilvaithwy and remind him of who had confirmed him as oligarch of Cardigal.

"By rights this man should be tried by me," the young man said, "and hanged right here in Cardigal. The people are exceedingly angry, and that's what they want."

"Nevertheless," said Chutt, "the man is under my command, and this responsibility is mine. You may assure your people that justice will be done. Surely you can do this for me."

Gilvaithwy agreed, but didn't like it. "We thought we'd seen the last of Wallekki freebooters," he grumbled. "This incident reopens our wounds, my lord."

Amid jeers and curses, four of Cardigal's militiamen brought the prisoner back to Chutt's camp. Advised by Gallgoid, Chutt proceeded instantly to judgment.

Captain Born's men cleared a space while Ilfil explained to his followers—not without blows—that all of this was necessary and their comrade had only himself to blame. "By the Moon God's horns," he said, "the next man of you to disturb the good order of this camp, I'll slit him open with my own hands! Do you want to go back to being thieves and wanderers in the country of your enemies, starving, to be hunted down and killed like dogs, one by one and two by two? Let any man who won't obey me leave this army now!" But no one left.

Gilvaithwy had the two drovers brought as witnesses, to be questioned by Chutt. The judge sat on an oaken chair brought out from town and placed atop some sturdy crates.

The prisoner stood before him with hands tied behind his back. Beyond Born's cordon of spearmen, the whole town watched and listened.

"There being no doubt whatsoever of your guilt," Chutt said, "I sentence you to be hanged tomorrow at noon, here in the camp." He raised his voice. "And let every man know, who may be tempted to do as you have done, that he shall likewise perish."

In the evening Gallgoid found a chance to speak with Chutt alone.

"My lord, you have acted wisely in this matter," the spy said. "But I tell you now, as your friend, that sooner or later you must separate yourself from these Wallekki."

"But they've served me very well, on the whole," said Chutt, "and besides, King Ryons' army was full of Heathen, and people accepted it."

"If they had accepted it wholeheartedly, my lord, the king's chiefs would not have had to withdraw that army from the city. You were not in Obann then, but I was. Had the Heathen stayed, the city would have risen up against them. That's why they're forced to make their nest in Lintum Forest."

"Maybe so. For the time being, though, I need Chief Ilfil and his men—at least until I've brought my gold back to the city."

"Don't wait too long, my lord," said Gallgoid. And by Chutt's silent nod of assent, he knew he'd planted the seed of betrayal.

Ysbott attended the trial, unnoticed in the crowd of townsfolk. He saw the prisoner marched off and placed under guard in an unused chicken coop just outside the camp, part of an abandoned farm.

Ysbott would have dearly liked to rescue the fellow—a man after his own heart, he supposed—but four able-bodied men with spears presented too much of an obstacle. It might be better, after all, to let the Wallekki watch the hanging and resent it.

"But all is not lost!" he whispered to himself. The whole town would turn out to see the hanging, creating a splendid opportunity for him to break into a nice house and steal the clothes he needed. It would be dangerous, doing it by daylight, but perhaps the mask would see him through. He cradled it in his arms like a baby and spoke to it.

"You have your own plans for me, don't you?" he said. For he now believed the mask had chosen him. It hadn't let Chutt's diggers find it. No, it had waited for him. It had been waiting for him all along.

"The Thunder King can't die—everybody knows that," he whispered. "I know your secret now. Whoever wears the mask becomes the Thunder King."

It never entered his mind that the mardars had raised up a new Thunder King, claiming that the one that died in the avalanche was but a servant and that the master, the true King Thunder, had never left his fortress of Kara Karram. Ysbott had never heard of Kara Karram and knew nothing of the mardars.

"But I have you to guide me, haven't I?" he said to the

mask, concealed in coarse burlap. “And am I not Ysbott the Snake, the slyest man in Lintum Forest? Between us we will do great things!”

CHAPTER 14

A Message from the East

Lord Orth heard no news from the west, and hardly any from the north, but from the east came tidings that surprised him.

From the valley of the Green Snake River came three chiefs of the Fazzan, alone, under an antelope skull hanging from a pole, their nation's sign of peace and submission. Some Abnak warriors whose feelings ran high tore off and trampled the chiefs' wolf's-heads that they wore and followed after them, cursing and threatening. But they did them no other harm, and the three chiefs continued stoically on their way until they arrived at Foxblood's camp. There they asked to see the holy man from Obann.

But first Foxblood questioned them. "I remember you," he said to one of the three. "You spoke for the Fazzan at the fort where they killed their mardar and surrendered to us without a fight." He nodded to Orth, who stood beside him: "And at this man's urging, because he said it would please God, we let you go in peace. Why do you return?"

The Fazzan extended their arms, palms upward, to show respect. Orth had not yet learned enough Tribe-talk to follow the conversation word for word, but he got the gist of it.

"O Foxblood," said the spokesman, "we salute you as a

great war chief and a man of wisdom.

"All the tribes of the Fazzan know that the Abnaks have expelled the Thunder King's armies from their country and are free of them. We know this happened because the God of Obann fought for you.

"King Thunder, claiming to be himself the greatest of gods, took away our gods and enslaved us. We three, when we returned to our country, became fugitives. You see only the three of us because the mardars killed the other chiefs, and most of the men, who came home with us. Nevertheless, now all the Fazzan know what the God of Obann did for the Abnaks.

"We three have come here to learn about this God and to petition Him to help our people, too. If God will send your Abnaks to lead us against the Thunder King, we will become His people, too. And we will become your servants. So say we all."

"They submit to us," Foxblood explained to Orth in Obannese, "because they seek our help against the enemy. They are offering to become God's people."

Orth's heart began to race, but he only nodded, leaving it to Foxblood to give an answer.

"Chieftains," he said, "we Abnaks want nothing that belongs to the Fazzan. Why should we wish to rule you? We have everything we love right here, and we've fought hard to keep it. I myself have never once laid eyes on your Green Snake River. Why should we want your people for our servants?

"But if you'll agree to become God's servants, as we are—well, that's different. I think God will help you. As He has fought for us, He will fight for you. But you must be true to Him. No going back on your pledge!"

"Why should we ever turn against the God who saves us from the Thunder King?" the spokesman said. "Tell us what the God of Obann requires of us, and we will give it."

"You tell them," Foxblood said to Orth, "and I'll make sure they understand."

Orth felt like a man for whom many doors were opening at once, all unexpectedly. It took him some moments to find the right words.

"What does God require of you?" he said. "To love Him and to keep His laws, to live in peace with one another, to love mercy and truth-telling and justice. You must have no other gods but Him, and put away your idols. As for your lives and your treasures and your land, God has given you those for your enjoyment—so be thankful."

The three Fazzan exchanged puzzled looks with one another and stared at Orth.

"That's really all He asks of you," Orth added.

One of the chiefs blurted out, "How is it that we have never heard this good word before?"

Foxblood smiled at him and said, "You're hearing it now."

At Prester Jod's direction, reciters gathered small groups of people here and there throughout the city to read the Scriptures to them, preach, and teach. Jod himself preached to large assemblies in market squares or on the grassy fields outside the walls. As the First Prester's vicar, and in the absence of the king, Jod had authority over both the clergy of Obann and the troops remaining in the city with General Hennen in command.

"Preach as if the life of the Temple depended on it," Jod exhorted the reciters, "as it very likely does. For most of the people it will be the first time they've ever heard God's word—and shame on us for withholding it from them for so long." He himself preached Orth's message: "You, God's people, are the Temple now—a temple not made of stone and timber, but by the everlasting power of God's word." And all the while, Constan's scholars and students at the seminary turned out copies of the sacred writings.

Hennen had recently escaped from being held prisoner by Lord Chutt in North Obann, and Jod spent much time in conference with him. Hennen knew Chutt was coming with the gold and bent all his thought to ensuring the army's loyalty to the king.

"The men who've seen King Ryons, and marched with him and fought for him—they're solid; we can depend on them," said Hennen. "Together we've won battles that we had no business surviving! They believe in God and in the king God has given us. It's too bad there are only some four hundred of us left. But no amount of gold will buy those men."

"We have, I believe, some three thousand spears, all told?" Jod asked.

"At last count, yes: most of them recruited from the west and from the north—men who've never seen the king. I think the men from the west will be loyal to you, at least, if not to the king."

Jod shook his head. What would Hennen say if he knew that the boy Jod had protected in Durmurot, and later in Obann, was not King Ryons, but a double? But that secret was not his to share with anyone, not even Hennen.

"I'm uneasy for the clergy, Hennen. If the First Prester were here, I'd have more confidence. But there are too many of Lord Reesh's creatures among the presters. It won't be hard for Chutt to turn them against us."

"You're too modest," Hennen said. "You are the most respected man in all Obann. Where you stand, many will stand with you."

"I grope in shadows, General," said Jod. "If only we had word from Gallgoid! How he would manage to send us any kind of message, of course, I don't know. If he's traveling with Chutt, I suppose it would be difficult. But Preceptor Constan trusts him, and he's a better judge of character than I am."

"Him? Half the time you'd think he was asleep—with his eyes open!"

"If you come to know him better, General, you'll see how wrong you were."

Roshay Bault set out for Cardigal with Martis and a dozen mounted men. Vannett's message to Prester Jod had gone out as soon as the ink was dry.

"Be careful," the baroness said to her husband, just before he swung himself into the saddle (it had taken him some months to learn how to do that gracefully). "That man Chutt let you get away from him once. He's not likely to do it again."

"Send for the king's men in Lintum Forest if you need them," Roshay said.

"You may need them before I do."

The baron turned to his children. "Be good to your mother and help her in any way you can," he said. Ellayne reached up to kiss his cheek. Jack couldn't see his way to anything like that: he didn't yet understand how much his adoptive father loved him. But the baron understood Jack's mind and pulled him into a hug.

"We ought to be going with you, Father," Ellayne said. "And Wytt, too."

The baron laughed out loud. "Not on your life, miss! You stay here where your mother can keep an eye on you. There'll be plenty of work for the both of you. I wish Dib and Josek were here, too." But his two grown sons were busy among the logging camps along the upper reaches of the river. The family's business had to go on, and they would see to it.

Ellayne kissed Martis, too. "Don't worry about us," she said. "Just don't let my father get himself in trouble."

The company was not long out of Ninneburky, along the River Road that was the shortest way to Cardigal, when Roshay turned to Martis.

"You don't like being away from the children, do you?"

"It's my oath," said Martis. He'd sworn it on Bell Mountain, to protect Jack and Ellayne with his life: for he knew God had spared his life for that very purpose and no other. The baron knew all about it.

"They're growing up, Martis," he said. "Before you know it, life will turn the other way around, and they'll be taking care of us. You and I will sit on the porch with blankets on our laps and smile when they bring us tea."

Martis, whom Lord Reesh had raised to be an assassin, laughed quietly. "That's one end for me that the old villain never had in mind!" he thought.

"Do you think Lord Chutt will put us in irons?" Roshay said.

"Baron, I never knew him well—only that Lord Reesh had little respect for him. I expect Gallgoid knows more. Chutt could have had you killed at the Golden Pass, and didn't—which makes me think he'd rather not. Still, it wouldn't surprise me if he used some forceful methods on us."

"He wants to buy Obann, not fight for it," the baron said. "This is my order to you, Martis: if Chutt puts us under arrest, make sure that you escape to bring word to my family. Don't let them take you, too—not even if they try to kill me."

Martis nodded, appreciating Roshay's wisdom.

"We should have gone with him," Ellayne said, when she and Jack were alone behind the stables.

"Just what he would need—something else to worry about," Jack said.

"Are you getting stodgy, Jack?"

"Oh, talk sense! What could we do? How do you think the baron would like it if Chutt got his hands on us?"

"I guess he wouldn't," Ellayne admitted. "I just wish there was something we could do. I won't feel right until father comes back safe and sound."

"Leave it to Martis," Jack said.

CHAPTER 15

A Change in Plans

Ordinarily Gurun wouldn't venture to advise the king's chieftains. What did a Fogo islander know of war? "There are not enough of us to have a war," she said. "Even so, I hope you will not mind if I tell you what I think."

"A queen may always speak her mind," said Shaffur. She thanked him, took a deep breath, and spoke her piece.

"That fellow Greyr will go back to Kara Karram as fast as he can and tell everything he's seen and heard of us. So we must act quickly.

"The time has come for us to return to the land. Our great strength is in men on horseback, but those horses can do nothing for us while we're on the water. We had intended to land on King Thunder's doorstep. If he is wise, he'll be prepared for that. So we should land somewhere else and complete our journey as we started it, on horseback and on foot.

"I fear that wherever we sail on this lake, we will expose its people to danger. To destroy us, the Thunder King will burn every island in the lake—if he is able to do it—and all the people, too. We would be to blame for that."

Shaffur grinned. "That's a plan that appeals to me!" he said. "Now that he knows we're all on boats, the Thunder King will know we can't defend ourselves."

"We must do all we can to draw his attention away from the islands," Obst said. "We've already crossed most of the distance to Kara Karram. The rest of it won't amount to much."

Ghur Manyan and the elders of Shurk were troubled.

"If he comes here," Ghur said, "it will be to kill us all. We might scatter to a score of smaller islands, but that would mean abandoning our cattle and our crops. What can we do?"

"If he's chasing us, he'll leave you for later," Uduqu said. "The only way to be safe from the Thunder King is to put an end to him, once and for all. If we can't, he'll surely put an end to us! Anyhow, I've had my rest. I can walk the rest of the way to Kara Karram."

"Many of our best men will walk with you," Ghur said.

Before the night was over, the whole army was ashore on the mainland. From there, said Ghur, they would have to march around the northern arm of Lake Urmio, the greatest of the lakes, and then along its north shore until they came to the earthen cliffs of Kara Karram.

No one in all the host had ever seen the fortress from the lakeshore, but some of the men from Shurk had heard it described by others.

"From the water's edge to the foot of the cliffs is hardly the distance a healthy man can throw a stone," Ghur said. "Not much room for an army to stand or for two armies to fight a battle."

"Can the cliff be climbed?" asked Jiharr the Zephite.

"I never heard of anyone who climbed it. I suppose you

could get up that way, if you weren't being pelted by spears and stones and boiling tar, but it's a long way up, they say. If all you had to do was climb, you could cut your own steps. Those cliffs are earth, not rock.

"But the hardest thing will be to get there at all. King Thunder has settled Zamzu on the lands above Lake Urmio, and they will fight you all the way."

The chiefs fell silent. They'd defeated Zamzu before—but what was the nation that didn't dread the Zamzu, eaters of men? Of all the peoples under the rule of the Thunder King, only the Zamzu, his favorites, had never turned against him.

"Ah!" sighed Xhama. "If only we had three full regiments of Hosa! My Reds, Hawk's Ghosts, and the Starved Hyenas, who have never lost a battle! We would feed those Zamzu to the crows."

"Our horsemen will have to suffice," Shaffur said, nettled by Xhama's words. "The Zamzu have no cavalry."

"Nor bowmen," added Looth.

"But I do wish Helki were with us!" Ryons thought. It was Helki, with his rod, who felled the Zamzu champion, Shogg the Giant, on the way to Obann. It was Shogg's sword that Uduqu carried. But Ryons didn't think the Zamzu would be daunted when they saw it.

"Just think how scared the Thunder King will be when we defeat his Zamzu," Uduqu said. "And he's afraid of us already, or he never would have offered peace."

Jiharr stepped forward.

"I speak as a man who should have died, but lives—and that by the mercy of God," he said. "The Zamzu are big and strong and fierce as crocodiles—but also slow and proud and stupid. Did God raise me from death just so I could be eaten by the Zamzu? I don't think so. I'll stand face to face against them, while you horse pamperers break their flanks and take them in the rear." For the Zeph, horses were not for riding, but for dinner.

Chagadai grinned at him. "You'll think more of horses, brother, before we're through!" he said.

Ysbott the Snake had spent very few days of his life in towns—let alone a big, important town like Cardigal with a stone wall around it. Fires set by the enemy had gutted much of Cardigal, but by now much of it had been rebuilt. The main gate, battered into splinters, with some of the adjacent wall knocked down, had been cleared and left as a wide gap so that rubble could be carted out and loads of building material brought in. Ysbott passed through the gap early in the morning.

As noon drew near, everyone put down his work and went out to see the hanging. The new oligarch went out with guards in armor. Mothers brought out their small children, not to watch the execution, but to have a picnic by the river: it was a nice day for it. If he were a boy, Ysbott thought, he'd sneak away to see the hanging.

"They ought to hang all of those Wallekki, while they're at it," he heard a workman say. "What do we want with a lot of murdering Heathen?"

Ysbott reasoned he would find fine clothes in a fine house. It looked like half the homes in Cardigal were still charred timbers, but there were still big houses here and there.

He lurked in a ruin until it looked like he would have the street to himself. It made him edgy when he ventured into the open. "Best to get it done quickly!" he whispered to the mask.

At the first likely-looking house, he tried the door. It was locked, of course, and he was afraid to make noise breaking it down. But there was a ground-floor window that swung open to him when he tried it. He climbed in and pulled the window shut after him.

Every nerve in his body tingled. He found it hard to believe that any place could be so silent. He marveled at the furniture—even sat on a couch for a moment, to see what it was like. But he mustn't dawdle.

Parlor, kitchen, dining room—but no clothes, not downstairs. Plenty of nice things to steal, if only he had time. Alas, he didn't.

For the first time in his life, Ysbott climbed a flight of stairs. If anyone were to jump out on the landing above him, Ysbott would have fallen backward down the stairs.

He entered a room with a big bed that was like nothing he had ever seen before. Someday he would have a bed like that! But the most important thing was the two wardrobes that occupied two corners of the room. He didn't recognize them as wardrobes, but they had doors and something told him that the clothes would be inside, if they were anywhere.

He opened one and caught his breath.

Fine clothes! Beautiful clothes, just what he needed—long, soft, and brightly colored.

These were women's dresses, but Ysbott didn't know that. To him they were just the finest robes he'd ever seen. He selected a bright scarlet gown and, with some difficulty, tried it on. There was no mirror in the room, and it didn't occur to him to look for one: he barely knew what a mirror was. From what he could see of it, the robe was exactly what he wanted. He took it off and rolled it carefully into a small bundle. Resisting the temptation to take another one—someday he'd have all the robes he wanted—he went back down the stairs and let himself out the window.

"Your father is on his way to do something that I think will be dangerous," Vannett told Jack and Ellayne. She sat at the desk in Roshay Bault's office, with the children standing beside it.

"Martis will protect him," Ellayne said. She didn't know that Martis had already told her mother and father all about his career as Lord Reesh's pet assassin.

"Martis will come straight back here to warn me if Lord Chutt arrests your father," said the baroness. "But I've been thinking about this, and I'm afraid that won't be enough. Under no circumstances must that man get his hands on either of you.

"How would you like to go and stay in Lintum Forest for a while?"

Ellayne could hardly believe her ears. Was this her mother talking?

"The baron wants us to stay here with you," Jack said. Ellayne repressed an urge to kick his shin.

"I'll find secretaries to help me with the baron's messages," Vannett said. "Meanwhile, I'll be much easier in my mind if I know you're out of Chutt's reach. And it'll help your father if he knows it, too."

"Mother, we would love to go to Lintum Forest!" Ellayne said.

"But we'd miss you," added Jack—and he meant it. Every day the baroness read to them from the new book of Scripture that Queen Gurun had sent them as a present. Yes, he would miss that very much. His own mother had died while he was still a tot.

"You can come back when the danger is past," said Vannett. "You can take that little hairy creature with you, and I'll send two men as an escort. I wish we'd sent you down with Helki when he was here, but I never thought of it at the time. Do you think you can set out tomorrow morning?"

Both children nodded.

"You've made the trip before," Vannett said, "and now you're older, and the king's men have cleared the plain of slavers and brigands. You've already done more traveling than I'll ever do, and one more trip won't hurt you."

"Why don't you come with us, Baroness?" Jack said.

Vannett laughed aloud. "Heaven forbid it should ever come to that!" she said.

Later, after they'd packed their things and hunted up and down for Wytt until they found him, and made sure their own donkey, Ham, was fit to make a journey, Jack and Ellayne had time to wonder what the baroness was really thinking.

"What does she think is going to happen?" Jack said. "She must think something is going to happen, or she wouldn't send us away. But whatever might happen to us could happen to her, too. She'd be safe in Lintum Forest."

"Don't be simple," Ellayne said. "If my father's not here, then she has to be. She's the baroness."

"But what do you suppose she thinks might happen?"

They talked that question up and down, but couldn't find an answer.

CHAPTER 16

The Return of the Thunder King

It was all Ilfil could do to keep his men in line, Gallgoid noted. The hanging had unsettled them and reminded them that they were strangers in the country of their enemies. Ilfil himself had great expectations, but without his Wallekki's swords and spears, Lord Chutt would have no use for him.

"Those Wallekki are going to bear watching—depend on it," Gallgoid confided to Captain Born, when he found a chance to speak with him alone. "To them, to be hanged is the most disgraceful death a man can die. There will be hard feelings."

"Let them feel what they feel, and the devil take them!" Born said. "The closer we get to Obann City, the less those Heathen will matter to our plans." Born had spent his life doing hard soldiering in North Obann and had leaped at the chance to end his days in luxury, courtesy of Lord Chutt. He wouldn't let any number of Wallekki jeopardize that chance, thought Gallgoid. He was tough and hard, but now the soft life beckoned to him. Gallgoid doubted he could resist it.

As Born and Gallgoid spoke, Lord Chutt was in his tent

with Ilfil, trying to mollify him. The chieftain was hardly in the mood for it.

"The Obannese are shifty, slippery, and treacherous!" he complained. "All was well with us when it was just our army up on the Golden Pass. My people fear it will go ill with us in Obann City. We have a proverb about people who live in cities: crooked streets make crooked minds. There are those of us who'd just as soon you paid us our share of the gold right here and now and let us part from you in peace."

"Are you one of those, my friend?" asked Chutt.

"Faugh! I am a wiser man that that, my lord. I know that if we are not the core of your army, we can never hope to be anything better than a mass of brigands. What good is gold to us, if we can't spend it? But I tell you this, my lord—there must be no more hangings."

Chutt sighed. "I've already decided we must move on from here tomorrow, Chieftain. I won't be happy until the gold is safely stored in some strong place in the city and we're well on our way to restoring the Oligarchy.

"I'm afraid your men are going to have to get used to city life. They'll feel differently, once they learn what gold can buy them in the city. You'll be my personal troops, loyal to me as governor-general. Your men will live in houses of their own, with servants to wait on them. As their commander, you'll have a fine townhouse of your own and an estate beside the river. You'll own the finest horses—racing stock, if you like—and sleep in silken sheets. All it'll require is just a little more patience. And maybe a little more fighting, if it's necessary—although I do hope to avoid that. I daresay you'll never have had it so good."

Chutt was no scholar, but he knew what things were

most prized by a Wallekki chieftain: horses, weapons, sumptuous feasts with many guests praising his name, and, above all, the esteem of other chiefs. "You'll be the envy of every chief who lives in poverty because he didn't have the opportunity to link his future to mine," he added.

Ilfil made himself smile. "I see in you, my lord, a man who knows what he wants and who will use wisdom and subtlety to get it," he said. "By all means, let us leave this place tomorrow! My people will be easier to control when we're on the march again."

So Chutt and his gold weren't there anymore when Roshay Bault arrived at Cardigal. The baron had wanted to rush on and overtake him or, better, to reach the city first and stir up opposition.

"We ought to stop and see what Cardigal thought of him," Martis said. "We can easily get to Obann days before he can."

When Cardigal's new oligarch heard that the Baron of the Eastern Marches was in town, he invited Roshay to meet him at the newly built town hall, the old one that Roshay remembered having been destroyed by fire.

"Wait for me outside," he told Martis, "and if I come out under guard, or don't come out at all, you know what to do."

Martis nodded. "Chutt has already begun appointing oligarchs," he said. "That's bad."

Roshay had once been a guest at the house of the old oligarch, Gilvaith, and remembered Gilvaithwy as a towheaded little boy. Now the father was dead and the son governed in his place, despite the king's abolition of the Oligarchy. When Roshay reminded him of his visit years ago, Gilvaithwy said, "I'm sorry, sir, I don't remember."

They sat by themselves in a small chamber off the meeting hall. Gilvaithwy had dressed to impress him, but the baron was still in his rough traveling clothes.

"To what do we owe the honor of your visit, Councilor?"

"Councilor no more," said Roshay, "but Baron of the Eastern Marches by appointment of His Majesty the King. But you knew that, sir."

"No discourtesy intended, sir," Gilvaithwy answered, with a cold, hard smile. "But I know of no law that establishes a monarchy in Obann, so as far as I know, you're still the chief councilor of Ninneburky."

"I've only stopped here on my way to see Lord Chutt," the baron said. "And I know of no law that makes an oligarch's seat hereditary."

"I have received my appointment from the only survivor of the High Council of the Oligarchy, pending confirmation when a new High Council is elected by the oligarchs."

"Many of them raised to that rank by Lord Chutt himself and owing their position to him—plus whatever votes his gold can buy."

Gilvaithwy showed his teeth in a grin. "We aren't exactly hitting it off, are we, sir?"

"Do you reject King Ryons—the descendant of Ozias?"

"I stand by the laws that have governed Obann for centuries and have never been repealed."

"Then I would say we don't have much to talk about," the baron said.

"As you wish. But I think it would be unwise to go against the laws."

"And more unwise to go against the king!" Roshay fought to control his temper. "Or haven't you heard, my boy, how King Ryons personally delivered the city when the Heathen were on the point of taking it? And haven't you thought about where you and your people would be now, if he hadn't?"

"I could have you arrested, Councilor," Gilvaithwy said, "but I think Lord Chutt will do that when you see him."

Martis idled—or so it would have seemed, to anyone who didn't know him—by the door of an ale-house from which he could watch the front of the town hall. He nursed a cup of ale from which he sipped occasionally to keep off the heat of the afternoon.

He almost spilled it when a townsman jostled him. Muttering an apology, the man went on his way, but now Martis had a folded piece of parchment in his hand. The man had very deftly placed it there.

Waiting until the man was out of sight, Martis pretended to take the parchment from his belt. When he unfolded it, he found a letter. Feigning indifference, he read it.

"Gallgoid to Martis—

"Chutt's position is strong, but his character is weak. Advise Prester Jod to resist him. He is coming to Obann to make himself governor-general. I will work against him from within. Advise all the king's friends: use up time. Delay is better than swords."

For a moment Martis suffered a twinge of jealousy, just as if he and Gallgoid were still working for Lord Reesh, and Gallgoid had been entrusted with an important task that should have gone to him—the assassin with the knife, rather than the plotter with the poison.

"Am I still such a villain as that?" he wondered. But by now he was far enough removed from his old life that he could summon up a smile, even as his conscience rebuked him.

Roshay Bault emerged from the town hall alone and unmolested, but visibly annoyed. Martis met him on the street.

"Chutt's bought himself a loyal oligarch," said the baron, and went on to describe his meeting with Gilvaithwy. Martis let him rumble on, uninterrupted, as they rejoined their escort. Only when they were all mounted and ready to leave did he mention Gallgoid's message.

"It won't help us to catch up to Chutt," he said. "We ought to go straight on to Obann, to Prester Jod, and show him this." He handed Roshay the letter.

Roshay nodded. "I suppose we'll do better if we put our heads together," he said. He called for one of his riders. "Go back to Ninneburky and tell the baroness that we're going on to Obann to meet with Prester Jod. I'll send her further tidings when I can."

Ysbott hurried after Chutt's wagon train. The scouts paid no attention to him. To them he was just another traveler on the North River Road.

The time had come, he decided, to reveal himself to Chutt's Wallekki. That hanging in Cardigal hadn't sat well with them: he'd heard several townspeople say things like, "Look at their faces! How they'd love to cut our throats!"

Some miles out of Cardigal, Chutt made camp for the night. His great concern was to guard the gold. He parked the wagons within shouting distance of his tent and detailed several hundred men as sentries all around. Another hundred had to guard the animals: it would be a calamity if those were stolen or stampeded. That left only a few to watch the camp's perimeter—Wallekki riders who would have to be relieved at intervals. If he put any more men on guard duty, they wouldn't get enough rest to continue the journey in the morning.

Ysbott waited for the middle of the night, selecting a spot that was only thinly screened by horsemen.

He shed his rags and put on the scarlet dress, then the golden mask. It gave him a surge of confidence. It was the mask that made the Thunder King, he thought.

He waited a little longer, crouched behind a stand of inkbushes, counting the riders as they made their rounds. He estimated it was at least fifteen minutes between the appearance of each sentry. Was that enough time? But it was all the time he'd have.

He was ready. When he heard the soft clop of a horse's hooves on grass and the quiet jingle of the rider's gear, he stepped out from behind the bushes and strode forth to meet the sentry. His heart hammered in his chest. Happily, there was enough moon tonight for the rider to see him clearly—but not too clearly.

Here came the Wallekki. Ysbott raised his voice, imitating the call of a Lintum Forest dog-fox. To a foreigner it would sound like a woman getting skinned. It got the rider's attention and made him rein in his horse so he could sit and listen. He heard Ysbott coming and sat up straighter in his saddle.

At first he couldn't quite make out who or what was coming toward him, and he drew his sword. Ysbott heard it slide from the scabbard.

"Who goes there?" barked the sentry.

Ysbott kept on coming, and then the rider's body stiffened and Ysbott knew the man saw him now, with the moonlight glinting off the mask of gold.

You might think a man would laugh at the sight of another man advancing toward him in a woman's formal gown. But what would a Wallekki know of women's costumes in Obann? And the gold face of the Thunder King himself was staring at him with black holes for eyes—eyes that saw everything.

"I live!" said Ysbott, spending two of the very few words he knew of Tribe-talk.

Those two were enough. The rider gave a shriek and fell out of the saddle in a faint. The horse neighed once, then bolted. And in the dark, not far away, two other sentries cried out to their unseen comrade. Ysbott snatched off the mask and ran away, fleeing into the refuge of the night.

So he wasn't there to see two riders trot up to help their friend or to hear them gabble to each other in Wallekki. One dismounted to see to the fallen man, and the other rode off to catch the horse. But it would have surprised and gratified him had he been able to understand the language, to hear what was said when the man who'd fainted came around.

"Affad, what happened?"

"The Thunder King! He lives!"

"Of course he lives. He cannot die."

"No, no—he is here! I saw him! And he spoke to me. To me!"

"What are you saying? Have you gone mad?"

"Wullah! I saw him! He came out of the night, out of nowhere. Right in front of me! And he said, 'I live.' O, my mother! We are lost!" He wailed like an infant.

The other rider came back with the horse, which hadn't gone far. "What's all this trouble?" he said.

"Affad fell asleep in the saddle and had a scary dream."

"I tell you it was no dream!" cried Affad. "I have seen the Thunder King—he's here! He's watching us. I have heard him speak. It was no dream—I swear it by my father's head!"

No Wallekki swears this oath lightly. The two abruptly ceased their mocking.

"Can you ride, Affad? You must tell this to Chief Ilfil."

"Who will gut you for it," muttered the other.

CHAPTER 17

A Battle by the Lake

Gurun's personal bodyguard needed comforting.

They were Blays, eighteen of them, squat, solid little men from far out in the East. They were all that remained of hundreds of their countrymen forced by the Thunder King to join the invasion of Obann—a place they'd never heard of, at the ends of the earth. Gurun met them in the wilderness and they took her for their queen, because the Thunder King had taken away their gods and they thought this tall, fair girl might be able to stand between them and the wrath of Obann's god.

At the time, theirs was an act of desperation. But now their head man, Shingis, sat among King Ryons' chieftains; and strange to say, the king's own bodyguard, the Ghols, the Blays' hereditary enemies in the East, were now their closest friends. And it would have mortified both Ryons and Gurun to hear their devoted warriors gossiping about when the two of them would marry.

"It's too bad, my queen," said Shingis, an intelligent man who'd practiced hard and mastered Obannese and Tribe-talk, "but we're afraid to fight the Zamzu. They eat people. When we were in the big army, we saw them do it many times. And yet we would be ashamed to hang back from any battle. We all feel like there is a shadow on our souls."

"Have you not yet learned that God protects us?" Gurun answered. "Not one man in this army would be standing here today, alive, without that protection. He would not withdraw it from us now."

"Even so, my queen, it would be good for us if you prayed a special prayer with us, like you used to, when we first knew you and didn't know much else."

Gurun was taller than any of the Blays. She smiled down at them.

"I thought you understood by now that God hears your prayers as readily as mine. He is All-Father, and we are all his children."

"Oh, we do!" said Shingis. "But sometimes it's hard for us to understand a God like that. We want you to pray for us today, and we will all pray with you."

So Gurun led them in a prayer, and they were comforted.

"We don't have far to go to reach Kara Karram," she said, after the prayer. She saw tears in the eyes of several of the Blays; they stirred her heart. What were they but peaceful villagers and farmers—not so different from her own people—who'd been swept up in great events too big for them to comprehend? "A storm brought me down from the north, from an island that not one person in Obann had ever heard of. I know how hard this has been for you; it's hard for me, too. My home is far away, like yours, and I miss it and long for it as you long for yours.

"Sometimes it seems like a dream, that God has chosen me and brought me to all these strange and distant countries in His service—just as He has chosen you. Sometimes it's like staring up at the face of a great cliff and thinking it might fall down on me. It's hard, but it's also a thing that I wouldn't give up—not for anything. So I have no doubt at all that you and I will stand before Kara Karram and do God's will."

By the northernmost tip of Lake Urmio was a narrow place where the hills came down almost to the water, as if to soak their feet in it. There the Zamzu waited, blocking the road with their bodies. Looth's scouts had already looked down on them from the heights.

"They are fools," the Attakott chief reported, "to think we'll throw ourselves against them and be crushed."

"They're like a cork in a bottle, eh?" Shaffur said. "I marvel that they had no guards posted on the hills. How many of them, Looth?"

"Enough to fill the gap."

Looth was more interested in something else—an ancient structure that crowned the highest hill.

"The top is broken off," he said, "and what's left of it is very strange. I would say the top was burned off, somehow: all the rest is scorched. The strange thing about it is, it looks like it was all carved out of one single great stone—maybe carved out of the rock that lay beneath the earth. How that could be done, who knows? It must be very old. Its walls are thicker than a man is tall, and every line of them is exceedingly straight. There are many cracks in it, though; and inside some of the cracks, you can see the remains of metal rods, all rusted. How they got those into the rock, I don't know. Maybe by magic."

Of them all, only Obst had ever seen such things before.

"It seems you've discovered the ruins of one of Obann's

outposts, burned up in the Day of Fire long ago," he said. "The Empire reached all the way out here to these lakes. But it wasn't magic that built such places, but arts and skills that men have forgotten since those days—that, and pride that made them blind to God's displeasure."

"All very interesting," Shaffur said, "but how are we to dispose of those Zamzu?"

"Can our horses climb those hills, Looth?"

"Yes—if they start from here, where the ground is not so steep. We know the way."

Chagadai smiled. "Then it ought to be easy to send horsemen around to take them in the rear, while archers on the slopes rain arrows on them, and the rest of us press them from the front. It doesn't seem the Zamzu have much generalship."

"They're used to crushing their enemies with clubs, by main force and terror," said Jiharr the Zephite. "They don't bother much with tactics—not when some armies run away at the very sight of them."

Ryons listened, dismayed by the thought that some of his men would die in yet another battle. They were few enough already. And if they did get past the Zamzu, what would the Thunder King have prepared for them at Kara Karram?

"I warn you all," said Ghur Manyan, "the Zamzu never run from battle, nor do they stop fighting until all their enemies are slain or else they're all slain themselves. Even if we win, the cost will be high."

"If they do not run," said Xhama, "then we shall kill them all."

Singing the anthem so that it echoed in the hills, with the waters of the lake shining on their right, the foot soldiers of King Ryons' army approached the narrow passage where the Zamzu awaited them: the Hosa in the front line with their big shields scrubbed a dazzling white, and behind them, under the command of Uduqu, the Griffs, Zephites, and the Dahai from the islands in the lake. The Wallekki were already up in the hills, out of sight and silent. You couldn't see the Attakotts or the Ghols, either, but they were up there, too.

Riding beside Gurun, behind the line of battle, Ryons saw the Zamzu packed in a solid mass between the water and the hills. They were all big men, armed with clubs and maces.

The Blays clustered around Gurun, busily fitting round stones to the pockets of their slings. They would move up to the front line when they came within range. Their accuracy, Gurun assured the king, was something to behold—"Not that they'll even have a chance to miss," she added, "with so many men in such a crowd."

"If only I could stop it!" Ryons thought. What if the Zamzu charged before his cavalry could come down from the hills? Could even the Hosa hold them back?

Beside Ryons' horse, Cavall howled once, adding to the din of the anthem. Behind him, Perkin had both hands on Baby's leash. "I won't be able to hold him, Your Majesty, once the fighting starts!" he gasped.

Angel the hawk flew overhead, round and round in circles.

And then—Ryons could just barely see him—a man

came running and stumbling down the slopes as fast as he could without falling. All the Zamzu turned at once to watch him. Straight into their midst he ran, flailing his arms.

And by twos and threes, and fours and fives, the Zamzu turned and ran.

"Come back here, you cowards!" roared Uduqu, brandishing the giant's sword.

"So they did have at least once scout up there, after all," said Gurun, "and it seems he has advised them of their peril."

"Look at them go!" cried Shingis. "I never knew Zamzu could run so fast!"

It was a stampede. Those few men who fell were trampled by the rest; no one stopped to help them up. A great cloud of dust rose over them. Ryons watched in amazement as, for the first time in human memory, the Zamzu ran from battle.

"Steady! Steady there!" Uduqu bellowed. "Xhama, hold your men—no chasing!" Xhama raised his spear to show that he'd heard the command. The black warriors continued their advance, but never broke into a run, maintaining the good order of their formation. There was no room for anyone else to get around them.

Looth and his men rose up from concealment and loosed some arrows, but not many. The Zamzu were already getting out of range. Anyone could see that the Wallekki were still up in the hills and unable to give chase. When they did come down, Shaffur held them back. As long as they were running, he wouldn't provoke the Zamzu to turn and fight.

From where Ryons sat, the enemy was already out of sight. He let out his breath in a long sigh.

"What got into them?" he wondered. "Ghur said they never run away."

"I think there must be fewer men, these days, who are willing to stand fast and die for the Thunder King," said Gurun.

High up in the sky, Angel followed the fleeing Zamzu. Before they stopped running, she flew back to King Ryons.

It seemed to both Jack and Ellayne like a lifetime ago, the first time they'd set out across the plains, just the two of them, on their journey to Bell Mountain. They'd each grown several inches since then, and it was getting much harder to disguise Ellayne as a boy. This time they didn't bother to try—not with two armed men to protect them. The baroness would have lent them each a horse, too. "Not much point in walking all that way," she had said.

"I get saddle sores!" Ellayne confided in her mother. Jack just shrugged and said they were used to walking. "We can ride behind the soldiers if we get too tired," he said.

Their donkey, Ham, who'd been to Bell Mountain with them, came along to carry their spare clothes and camping gear—not a very heavy load. And Wytt, when he wasn't perched atop Ham's pack to sniff the air, scampered on ahead, catching insects for himself and finding birds' eggs for the humans. The two riders, Dan and Otha, needed a couple of days to get used to Wytt's company: Obann's folklore is full of tales of the Little People who can put a hex on a man and lure him into destruction. But Wytt didn't know any of those stories.

The trek would have seemed more like a holiday if the children hadn't known their father was riding into danger. They were old enough now to find that hard to forget. Still, they'd had some good times in Lintum Forest, and they had friends at Carbonek: they were happy to be going there.

"I'd love to see the knuckle-bears again," Ellayne said, as they hiked along. "But they don't like to show themselves, Obst says. They're mighty shy for such big animals."

"Obst says there aren't many of them," Jack said. "What I don't want to see are any of those giant birds."

But on the second day out, late in the afternoon, they caught a glimpse of one. It watched them from a distance and didn't come any closer. The two grown men could hardly believe their eyes.

"It's taller than a horse!" said Otha.

"I'm glad there are two of us with spears," Dan said. "I wouldn't give much for my chances if I had to face a monster like that on my own."

The southern plain was dotted with large, eroded hills that weren't hills at all, but the remains of Obann's ancient cities destroyed in the Day of Fire. Their first time out, Ellayne and Jack had sometimes camped on top of them. That was how they'd met Wytt: the ruined cities were the Omahs' favorite habitat. But they didn't think it would be wise to camp there with Dan and Otha. If one Omah could unsettle them, what would it do to their courage to meet a hundred Omah?

"It's in the Scriptures," Ellayne said. "God gave those places to the Omah."

"You fellows wouldn't like it up there," said Jack. "Sometimes you'll find great big heaps of dead men's bones. We did."

"Bones can't hurt us," Otha said, "but I wouldn't like to wake up some night with a lot of those little people crawling over me!"

"They wouldn't do that," Ellayne said. "They've always been friendly to Jack and me. The old stories about them are mostly a lot of bosh."

"We wouldn't know about that," Dan said. So they camped each night on low ground, at places selected by Wytt, who always knew where to find good water. The men made big campfires to keep beasts away.

It took just five days to come within sight of Lintum Forest. Two of the king's Abnak scouts came out to meet them. One was a warrior named Bandy, whom they'd met before.

"King Ryons' friends!" he said. "You are welcome, but too bad the king not here. You want to come to Carbonek?"

"That's why we're here," Jack said. "How are things at the castle?"

"Right-o good enough," said the Abnak, "but better when the king comes home. You heard anything of him?"

"We saw him when he passed through Ninneburky," Ellayne said, "and from there he went up the mountains and crossed into the East, by way of the Golden Pass. Nothing since! We miss him, too."

"Well, Helki be plenty glad to see you," Bandy said, "and Fnaa and Jandra, too. Fnaa's mother, she married to Trout now."

They all camped together that night under the eaves of the forest. In the morning Dan and Otha turned back to Ninneburky, and Jack and Ellayne, guided by the Abnaks, went on to Carbonek.

"Have you heard any news from Obann City?" Ellayne asked. Roshay Bault must be there by now, she thought.

"No news from anywhere," said Bandy, with a frown.

"But holy man Jod, he send word to us if anything go wrong." His frown turned into a bright smile. "Then we go to put it right!" he said.

CHAPTER 18

How Gallgoid Used a Gift from God

Lord Chutt's camp was troubled. Indeed, it was all Chief Ilfil could do to keep his men from breaking into mutiny.

"This is bad," he admitted. He'd had to clout some of his men into silence. "One of my people swears he saw King Thunder himself—in the flesh—and the rest are terrified."

"Oh, but that's impossible!" Chutt said. But he knew the Wallekki were famous for their superstitious souls.

"It's not the kind of thing any of us would lie about."

"No, of course not, but still—" Chutt paused. Gallgoid, better than anyone else, could have told him that there was no Thunder King, that it was all a pretense by the mardars: a colossal hoax by which they'd enslaved whole nations. But Lord Chutt didn't know that. He'd been in the north when Gallgoid had made his discovery known to King Ryons' advisers.

"It makes no sense!" Chutt argued. "If the Thunder King were going to come back from the dead—"

"He cannot die," Ilfil interrupted.

"Well, then, back from wherever he was! Buried under the ruins of his golden hall, I'd say. But if he were going to show himself to you Wallekki," Chutt said, "why here? Why wouldn't he appear at the top of the pass, where all the gold was? Why wait until we got all this way down here, practically to Obann?"

"How in the world would I know?" Ilfil cried. "Am I a mardar, to know the mind of the god?"

Chutt put out his hands, but didn't touch the chieftain. Ilfil was getting himself into a state and needed calming.

"My friend, my chieftain—please!" Chutt spoke soothingly. "We are men of the world, you and I. We've been to many faraway places and seen many things. We aren't easily frightened. Come, now—do you truly believe, with all your heart and mind, that the Thunder King is here? Here in Obann, wandering around all by himself—alone? Are you thoroughly convinced of that?"

Ilfil snorted. He shook he head. If it was true, thought Chutt—if Ilfil believed it to be true—then he might easily believe he had betrayed his fierce and unforgiving lord, and all his dreams of acquiring wealth and honors in Obann, well, those would have to be abandoned, and quickly. Chutt perceived the chief's dilemma. Ilfil didn't want it to be true. Right down to the bottom of his boots, he didn't want it to be true.

"O, Chutt," he said, "no man of the Wallekki would ever dare to invent a lie like this. And yet a man might be deluded in his mind.

"You know nothing of the fear engendered by the Thunder King—years and years of it! His mardars took away our gods. Through the mardars, he made our wells go bad. Our flocks dwindled. Any man who spoke against him died. There was no defense. By magic and terror and starvation, we were forced to obedience.

"Do you think so much fear can be dissolved? It has deep roots! We Wallekki go into battle cheerfully, no matter what the odds. But we never found a way to fight against King Thunder."

"But how could he be here?" Chutt said. "If I had asked you this afternoon, 'Where is the Thunder King,' you would have said, 'In Kara Karram, in the midst of his mardars and his slaves.' He never walks alone. So how could he be here? Have you ever heard of him going anywhere alone?"

"No—he has never done that," Ilfil said. "Why should he, when he has countless hosts of men to do his bidding?"

"Then in all likelihood he hasn't done it now," said Chutt. "Who knows what this man of yours has seen, or thinks he's seen? The thing for us to do is to get on to Obann City with all speed, which we will do as soon as we break camp tomorrow. Indeed, the night is so far gone already, we may as well get started now. We'll get away from this place, Ilfil. There may be something wrong with it."

"I'll give the order to my people," Ilfil said. "You are a man of wisdom, my lord."

"God has given us a gift," thought Gallgoid. "And how are we to use it?"

He spoke Wallekki fluently, a fact that he'd concealed so far. As he moved about the camp, he soon learned why none of the Wallekki was sleeping anymore.

Someone claimed he'd seen the Thunder King. To Gallgoid that could only mean one thing: someone had found the golden mask and was wearing it. Someone in Chutt's army must have found it while they were digging up the hall and somehow managed to keep it a secret—until now. "That's a man I'd like to meet!" Gallgoid said to himself.

The man with the mask, he reasoned, would seek the overthrow of Chutt and all his officers so that he could take possession of the gold. He would have to act before the army reached Obann. He would turn the Wallekki against the Obannese, and against their own chief who'd supported Chutt. It would be a bloody business.

By now the whole camp was astir, Wallekki and Obannese alike, striking their tents, hitching oxen and horses to the wagons. Ilfil was like a man possessed, rushing here and there, shouting orders, and lashing at warriors with his quirt.

Gallgoid hastened to Chutt's tent, which was already being taken down.

"My lord, what's this?" he asked.

"We're moving out, Gallgoid. No time to explain!" Chutt said. "But ride with me, once we're under way. I want your advice."

"And you shall have it, my lord," said Gallgoid. But it won't be good advice, he added to himself.

The wagon train was on the move by the grey light of dawn. By then Ilfil was hoarse from threatening and cursing. Born and his spearmen, who had as yet received no explanation of the tumult among the Wallekki, nor any reason for starting the caravan before the sun was up, kept close together as they marched. Let just one alarm be given, Gallgoid thought, and those spears would be at the throats of the Wallekki.

He rode beside Chutt and had to strain to hear, because the oligarch wouldn't raise his voice and the wagons behind them made a racket.

"I don't want the men to overhear," Chutt said—not that he was able to explain what had happened, or make any sense of it, or even be sure that it had happened at all. "But what are we to do, Gallgoid? I need Ilfil and his men to get the gold safely to the city. Once there, they'll have no option but to be personally loyal to me. But first I need them kept under control, and only Ilfil can do that. This rumor—this foolishness!—of the Thunder King walking around our camp by night: I can only believe it's a delusion. But it's pushing the Wallekki into panic. I'm not sure Ilfil will be able to control it. And all because of the feverish prattlings of just one man! No one else saw anything, Ilfil says."

"My lord," said Gallgoid, "these men will surely mutiny before we reach the city. You must get rid of them before that happens."

"Yes, that thought has crossed my mind," Chutt said—a mind, thought Gallgoid, sharp but not deep. "But how do I get rid of them? Ilfil will never leave the gold. I wish I could send them into a battle, but there's no one for them to fight but my own infantry."

"Nevertheless, my lord, you must send them away. Ilfil may not like it, but I think his men would be glad of something else to do—especially something that would put some miles between them and their Thunder King."

"You'd think the miles between here and the Golden Pass should have been enough!" Chutt said. "They think he's a god—and how do you run away from a god? Oh, it's all such superstitious nonsense!"

"Lord, tell them you've received a message that King Ryons' forces are somewhere in the area, looking to intercept us before we can get to the city," Gallgoid said. "By all accounts, they have an army in Lintum Forest. Tell Ilfil that that army is on the move. And meanwhile, send messages to all the towns along the river, and to the city, asking them to reinforce us with militia."

Chutt gave that some thought.

"Let's try it," he said. "If nothing else, your plan will buy us some time. Only—" he hesitated, then added, "only if it wasn't the Thunder King that the sentry saw last night, then what was it? What could it have been?"

"A figment of the man's imagination—who knows?" Gallgoid said. "But I do know that imaginary fears can be every bit as potent as real ones."

Chutt waited until sunup to summon Ilfil. The chieftain looked weary, Gallgoid thought, but too wrought-up to rest.

"Are your people fit for duty, Ilfil?"

"They obey me still, my lord. If not, they get a taste of this." Ilfil shook his quirt.

"I hope so," said Chutt, "because now we have need of them. A report has reached me that a force serving the false king of Obann has come out of Lintum Forest, and by dint of forced marching, they mean to get between us and the city, and to take the gold. They're somewhere south of the river, and they're all on foot—no cavalry. Even so, they're faster than our wagons."

"How many?" Ilfil snapped.

"A thousand, at least. Maybe as many as two thousand. Mostly Abnaks, with some Lintum foresters. That's all we've been told," Chutt said. He and Gallgoid had rehearsed the story. “Your horsemen must defeat them if you can. If not, harass them, slow them down, and don’t let them get across the river.”

“And you’ll march on without us?”

“Chieftain, your riders are swift. You’ll easily rejoin us before we reach the city. A good fight will brace up the men’s courage and take their minds off the Thunder King. And besides,” Chutt added, “King Ryons is your king’s great enemy. If your king is watching, he’ll be pleased when you shatter Ryons’ army.”

“If there is an army!” Ilfil said.

“Chieftain, if your fighting men won’t fight, then I don’t know what to say. We can’t let anyone get between us and the city. If the city forces join with them, then we’ll be very badly outnumbered. And we’ll lose the gold that’s cost us so much labor—and our lives, too, probably. There are those in the city who would jump at the chance to destroy us. I’d send Born’s spearmen, too, only speed is of the essence and they can’t keep up with you.”

Ilfil pondered the order for a long moment—long enough for Chutt to get uneasy.

“I’ll do it, my lord,” he said. “But if we come back without a fight, our partnership is at an end.”

“I hope not,” said Chutt. “I prize your friendship, Chieftain. Without your warriors and their loyalty, our whole enterprise would be undone.”

Within the hour, two thousand Wallekki rode off in a cloud of dust to seek the nearest ford across the river. Chutt lost no time ordering Born to send out for reinforcements.

“I knew it would come to this,” said Born.

And Gallgoid was content. Who knew what the Wallekki would get up to on their own? But Chutt needed them, and now he wouldn't have them. And to the people of the city, it would look like Chutt had sent out raiders. That would damage his standing and give his supporters second thoughts.

CHAPTER 19

Skipping Stones

Since Ryons' army had recaptured Silvertown, peace reigned in the hills. Even with his wife and child, Hlah made good time on his journey back to his homeland.

Their reunion with their old friend Sunfish at Foxblood's encampment was a merry one. The First Prester wept for joy when little Wulf ran to him with outstretched arms.

"He remembers me!" Orth said, as he picked up the babe and kissed him. "I never thought he would."

"You aren't an easy person to forget," said May. Then it was her turn to kiss him, and then Hlah's.

"You are welcome, my son!" Orth said, beaming at the young man. "I really do think of you as my son, you know—a son begotten not of the flesh, but in the faith. And yet at one time, when we first met, I was like a son to you, a helpless little child who didn't know anything—not even my own name. I hope you've come to stay. There's much work to be done."

Orth didn't explain what he meant by work until they'd had their supper, stewed squirrel with wild onions, in Chief Foxblood's birchbark wigwam. Foxblood himself said a prayer of thanks over the food. "A miracle!" Hlah thought: an Abnak man giving thanks to God. Only after they were all well-fed and well-rested did Orth speak of his plans.

"Very soon, Hlah, I'll have to go east, to the Fazzan in the valley of the Green Snake River, to preach among that nation. Their chiefs have requested it, and so I'll go.

"Meanwhile, there are men on their way here from Obann with copies of the Books and a few young scholars to help with the teaching. If you're willing, I wish to ordain you a reciter, by the ancient custom of laying on of hands, with all the Abnaks here to witness it, so that you may carry on the work of bringing this people to the Lord."

"My lord First Prester! I'm a very poor reader, and an even worse reciter!" said Hlah.

"You'll get better with practice, my son. There is no doubt in my mind that this is why God brought the two of us together in the first place."

May interrupted. "But isn't that country very far away?" she cried. "And won't it be very dangerous for you to go there?"

"He'll be escorted by one hundred of my bravest warriors," Foxblood said, "and each of them a servant of God. There might be some fighting when they get there. Having lost the Abnaks, the Thunder King will try to keep the Fazzan under his yoke. But if God fights for them as He fights for us, Fazzan will soon be free."

"But we came here to be with Sunfish!" May said.

"I won't stay away for long," Orth said. He had no memory of how May used to take care of him when he was a poor witless madman, but Hlah had told him all about it. These two, with their little son, were the people he loved most in all the world. "Besides, the Abnaks would only come and get me if I stayed too long." Foxblood laughed at that and said, "Too right!"

"Nevertheless," said Orth, "I must go where God calls me. It's been thousands of years since anything like this has happened! We are living in a very special time, my friends, and being called to a very special purpose. The spirit of the Lord is reaching out to whole new nations, to bring them into His family. We mustn't flinch from any hardship it entails."

"Et-taa-naa-qiqu says we Abnaks must all learn to read and write," Foxblood said, "so that we can learn God's word and pass it on to others. Imagine that!" He grinned at Orth. "This man won't forget what a time he had, just teaching me to write my own name."

"We'll need many Abnaks to be teachers of the Abnaks," Orth said. "Obann will send some help, but it's not a work that can be left up to Obannese. The people will need teachers who understand them and their ways."

"And you rely on me to start all this?" said Hlah. "But I'll be surprised if anyone will listen to me!"

"They will," said Foxblood. "They will."

The night following the rout of the Zamzu, Obst, stretching his legs, found Chief Shaffur all alone beside the lake, kicking pebbles into the water.

"Are you well, Chieftain?"

"Hah! Not much of a battle today, was it?" Shaffur said. "Enemy gone before we could ride down from the high ground."

"You're disappointed?"

"No—I can't say that. We made the Zamzu run, and no one ever did that before. There's something to be said for winning a battle without having to fight it."

"But something's weighing on your mind," Obst said. "What troubles you?"

"That's told easily enough," Shaffur said. He kicked another stone. "Simply put, it's this.

"At the end of our journey, we'll find ourselves looking up at a mighty fortress on a cliff. Our main strength is in horsemen, but what good will cavalry be in such a place? We have no siege equipment, and even if we did, how could we get it up the cliff? And the Thunder King has all the nations of the East from which to draw his forces."

He frowned. "I was there," he said, "the day our mardar would have sacrificed a slave to read the future in his entrails. And you forbade him to do it, and God struck him dead, right before our eyes. That slave is now our king, and you're our teacher.

"But to have come all that way, from that moment on, just to put ourselves in a position in which our very survival—let alone victory!—is plainly impossible: well, what need I to say?"

Obst hadn't thought along those lines. He didn't know how to answer.

"There won't be any miracle this time, Teacher—no great beast to scatter the enemy's armies," Shaffur said. "A thing like that can only happen once. I say again, we ask too much of God! And I dare to say, He asks too much of us."

Obst picked up a flat stone and skipped it on the surface of the water—a thing he hadn't done since he was a boy.

"How did you do that?" Shaffur snapped.

"What? Oh, you mean the stone?" Suddenly it seemed a very silly thing to have done. But Shaffur wanted to know how he did it, so he picked up another stone and showed him. "Like this." And the stone hopped three or four times before it sank. "I didn't know I'd remembered how to do that."

Shaffur threw a stone, but it didn't skip. Obst showed him again, and this time the chieftain managed it. A grin broke through his black beard.

"Well, well!" he said.

"Chieftain," said Obst, "we've been through many impossible situations. When I defied the mardar, it was just something that I couldn't help doing. I loved the boy and I had to save him. I couldn't do otherwise; it just came out. I never thought the man would fall down dead. And when he did, if my memory is right, I fainted."

"So you did. For a moment we all thought you were dead, too."

"Ryons and I both should have died that day, but we didn't. And I suppose what I want to say to you is that the hand of God has been upon us ever since and that we have no reason to believe He will withdraw it now. I don't know how He will empower us to take the fortress, but I believe with all my heart He will."

"I wish I could believe it," Shaffur said.

"But you will follow the king there, regardless?"

"I will."

"Then I don't see what more God will ask of you, my lord," said Obst.

"Just go on and on, whether it's impossible or not?"

"I'd say so. What else can we do? We have only a little ways to go, and then we'll get there. And when we do, a righteous and almighty God will decide what happens next."

Shaffur picked up another stone and slung it at the lake. This one skipped five times.

"Ha! I've mastered it!" He turned to Obst and smiled. "And you have mastered me, old man. I'm ready to go on, cliff or no cliff, fort or no fort. Someone has to do it, and as we've come so far already, it may as well be us.

"Now, let's see if you can beat my stone!"

CHAPTER 20

A Holy Place

When the Wallekki suddenly galloped off before the sun was over the horizon, Ysbott's heart stopped. If the sight hadn't paralyzed him on the spot, he might have run after them. But they would have only left him in the dust.

Ysbott didn't dare enter Lord Chutt's camp, but he crept close enough to it to know he'd caused a commotion. When they broke camp and went on the march while it was yet dark, Ysbott followed at a safe distance. But then the Wallekki went tearing off to the south, and all he could do was stand there with his mouth open.

The mask and the dress were safe inside the burlap sack, and no one would take Ysbott for anything but a poor gadabout trying to find work. Obann's roads were full of people displaced and impoverished by war. This enabled him, around midday, to pass time with a few of the Obannese spearmen when the wagon train halted for an hour's rest.

"What got into those Heathen that they all rode off like a host of devils was chasing them?" Ysbott asked. "I was sleeping in a ditch, and they woke me when they thundered past. If I hadn't been in a ditch, they would have run me down."

"They think their Thunder King is after 'em!" laughed one of the soldiers. "One of them saw a spook, so now they all see spooks. Good riddance!"

"They've deserted?" cried Ysbott. He couldn't suppress a note of panic in what should have been a casual question, and it made the soldiers take a closer look at him. He laughed nervously and tried to shrug it off. "I mean," he added, "aren't they bound to make a lot of trouble, running all around the countryside?"

"Who knows?" said a spearman. "All we've got to do is get these wagons to the city—"

"Loose lips!" a man interrupted, and the speaker said no more.

Ysbott cadged a ration from the men and went his way, at a loss for what to do. He couldn't possibly catch up to the Wallekki, and the Obannese would only arrest him if he tried to make them think he was the Thunder King.

"Think, think, think!" he goaded himself. But wise thought was slow in coming.

Roshay Bault and Martis were already at the city, conferring with Prester Jod at his townhouse.

"Most of the surviving oligarchs are here by now," Jod told them, "waiting for Chutt to arrive with the gold. He's sure to convene an assembly and proclaim the restoration of the Oligarchy. But first he'll take some time to buy their votes."

"And buy them he will," Roshay said. "If only the king were here with his army! And the First Prester, too."

"He will propose the rebuilding of the Temple," Jod said, "and I'm afraid that will win the people to his side. We need to discuss this with General Hennen."

"If Hennen and his men hold out for King Ryons, there may be fighting in the city," Roshay said. "What's Hennen's strength?"

"Two thousand spears, at most. But some of them will go over to Lord Chutt and the oligarchs."

"Civil war," said Martis. "Sir, you'd better go back to Durmurot before Chutt comes here."

"I am the First Prester's vicar, and here I stay," Jod said. "But you, Baron, had best return to Ninneburky and do what you can to hold the eastern reaches of the river for King Ryons."

Roshay's mustache bristled. "I ran away from Chutt at the Golden Pass," he said. "I wouldn't like to run from him again."

"The Baron of the Eastern Marches ought to hold the Eastern Marches," said Jod, smiling as he said it. "God has not been pleased with the City of Obann, where Judge Tombo hanged the prophets and the people consented to it. First the Temple, then the Palace: the Lord has turned them into mountains of rubble for everyone to see, every day. He is taking away this city's pride and glory piece by piece. Someday the whole place will lie in ruins, just like the ruins of Old Obann across the river."

Martis nodded. He'd been in what was left of the Old City. With Ellayne and Jack he was in the cellar beneath the cellar of the Empire Temple, where King Ozias hid the Lost Book of Scripture, written in his own hand. It was not a place Martis would ever like to see again.

"What will you do, Prester, when Chutt tries to bring back the Oligarchy?" Roshay asked. "Do you have a plan?"

"I'll oppose him, of course. Beyond that, no, I have no

plan," Jod said. "Gallgoid has advised us to play for time. There are many ways of doing that.

"Tonight I have called for an assembly of all the people, gathered in High Market Square, to pray for King Ryons' safe return. They must be reminded that their king has gone into grave peril for their sakes. We shall pray for our First Prester, too, who labors to bring peace. It may be God will spare this city, after all, because it is precious to His servants."

"The people won't remember anything else, once they clap their eyes on Chutt's gold," Roshay said. "If only Hennen had more men! He might be able to keep the gold out of the city."

"Not without a fight," Martis said. "And Chutt's force is the stronger."

"Whatever we decide to do," Jod said, "we must not spill the blood of our own countrymen."

"It still might come to that," said the baron.

In Lintum Forest, Fnaa showed Jack and Ellayne his favorite place for catching lizards.

"Trout's been teaching me how to find my way around the woods," he said, "so I'm not likely to get lost. I've learned a few things from Helki, too. If you got lost, I could probably find you and bring you back to Carbonek."

He led them cunningly through thick and thorny berry patches, finding paths they wouldn't have found on their own, and around low spots where water seeped into the leaf litter and turned it into sticky black muck. "He's right," Jack thought, "we'd never find our way back through all this." It only took some twenty minutes to get there, but by the time they did, the castle and the settlement seemed miles away. Gnats swarmed all around them, but Fnaa had learned which plant juices to rub on their skins to keep the insects from biting.

Then the underbrush thinned out, and the sun shone through the trees, and they were there.

"Is this a shrine?" said Ellayne, when they saw it.

"Helki thinks so, but he says Obst would know for sure," Fnaa said.

A great grey stone stood overlooking a quiet little pond with mossy banks and pale green peace-pipe plants in clusters all around it. Lichen dappled the stone, but you could still see, almost worn away, the figure of a man carved in relief, with some indistinct lines of writing incised in the rock below the man's feet. His face was gone, but in one of his two upraised hands you could still make out the remnant of a shepherd's crook—Obann's most ancient symbol of royalty.

A few green lizards, as bright as living jewels, basked in a sunny spot above the man's head.

"I don't suppose you can read this writing, can you?" Fnaa asked.

Ellayne and Jack moved up for a closer look, Ellayne tracing some of the letters with a finger.

"We can't read it," she said. "These are old letters that people don't use anymore." She almost added that they'd seen a stone very much like this one on the shoulder of Bell Mountain, erected by Ozias and his men on their way to the summit. Obst was with them then, and he could read the writing on the stone.

"Whoever this is," Jack said, "he was a king. That's why he has a crook in his hand."

"I thought he was a shepherd," Fnaa said.

"Don't be silly," Ellayne said. "Nobody would put up a shrine to a shepherd. The crook means he's a king."

"Which one, though? Hasn't Obann had a lot of kings?"

"But only King Ozias was born in Lintum Forest," Jack said. "It must be him."

A feeling of reverence came over them. Ozias was the last anointed king of Obann, and a prophet—a king loved and blessed by God. And he was King Ryons' ancestor. Suddenly it seemed very childish to come here just to play with lizards.

"They ought to make a path to this place," Jack said, careful not to raise his voice, "so people could come here to pray."

"Is it a holy place, then?" Fnaa said. "Ought we to pray to King Ozias?"

"Of course not!" Ellayne said. "You only pray to God. Still, it was Ozias who wrote most of the Sacred Songs." That made her think of her mother in the parlor, reading the Scriptures from the book Queen Gurun sent them. It brought a lump to her throat.

"I wonder if the whole forest is a holy place," said Jack.

And Ryons, who had supped with the ancient kings of Obann one night in the forest, could have told them that it was.

But Ryons wasn't there.

CHAPTER 21

A Wagonload of Melons

Wytt wasn't there, either. He was up in the topmost branch of the tallest tree for miles around and had no time for chasing lizards.

Today it was birds that claimed his interest. Not the ordinary tribes of blue bawns, red cappies, jays, crows, and goldies that inhabited the forest: he didn't care about them. Jandra's toothed bird hissed and tried to bite him today, but he didn't care for that, either. He knew where there was a whole nest of them; and unlike a human being, he never asked why such bizarre creatures were now appearing in his world.

If you could have climbed up to where Wytt sat, you would have seen all Obann laid out like a map unrolled on a table. There stood the mountains like a purple wall, hiding the countries of the East. There rolled the plains in waves of green and amber. But Lintum Forest was dark green here and a bright green there. From up this high, distances might fool you. Places that were many miles away seemed invitingly near, just an afternoon's hike. And of course you couldn't see all of Obann, because God had made the world a sphere and you could never see but a little piece of it at once, thanks to the curvature of the surface.

But Wytt was watching birds.

He saw a couple of them close-up yesterday, resting on a tree—birds that didn't belong in Lintum Forest or anywhere else west of the mountains. They were robin-sized, a muted orange with black wings and little crests atop their heads. The birds he'd seen in the little woods by Ninneburky had come from the west slope of the mountains, from the Golden Pass; but these orange-and-black birds had come from farther away than that—from so far away, indeed, that Wytt understood nothing of their speech.

What were they doing here? They were very tired, he perceived that much. And some small residue of fear clung to them: he'd never seen any birds as fidgety as these. When he tried to communicate with them, they stared at him as if he were a wild cat about to pounce, and hastily flew out of sight.

From high up in the trees Wytt saw more birds flying in from the east—not in any great flocks such as a human being might notice, but singly, by twos and threes, no more. By their style of flight he recognized that these were strange birds, too: foreigners.

Birds, he knew, don't make such long journeys—out of season, no less—without good reason. It reminded him of the mice and insects that had abandoned the Palace of Obann before it was destroyed and the spiders in the Palace that had woven crazy webs.

It didn't occur to him to mention this to Ellayne or Jack. They wouldn't understand. When it came to the world around them, they were only a little more observant than tree stumps. He would have to find some of the Forest Omah and see what they thought. There were quite a few of them around the castle, guarding it as a favor to Helki, but the settlers very seldom saw them.

Far to the east, as a new day dawned, Angel was aloft again.

Something drew her to Kara Karram, the great nest on the cliff beside the water. Her king was determined to go there, so Angel went, too—a scout who had no means of reporting what she saw. Cavall, who had good sense for a dog, understood only a tiny fraction of what Angel had to tell. Wytt would have understood much more.

Today she could not bring herself to fly directly over the fortress. It was nothing she could hear or smell, nothing for even a hawk's keen eyes to see. Nevertheless, there was something there that warned her off. And it ought to warn off Ryons, too, if only she could tell him.

It was almost like flying into a barrier—but not a barrier of heat or cold or contrary wind. This barrier she could have crossed with one more flap of her wings. It wouldn't even ruffle her feathers.

She let out a shrill cry of frustration. The men in the fortress heard it, and some of them looked up. She saw their faces as pale dots, and didn't like what she saw. She was out of arrow range, but it wasn't arrows that she feared.

If Angel could have put it into words, she would have said that death hung over that place like a heavy cloud. It was not a cloud that any wind could shift aside.

Angrily she turned away, unable to fathom what was troubling her. The bits of meat that Ryons had fed her first thing in the morning now stirred uneasily in her craw. If she stayed a moment longer, she would be sick.

She flew over a body of men marching along the lakeshore, marching to meet King Ryons' army. They toiled along like beetles on a chilly morning, unable to take wing and fly away. She swooped a little lower, then abruptly up again: these men had an evil odor on them.

Angel shrieked a protest, then flew back, straight and swift, to Ryons.

Ysbott had no choice but to follow the Wallekki. Unless they turned back, or stopped and stayed somewhere, he'd never catch them. But at least anyone could follow the trail two thousand horses made.

Why had they separated themselves from the gold? Where were they going? He wondered if they were frightened of the Thunder King and trying to escape.

He found the place where they'd swum their horses across the river. The Imperial ran wide here, with a slower current. But Ysbott had never learned to swim, and with the golden mask to weigh him down, he was not about to try. He had to slog along the riverbank for two or three miles before he found a ferry, and then he didn't have any money for the fare—he, who had seven great sheets of gold cached in the woods below the Golden Pass, couldn't afford a ferry ride. But he could always afford a lie.

"I was robbed by some Wallekki," he told the ferryman. "Maybe you've heard about this: a great mob of them crossed over, a little ways upriver."

"And scared the dickens out of all the people in these parts," the ferryman added. "There's a village yonder that they could have attacked, but they didn't. You're lucky they didn't kill you just for fun."

"They took a whole wagonload of trade goods, though,

and all my money," Ysbott said. "And now I can't get back across the river and go home. Won't you take me across, as an act of kindness? I'll pay you double when I come this way again."

"Why not?" said the ferryman. "Everybody else is hiding from the Wallekki. I won't get any fares today."

So Ysbott crossed the river. He thought of robbing the ferryman as soon as they landed, but decided not to. He might need the man again, if he had to retrace his steps for any reason. He might need money, too, but there was sure to be someone else to rob along the way.

First he had to hike back upriver to pick up the Wallekki's trail, which was not difficult. Toward the end of the afternoon, he met a lone man with an oxcart.

"Say, mister!" said the carter. "Did you see any of those Heathen who came this way yesterday? A whole army of them! I didn't think there were even a few of them left around here, thought the patrols out of Obann ran them off. But heaven help any patrol that runs into that bunch!"

"I see your cart is empty," Ysbott said.

"That it is—I sold them my whole load of melons. Didn't get much of a price for them, but better than nothing."

"I'm surprised they paid you anything at all." Well, here was a man with money to rob.

"Oh, they warmed up to me when they heard that I could speak their lingo. I did a lot of trading up the river in my younger days, and some of my best customers were Wallekki."

Ysbott nodded. This man had seized children and sold them as slaves: that was the only kind of trading the Wallekki did when they used to come into Obann, before the days of the Thunder King. He'd had dealings with men like this carter, on the edge of Lintum Forest.

"So you speak Wallekki," Ysbott said. Here was something more valuable than money.

"I get by," the carter said.

"What would you say if I told you those Wallekki who bought your melons are guarding a whole wagon train of gold, bound for Obann City?"

"I'd say they ought to have been more generous to me."

"I know a way to get that gold, if I can just catch up to them again," said Ysbott. "My name is Tobb, and I'm looking for a partner. This is something I can't do alone."

"My name's Dotter, and you've found one." The carter grinned. He was a bald, round-faced, round-bellied man, almost as dark as a Wallekki.

They shook hands. Dotter would slit Ysbott's throat the moment he saw a profit in it, and thought he could do it without risk, and Ysbott would do the same to him. This was the kind of man that Ysbott understood and trusted.

"What are we going to do?" Dotter said.

"You are going to be the servant and the spokesman of the Thunder King," said Ysbott. "I'll explain as we ride after those Wallekki."

"Can't wait to hear it," Dotter said.

CHAPTER 22

Lord Chutt's Faithful Bodyguard

Ilfil sent out scouts for miles ahead, but not one of them saw or heard anything of Ryons' army marching up from Lintum Forest. There was no enemy in position to intercept Chutt's wagon train. It made for an ugly mood among the Wallekki captains.

"We've been had!" they grumbled. Ilfil tried to calm them.

"There are only two things that need concern us—our own lives and the gold," he said. "We can still overtake the caravan before it reaches the city, and then fight Chutt for the gold. If he has reinforcements from the city, we will either suffer great loss in defeating him, or else be defeated ourselves. Either way, we would have no future."

"But he's made fools of us!" cried one—and the others growled their assent.

"I don't blame you for being angry," said Ilfil, when he could be heard again. "But let's not make fools of ourselves.

"I say we ought to hide our anger, rejoin Chutt, and march into Obann with him. He'll have no choice but to take us back as if nothing has happened. He knows we'll make it our business to kill him if he betrays us."

"We'll be hopelessly outnumbered, once we're in Obann," a chief said.

"But we will see to it, from now on, that Lord Chutt is never out of reach of several Wallekki daggers," Ilfil said. "Wullah! Was there ever a westman who could outdo a Wallekki for subtlety? Chutt will never find himself without his faithful Wallekki bodyguard right at his side. He'll be true to us, or we'll kill him on the spot."

They bowed to their leader's wisdom and rallied their men for a swift return to Chutt.

But Chutt had received no reinforcements. Hennen had refused to send them.

"If he's afraid of his own Wallekki, it serves him right," the general said, reporting to Prester Jod. "He'll either have to fight them or bring them into the city with him. And the people won't like that!" He knew from his scouts that the Wallekki had parted from the caravan and gone south across the river. But he did not know why they'd done that.

"Even so, the people are eager to see the gold," Jod said. "They talk of nothing else, according to my servants. People are flocking in from farms and villages for many miles around. There's not enough housing for them."

Against the prester's counsel, Roshay Bault had not returned to Ninneburky. Now he was staying at Jod's house as his guest. He had not yet told Jod or Hennen that he'd given special orders to Martis. As far as they knew, the baron had sent him back to Ninneburky.

"Ellayne says you know this city like Helki knows the

forest," he said to Martis. That was yesterday morning. "And you were, for years, Lord Reesh's pet assassin.

"Martis, I want you to hide yourself somewhere in the city and see if you can do something to upset Chutt's plans. If Gallgoid is still with him, maybe the two of you can work together. Chutt's a traitor, and a menace to the king: waste no sympathy on him. If there's nothing else that can be done to stop him, then you must do what must be done."

Martis looked him in the eye. "Sir, I have abandoned the assassin's trade," he said. "I have killed in battle and to protect the children, once, when the Griffs first captured them. I'll do what I can to hamper Lord Chutt, and obey you in all things, except this one."

"You won't assassinate him?"

"Would you?"

Roshay glared at him, then softened. "No," he said, "I don't suppose I would."

By the time Angel returned to Ryons and landed on his outstretched arm, she felt weak and out of sorts, as if she couldn't fly another hundred yards. She scolded him repeatedly, trying to deliver her warning. Cavall pricked up his ears and whined: he understood the general sense of it. But Ryons, Gurun, and Chagadai only stared at her.

"Something is wrong with this bird," said the Ghol, "but I see no sign of injury."

"She looks unwell," Gurun said, "but there was nothing wrong with her this morning. I have seen this in my father's hawks. Usually they recover."

Angel uttered a series of high-pitched peeps. Cavall

barked, urging the humans to listen to her. This alarmed Ryons, who loved the bird.

"Maybe she's hungry," he said, and hoped it was true. But Angel refused to be fed and nipped Chagadai when he offered her a pinch of dried beef.

"Can't you make that dog be quiet, Father?" he said. "Between the two of them, my ears are ringing."

"Hush, Cavall," said Gurun, and he hushed. Angel made a harsh clatter with her beak.

"What can we do?" Ryons said. The hawk rattled her wings, frustrated, and resolved to draw blood if the old Ghol offered her any more food. At the moment the smell of food revolted her.

Cavall whined. The hawk had discovered some danger in the way ahead and was begging the humans to avoid it. Cavall sniffed the air but smelled nothing untoward. Whatever the danger might be, it was too far off for any scent of it to be carried to him on the wind. Nevertheless, he believed the hawk.

Angel panted, open-mouthed. Ryons had never seen her do that before. He stroked her feathers with his fingertips, as Helki had taught him, and after a moment or two, she stopped.

"Let her rest," said Gurun. "Sometimes that's all a hawk needs."

CHAPTER 23

The Last Words of a Prophet

Thanks to Jack and Ellayne, and to messages from Baroness Vannett, the king's chiefs in Lintum Forest knew much about Lord Chutt's actions and something of his plans. The baroness kept swift riders going to and from the forest, arranging for a change of horses to be provided when they reached the forest. Bandy and some of his Abnaks were entrusted with that duty. "You might teach yourselves to ride, while you're tending those Ninneburky horses," Helki said. Bandy laughed. "I ride the day after I see you ride!" he answered. But they took good care of the horses, although most Abnaks considered horseback riding a dangerous and unsuitable activity.

Chutt would have been surprised to know that the chiefs in Lintum Forest were eager to march out and try to take the gold, even if it would entail a major battle.

"We can catch him before he gets to Obann," said Chief Zekelesh. "We can run most of the way and still beat him when we get there."

Helki had to call them to a council to discuss it.

"What tomfoolery is this?" he said. "Chutt has at least a thousand Wallekki, or twice that many, and a lot of trained

Obannese foot soldiers. At best our strength is barely equal to his, but I think we'll find ourselves outnumbered."

"That's never stopped us from winning," said Tughrul Lomak. "Besides, the lads are spoiling for a good, stiff fight. They're tired of tending crops and building barns—and hunting down outlaws, who are getting to be increasingly rare." Quite a few of his Dahai cheered those words.

"Who's afraid of those Wallekki?" said Chief Buzzard. "All the good Wallekki are with the king. Even now, while we sit here in peace, he may be fighting for his life somewhere in the east. It's a shame to us to be doing nothing, while he and Shaffur and Looth do brave deeds in the Thunder King's own country." This sparked even louder cheers.

"I'm losing them!" thought Helki. He answered, "Boys, have you forgotten why we're here? We're here because King Ryons' throne is here, and God has given it to us to keep that throne. Here is where He has established it.

"What do we want with a lot of gold—gold of the Thunder King? Haven't I told you how Roshay Bault, a brave man if there ever was one, gave it up because it's blood money? No good will come to any man who tries to keep it, and we'd be crazy to bring it into Lintum Forest. Why, I wouldn't touch it if Chutt brought it here and dumped it at my feet!"

"We don't want it for ourselves," said Buzzard. "We just don't want that traitor Chutt to have it. He'll use it to make mischief against King Ryons, and no one will thank us for letting him do that."

Ellayne nudged Jack and said, "I hope they're not thinking of leaving us behind."

"You mean so we can fight in a battle and get killed?" Jack said. "Why won't they listen to Helki?"

"They've been wanting to march out of here all summer," Fnaa said. "Trout says their scalping knives are getting dull."

Everyone in the settlement had crowded around the chiefs, who'd set up their stools in a semicircle around the empty throne. The children found perches on a broken-down castle wall behind the throne, along with several dozen of the settlers' children. From there they could see and hear everything.

Jack was thinking that this army never fought unless God commanded it, or unless an enemy attacked and forced them to defend themselves. That was why they'd never lost a battle. But would God bless them if they fought because they felt like fighting?

"Those Wallekki who follow Chutt," said Ellayne, "are nothing but a lot of thieves and robbers. I don't think Chief Shaffur would want them in our army."

Buzzard rose to speak again, but he didn't get the chance. A blood-curdling screech rang out, and the throng around the chiefs parted hurriedly to make way for the toothed bird. Behind it came Abgayle, hand in hand with Jandra.

"The Lord will speak to you," Abgayle said, when she and the child stood before the chiefs. The toothed bird shrieked again. The people were afraid of it; they held their breath. But Chief Zekelesh took off his hat because he more than anyone revered God's prophets.

From the mouth of the little girl issued the voice of a grown woman.

"The Lord of Heaven will speak to you no more through this child. She shall have rest from me until she is a grown woman. Then my spirit will visit her again, and bless her.

"Hear my voice: the seed of my servant Ozias shall make his throne in Lintum Forest. I have placed it here; it shall not be moved. Here he shall be established forever.

"If he and his people will hear me, and do my commandments, I shall continue his throne until my righteous servant come. He shall save the people from their sins; his blood shall wash them clean. By his death they shall be given life, and he shall reign over them in righteousness and peace. I have spoken it, and I will do it.

"Remember my words and proclaim them to the nations, and to all your generations."

Jandra fell silent, her face as white as wool. She stood motionless, as if carved from alabaster. Somewhere far away, a single blue jay called. Other than that, there was no sound.

Abgayle picked up the child in her arms. Now they could all see she was sleeping. Followed by the toothed bird, Abgayle walked away to put Jandra to bed. It was some long moments before Helki broke the spell.

"Our council is ended," he said. His eye chanced to fall on the children on the wall. "Ellayne! Find some parchment and write down every word of what we've just heard. I don't think we'll be hearing any more."

"The words must be saved exactly as they were spoken," said Zekelesh. "Can anyone doubt we have heard the word of God?" He sighed and added, "But I can't say I understand what it means!"

Quietly, the chiefs took up their stools, and the farmers and the warriors of Carbonek dispersed without another word among themselves.

While all of Carbonek ceased work and pondered what they'd heard, a different kind of prophecy was being discussed elsewhere.

"You're going to convince them you're the Thunder King? You—a beggar in rags?" Dotter laughed so hard, he almost fell off the cart.

He stopped laughing when Ysbott seized his hair and held the sharp point of a knife just under his eye.

"You can do as I say, and become rich beyond anything you've ever dreamed, or you can die right here and now." Ysbott didn't need to raise his voice. The knife did that for him. "You know the Wallekki and you speak their language. I can use you, and it'll be well worth your while. But if you'd rather not—well, you decide."

Dotter stammered. "Easy, easy! I meant no offense. What do you want me to do?"

"Whatever I say. Agreed?"

"Abundantly!"

Ysbott released him and sheathed the knife. "You are to be my spokesman to those Wallekki," he said. "The Thunder King will be the ruler of Obann, so from now on, he'll speak in Obannese. He will also speak in other languages that no one else will understand. But when he speaks in Obannese, you will translate his words to the Wallekki."

"I can do that," Dotter said. His face shone with sweat. "But how—if you don't mind my asking—will you make them think that you're the Thunder King? I mean, he is supposed to be their god."

Ysbott chuckled. "They're already well on their way to believing it! I showed myself to one of them the other night, and by now they've all heard of it. I'm sure none of them has ever seen this god with his own eyes. But they have seen you, so don't be thinking you can kill me in my sleep and take my place."

"I wouldn't dare," said Dotter, and Ysbott believed him.

"I'll also need you to teach me all you know about them and advise me how to deal with them. It won't profit you to betray me. But if you deal honestly with me, you'll prosper. I can promise you that."

"You can trust me. But what will you do?"

"I'll show you," Ysbott said.

He brought out the mask and put it on. Dotter stared at him.

"Where did you get that?" he whispered. "That's enough gold to make ten men rich."

"It's the golden mask of the Thunder King, and it's worth more than the gold in all the caravan. I dug it out from the ruined hall at the Golden Pass. Chutt and all his men couldn't find it! But I did.

"This has power, my friend. The power to command. I've commanded beasts, and they obey me. Now I'll command men—those two thousand Wallekki with their swords and spears, for starters. But there'll be more after that. Many more."

Dotter couldn't take his eyes off the mask.

"First," said Ysbott, "we have to keep them apart from Chutt. The Obannese won't believe in me. It will take time before I can make a triumphal entrance into the city. But I will—I will! And then I'll reclaim the gold from the Golden Pass, which is rightfully mine. When the Wallekki see me in this mask by night, by torchlight, they'll believe."

Up until now, the most ambitious thing Ysbott had ever done in his life had been to propose a truce to a rival bandit chief, invite him to a feast, and cut his throat after rendering him helpless with poisoned venison. As the murdered man was a vassal of Latt Squint-eye, the self-styled king of Lintum Forest, Ysbott's feat required boldness; and achieving it without being killed by Latt was a testimony to his cleverness.

It was not that Ysbott consciously knew his limitations. No: it was a reservoir of fear, not yet depleted, that held him back from too much risk. He was afraid to go into the great city, where even two thousand fierce Wallekki couldn't guarantee his safety—not even with the mask in his possession.

"They'll never let you in," said Dotter.

"The mask protects me," Ysbott said. "You'll see! It's the mask that makes a man the Thunder King." He took it off and put it back into the bag. He didn't like for Dotter to see it like this, as if it were only some object that he'd happened to acquire. "Why else do you think the man who wore it had such power?"

"It didn't save him from the avalanche, though, did it?"

"Only because it was time for someone else to wear it," Ysbott said. "The mask chose me! That's why I was able to find it, when Chutt and his whole army couldn't."

Their immediate concern was to catch up to the Wallekki—not an easy thing to do, with an oxcart chasing men on horseback. But it would give them time to rehearse the early stages of their plan, and as it turned out, their meeting with the horde came sooner than expected.

CHAPTER 24

An Occasion for Thanksgiving

Ryons' chiefs sent out scouts in all directions, as far afield as possible, as the main body marched along Lake Urmio. It wasn't long before Looth came back with a report.

"Zamzu ahead," he told the chiefs, "but no danger. Come and see."

"What do you mean, 'no danger'?" Shaffur said.

"I mean that here is something that I don't understand. If I tell you, you won't understand it, either. You must see it for yourselves." He turned to Obst. "For this we need our teacher's wisdom."

"Where there are Zamzu, there is danger," said Ghur Manyan.

"Not this time," answered Looth.

He would say no more. Attakotts are a taciturn people, not given to long speeches, or even to short ones. The army marched on, with the Hosa out in front and Ghols and Wallekki riding above them atop the hills.

"What could it be?" Ryons asked Obst.

Obst shook his head. "We'll see when we get there," he

said. But he looked fearful, and that made Ryons a little fearful, too.

"If Looth says there is no danger, then there is no danger," Gurun said.

It took them most of the afternoon to get to the place Looth wanted them to see. Angel wanted to fly ahead, but on Chagadai's advice, Ryons kept her on a tether. In the morning she had eaten normally, a good sign. Now she showed impatience, fidgeting on Ryons' forearm. He would have liked to turn her loose, but Gurun advised him not to.

"She's used to flying whenever she likes," Ryons said.

"Tomorrow will be soon enough, my king."

Behind them, Baby halted suddenly and let out an astonishingly shrill cry for such a massive creature. At the same time, Cavall threw up his head and howled.

"He smells something, and he doesn't like it," Perkin said, wrestling with Baby's leash. Because the bird's head was so high off the ground, he usually caught a scent before Cavall did.

The horses began to get skittish, too. Gurun rode a mare provided by Shaffur, chosen for her gentleness and placid spirit. "You'll have no trouble with her," he said. "It's almost like riding a cow." But now the mare snorted, tossed her head, and went into a start-and-stop gait that would have unseated Gurun a few months earlier. Chagadai reached over and grabbed the reins, soothing the mare with a little song in Gholish.

"Don't be afraid, Honeysuckle. She won't try to throw you."

"She's never behaved like this before," said Gurun. She was more afraid of falling out of the saddle in front of all these men than she was of getting hurt.

Ryons kept his own horse under control, just barely. His Ghols had been his teachers, men who could practically dress themselves and cook a meal on horseback.

The front ranks halted.

"Look!" said Chagadai, pointing skyward. A dozen ravens circled overhead.

"We all know what that means," Uduqu said, shifting the great sword from one shoulder to another. "Maybe someone else has fought a battle for us."

Looth urged the chiefs to dismount and follow him on foot. Chagadai helped Ryons, then Gurun, and ordered a man to hold the horses. Cavall took his place close to Ryons' side.

Baby dragged Perkin forward. "It looks like we're coming with you, Your Majesty!" the wanderer said. "I can't hold him back without a fight."

"Let him come," Ryons said. The great bird would protect him.

Between the water and the hills lay a scattering of bodies—Zamzu warriors, all dead, with ravens picking at their flesh. A few bodies dotted the slopes, as if the men had died trying to climb the hills.

"You see now?" Looth called. "Come closer."

Shaffur was the first to stand over a body, peering down at it. "No wounds!" he said. "And no blood anywhere."

"Others tried to go back the way they came," Looth said, "but we found them dead, all dead. None of them went very far."

"I hope you haven't touched them," Obst said.

"We don't touch the dead except to take scalps, and then we purify ourselves afterward."

Ghur Manyan pointed to another body. "Do you see these badges that they wear?" he said. "These Zamzu came from Kara Karram itself. They belonged to King Thunder's household guard."

Everyone moved up slowly, studying the scene, Ryons and Gurun with them. Along Cavall's spine the hairs stood all on end, and he had his ears held flat. Angel nestled her head deep between her shoulders and was probably happy that Ryons had left her hood on and she couldn't see anything. But she could smell it.

Ryons had seen dead bodies strewn over battlefields before, but this was not a battlefield. As Shaffur had observed, there was no blood—no wounds on the bodies.

"What could have killed them?" Uduqu said. "Look at their faces, and their hands—rough red blotches everywhere. And here's one face gone almost purple. I'm a little surprised the ravens cared to dine on them." The ravens, meanwhile, disturbed at their feast, flew off with a rattle of wings and a chorus of angry croaks. They all flew in circles now, waiting for the chiefs to leave.

Baby wouldn't come any closer. "Can't budge him!" Perkin said. "I thought I was going to have to hold him back from trying to make a meal of these bodies—but it seems he wants nothing to do with them."

"These Zamzu struggled hard to get this far," Looth said. "Their tracks are the tracks of men already dying." He turned to Obst. "What happened here, Teacher? Did God strike them dead so that we wouldn't have to fight them?"

"It's happened before," Obst said, "in ancient times. In the days of Zan, a mighty host of Heathen came up from the south, too many of them for the Tribes of the Law to meet in battle. But the destroying angel visited them by night, and in the morning they were all dead of the plague—according to the Book of Disorder. So maybe that's what happened here."

"The hills are full of corpses, too," said Looth. "This time they were not about to let us slip our horsemen around them on the high ground. It would have been a hard fight for us."

"Then we must praise God for this blessing," Obst said.

The chiefs returned to the main body of the army, out of sight of the dead, and Obst prepared a service of thanksgiving. Ryons knew he should be grateful, but what he mostly felt was fear. What kind of God could do such things? Yes, the Zamzu were the enemy, and they knew nothing of mercy. The one dead man whose face the king saw clearly grimaced with a mouthful of teeth filed to sharp points. These were the favorites of the Thunder King, and his most ardent worshippers, feared by every nation of the East. But to smite them all like this? Ryons thought of a verse that Obst had taught him once: "Behold, I do terrible things under the sun, and my wrath is a consuming fire." And here God had done such a terrible thing.

They served a power against which all the powers on the earth were powerless. And yet that power loved them, and protected them.

Ryons' mind could hardly take it in.

With a hundred Abnak warriors to protect him, and the youngest of the Fazzan chiefs to be their guide, Orth set out for the valley of the Green Snake River. It wasn't terribly far away across the plain, but none of the Abnaks had ever been there.

Before they left, Foxblood had each warrior swear an oath to defend the First Prester and never desert him.

"Is that necessary?" Orth said, not liking the idea. Who was he, that any man should take an oath for his sake?

"These are all grown men," said Foxblood, "and I have no power to command them to do anything. That's our way. But they all have power to command themselves, and if they swear an oath, they'll keep it."

May shed tears to see Orth go, and Hlah made him promise to come back.

"You've ordained me, Sunfish, but it hasn't made me feel like any kind of man of God," Hlah said. "How will I teach the people anything, when I myself need so much teaching?"

"Let the Scriptures do the teaching," Orth said. The two messengers had just returned from Obann with four copies of the Book of Holy Scripture and a pair of Constan's young students to help Hlah with his reading. "God's words will teach you without your knowing it. And I'll be praying for you every day and night of my journey—my only son." He smiled at May: "And daughter," he added.

The open country between the Abnaks' hills and the Fazzans' river valley was part of the Attakott's hunting grounds, and was regularly crossed by Wallekki trading caravans; but the wars had emptied it of people. Well-watered by little rills that trickled down to feed the river, it reminded Orth of the plains of South Obann. Farms and herds would do very well here, he thought, if there could ever be peace.

A few of the Abnaks spoke Obannese, and by now Orth had learned their language well enough—and a fair amount of Tribe-talk, too—to be at ease with them. Used to wooded hills and forests, the warriors didn't care much for the plain and hurried to get across it. The Fazzan chief, Weshesh, took them by the shortest route he knew.

"We'll enter the valley where my own people, the Birch clan, have their villages," he said. "There were still Zamzu and Wallekki there when I left, but it won't take much to make the Birches rise against them."

By night around the fire, Orth recited Sacred Songs, rendering them into Abnak as best he could. Someday Hlah would do it better, he believed. The warriors liked best those songs that praised God's handiwork in the heavens and the earth—the stars, the trees, the waters, and the hills. Born and raised in Lintum Forest, King Ozias spoke of things that Abnaks knew and loved. And afterwards the men entertained each other with tall tales—the more incredible, the better. No one ever called anyone else a liar.

"I had an aunt who never got along with anyone," went one of the tales. "This was because she'd learned to speak the language of the trees, and every time their leaves and branches rustled in the wind, they told her people's secrets: for the trees see everything.

"One day they told her that her husband, when he went out hunting, always visited a nearby camp so he could enjoy trysts with a certain woman there. The trees told my aunt all about it, and she was the only one who knew. So she persuaded the trees, the next time that woman went out to gather berries, to hem her in wherever she turned so that she couldn't get back to her camp. She starved to death before anyone could find her.

"But there was one tree, a young oak that was out of favor with the other trees, that liked to do mischief. This tree told my uncle what my aunt had done, and he was so angry, he went out to chop down all the trees that had captured and destroyed his lover. And he would have done it, too, only the last of those trees, a huge beech with an evil temper, dropped a heavy bough on him and killed him. After that, the rest of the family sent my aunt away because they were all afraid of her. We never heard of her again."

Orth prized the truth, so for him these tales took some getting used to. But for the Abnaks it made for a pleasant journey to the Green Snake River Valley.

CHAPTER 25

The Wallekki and the Thunder King

In two more days the wagon train would reach the city. Scores of Obann's leading citizens had already come out to see the gold—even tender young women from the best families, in ornately decorated carriages with gold and silver trim. Lord Chutt made a point of personally escorting the visitors around his camp.

Gallgoid wondered if Ilfil and his Wallekki would return. If they were coming, they should have been back by now. Except for the troops inside the city and King Ryons' men in Lintum Forest, there was no force anywhere strong enough to meet Ilfil in a battle. But where was Ilfil and what was he doing? If he stayed away much longer, he would be locked out of Obann, and Gallgoid doubted Chutt would ever pay Ilfil an ounce of all that gold unless he had to.

Gallgoid watched the visitors come and go. As Lord Reesh's eyes and ears, he knew them all, though none of them knew him. Not one of these men, who now wanted to be oligarchs, had remained in the city to abide the siege. Now that that danger was past, they were back. Except for Reesh and Chutt, the whole High Council had died defending Obann. "Now we're to be ruled by cowards," Gallgoid thought.

Soon he would be able to confer with Prester Jod. It would be so ridiculously easy to poison Chutt and be done with him forever, Gallgoid thought. But he knew Jod would never agree to such a thing. "And I'm no more Reesh's servant," he added to himself, "but the king's."

"And God's," Jod would have said, if he were present.

Martis disappeared into the city as an ant vanishes into a hole.

He mingled with the buyers and sellers and gossipers in the market squares, with tipplers in the taverns, and listened to their talk. Jod had taught him how to contact Gallgoid's agents if he needed them, but he didn't need them yet.

Sometimes he walked past the mountain of rubble that used to be the Temple, where he'd spent so much of his life. "My bones would be mixed with all that," he thought, if God hadn't chosen him for better things: God's choice, not his, although he now consented to it. The sight brought back memories of Reesh, who'd brought him up as if he were a son—albeit a son whose life he'd spend without a second thought, should need arise. But Martis didn't miss Lord Reesh.

The talk in Obann was all about the gold, and how it would make possible the rebuilding of the Temple. The people longed for that.

Even so, they weren't longing for the restoration of the Oligarchy. Most of them had seen the conquering beast, with the boy king clinging to its shoulders, shatter the Thunder King's host at the moment of its victory. They hadn't forgotten that he'd saved their city and their lives, nor were they eager to rob him of his throne. But behind them lay many generations of bowing to the oligarchs, and Martis doubted they would refuse to accept a return to the old ways.

"But where is the king? That's what I want to know!" said a white-haired woman to a farmer who was selling corn.

"Off somewhere with his army, fighting the Thunder King," the farmer said.

"Nah!" said another customer. "I heard he was killed when the Palace burned down, the day he was to be coronated—and they're keeping it a secret."

Martis didn't intervene in any conversations. Soon Chutt would be here with the gold, and it would be up to Jod and Hennen to resist him. Roshay Bault should have gone back to Ninneburky, but no one could convince him to leave.

"Civil war," thought Martis. "That's what we're headed for."

Ilfil and his riders found Dotter on their trail, this time with no melons in his cart. They would have passed him by, but he beckoned frantically to them with both arms, and because Ilfil recognized him, he reined in and trotted to the cart.

"I see you have nothing to sell us this time," the chieftain said. "What have you to offer, then? Speak up, we're in a hurry."

"O my friends, I bring you tidings!" Dotter said, nervously kissing his fingertips to show respect. "I hardly know how to tell you this. But I have seen King Thunder!"

Ilfil's hand shot up, halting the riders and commanding silence.

"It's true!" Dotter added, stammering. "Indeed, he has made me his slave and sent me to you."

Ilfil scowled. "What mummery is this?"

"Mighty lord! What am I, that I should dare to speak of such a thing? I do it under compulsion." Dotter didn't have to pretend he was afraid: Ilfil looked like he would like nothing better than to run him through. "The god of gods bade me tell you to make camp wherever I should find you and to offer sacrifice to him. And then, this very night, he will appear to you—to all of you together."

Not one man of all those Wallekki hadn't heard that the Thunder King had already shown himself, while they were still with Chutt. Dotter made sure that all the men around Ilfil heard his message. Then Ilfil wouldn't be able to pretend he hadn't spoken it.

"Great chief," he said, "the Thunder King, who cannot die, has come down from the Golden Pass to accomplish his conquest of Obann and revenge himself against those impious Obannese who robbed him of his gold. He will permit you to see him, and so test your loyalty.

"Don't be angry with me for telling you this! What choice do I have? He has made me his slave, and there's no escape for me."

All of the Wallekki began to talk at once. Ilfil growled at them, but couldn't quiet them.

"Will you be silent!" he roared. "Dismount! Prepare to lay out camp—we go no farther from this spot today." He turned to Dotter. "Come down, you reptile. You'll stay where I can get my hands on you. If this is a sham, I'll have you roasted alive and fed to the crows."

Come nightfall, the Wallekki sacrificed Dotter's ox. He didn't ask for compensation.

He wrestled with the temptation of confiding in Ilfil, exposing Ysbott and his scheme. Suddenly King Thunder's gold had lost its attraction for him. He would be lucky to get out of his predicament alive. But he was sure Ilfil would kill him regardless, and that sealed his lips. His only hope was that they would believe Ysbott and submit to him, with Dotter as his spokesman. Later, maybe, an opportunity to run away might present itself.

They made a bonfire. Ilfil spoke barely a word for hours, except to bark out necessary commands. Dotter knew Wallekki ways, so he perceived that Ilfil was afraid, and furious because he had been made afraid. He was at this time a very dangerous man, thought Dotter.

They threw fuel on the fire, snatching up wood wherever they could find it. The blaze burned fiercely in the dark, and Dotter sweated and trembled with the thought that Ysbott might lose his nerve and not appear, after all. "And I'll be the next thing thrown onto that fire!" he thought.

The Wallekki howled and wailed, as was their custom when worshipping the moon. But an idol with the moon god's spirit in it was imprisoned in the Great Man's dungeons at Kara Karram, and the moon—as far as the Wallekki knew—had become an empty coach making a pointless journey through the sky.

As for Ysbott, Dotter's fears were anything but baseless. Many times throughout the afternoon and into the evening, he almost dropped his scheme and ran away, leaving Dotter to his fate. He had the mask and seven sheets of gold in a secret cache. What more did he need? He was already a rich man.

He spent most of the day hiding in a ruined shed on an abandoned farm; they'd met people that morning who had seen the Wallekki headed their way and fled. He parted from Dotter at the last possible moment, reducing his partner's chance to cut and run. From the shelter of his hiding place, he saw the dust cloud raised by two thousand riders.

Yes, Ysbott could have fled. "Bold is one thing," he thought, "but crazy is another." But when he reached into the sack and caressed the smooth, cool gold with his fingers, he had other thoughts.

When it was good and dark, he put on the scarlet gown, fitted the heavy mask over his head, and came out of hiding. He had the light of the Wallekki bonfire to guide him, and no more fear. He found it impossible to be afraid while he wore the golden mask. His nerves pulled themselves as taut as harp strings, each one humming with a secret music. Whoever wore the mask, that man was the Thunder King. The mask had deserted a skeleton in the ruins of the golden hall and chosen him, Ysbott the Snake. The mask had the power of command, and it was now his power—no one else's.

Ysbott strode eagerly toward the red glow of the fire. He heard the Wallekki wailing. That noise was for him. He almost broke into a sprint, but the dress was too long to allow it.

Out of the dark, with a triumphant shriek, appeared the Thunder King. His golden face gleamed in the firelight. He wore a glorious robe that was like nothing ever seen in the land of the Wallekki.

Ilfil's men fell silent. Ilfil himself stood stock-still with his mouth frozen open.

Dotter ran to Ysbott and, as they had rehearsed, prostrated himself on the earth.

"Get up! Face these people, and tell them I have adopted mortal guise so they can look at me and not be struck dead."

Dotter obeyed.

"Tell them I shall speak to them through you because I will not use their language. I have come to Obann to take possession of it, so I will speak in Obannese."

Dotter translated. The Wallekki dared not even whisper to one another.

"I have come down from the Golden Pass. I live! I rested under the ruins of my hall and waited to see what my servants would do. Imagine my displeasure when I saw them consorting with my enemies! But now they must serve me and become the conquerors of Obann. Let those who wish to die, speak now!"

No one wished to die. There was not a man among them who had not seen someone die because that person had displeased King Thunder's mardars, and the mardars were only his servants.

"Tonight you shall eat and drink and sleep," said Ysbott, "and every man of you shall swear his oath to me, starting with the chiefs. Obey! For I am King Thunder, god of war."

How many times had Ysbott imagined these moments?

All in vain—they were like nothing at all that he'd imagined. Everything seemed to be happening so quickly! And yet, at the same time, slowly, and with unnatural clarity. He felt as if he could, if someone were to shoot an arrow at him, pluck it out of the air as easily as he could pluck an apple from a tree.

"Oh, yes, the Wallekki are the most superstitious people that I ever saw," Dotter said yesterday, instructing him. "That mask will scare them half to death, just the sight of it. Just don't let them ever see you put it on."

Ilfil the chief knelt before Ysbott and pressed his forehead to the ground. The other chiefs lined up to follow his example. "I swear as my people swear," he said, "and may this oath kill me if I fail to keep it." And all the others said the same.

And then all the men swore, groveling, many of them trembling from head to foot and even shedding tears, because they saw the face of the Thunder King and were afraid. In all probability, according to Dotter, no one of them had ever come within a thousand miles of the Thunder King himself. They only knew him through his mardars, who doled out death to any man they pleased, be he ever so mighty a warrior. Their curses poisoned wells, slew whole herds of horses, and dried up women's wombs. No one had ever stood against them, not even the Wallekki gods. And the mardars were only servants. To see the Thunder King himself, even in mortal guise, was to feel the hand of death laid on their shoulders.

When they'd finished swearing their obedience, Ysbott spoke to them again.

"Stand up! Every man of you shall be a ruler in Obann, or else be cursed and die. You shall not speak to me yourselves, but only to my slave, this miserable insect of a man. You shall not spare my enemies.

"Now I command you to feast and dance and sing and celebrate with all your strength. I shall be with you from now on, watching. You shall have me as your god, and all of Obann as your prey."

And even Dotter, if only for that moment, believed he stood before the Thunder King.

CHAPTER 26

A Grave for the Zamzu

The horses rebelled against setting foot among the Zamzu dead.

"If we bury the corpses, it will take all day," said Shaffur. "Maybe we could just roll them into the lake."

"Never!" cried Ghur Manyan. "People drink from these waters! And fish them, too. How would you like to eat fish that have fed on these bodies?"

"Your Majesty," said Obst, turning to Ryons, "what would you have us do?"

For a moment Ryons had a flash of indignation. Not fair! Why should he have to decide? But he understood by now that Obst and the chieftains were training him for kingship, making him practice it whenever possible, so that he would be ready against the time when they couldn't help him anymore. So he tried to answer wisely.

"I don't think it's right to leave them lying here unburied," he said, "or to toss them into the water. I'd rather we bury them as best we can and heap some kind of marker over them."

"This thing that God has done should be remembered," Gurun said.

"The king has spoken," Uduqu said. "Let's get to work."

The earth at the foot of the bluffs was soft, easy to loosen with the heads of spears. The Hosa took the lead in the work, singing a song of their planting season, while others ranged far and wide to drag the bodies to the grave. They couldn't bring themselves to lift them.

All told, some two hundred Zamzu went into the trench. What portion these were of the force that had come here to do battle, no one cared to guess. The Hosa heaped a mound over them and thrust in Zamzu clubs and spears to mark the spot. They finished the work by sundown, and Obst then conducted a service of thanksgiving, reciting one of King Ozias' Sacred Songs.

"The hand that spread the stars throughout the sky has felled my enemies: behold, they are no more. They lie with their faces in the dust; they go down into the pit that they have dug for me.

"How mighty is the Lord, who has delivered us! The Heathen are withered like grass upon a housetop; the Lord has burned them as men burn thorns.

"I said in my despair, Lord, they are too strong for me! They are as many as the sands, as ravenous as wolves, as swift as eagles: but now their place cannot be found.

"My sword shall rest in its sheath: for the Lord has done valiantly against the wicked."

Later, when Obst sat down at the campfire to eat, Uduqu pointed to his face. "Look at that!" he said to Ryons, Gurun, and Chagadai. "This hard life of marching and fighting agrees with you, old man. There are more black hairs in your beard now than when we started out. By the time we get back home, you'll be in your prime again."

Obst's hands shot up to his chin, as if he could feel the dark hairs among the white.

"You're not getting sick, are you?" Ryons blurted out. Obst, who had been alarmed and embarrassed, now laughed.

"No, my king, there's nothing wrong with me," he said. "You know, I almost died up there, on the shoulder of Bell Mountain. Sometimes I think maybe I did die, for a little while. I never did go all the way to the top: that was reserved for Jack and Ellayne to do. And Martis, too. But whether I did pass briefly into the shadow of death, or only slept, I don't know. All I know is that, when I woke again, I rose up on my feet, full of strength, and eager to be about my work in the service of the Lord. I could have run a race!

"But this business with my beard—" he shook his head. "I know nothing about it! Whatever God is doing with me, He hasn't explained it. Nor can I."

"It is a sign that He is with us," Gurun said.

"That may well be, and probably is," said Uduqu. "But I wish He'd do the same for these old legs of mine."

Ahead of Lord Chutt's caravan rose the walls and towers of the city, and another day's march would see them through the gates.

Captain Born marched alongside Chutt, who was mounted.

"Do you know," Born said, "I haven't laid eyes on this place since I was a cadet. The greatest city in the world! And yet it doesn't look as I remember it. Used to be a sight to take your breath away, but I don't feel that now. There's something missing."

"Two things missing," Chutt said: "the great dome of the Temple and the domes and towers of the Palace. It'll be up to us to make them rise again."

"The Heathen burned down the Temple," Born said, "but I never did understand just what happened to the palace."

"I wasn't here, Born, so I don't know for sure. They say it was a sudden storm of fire out of nowhere—the finger of God, according to the credulous. But I would say lightning. There was a terrible storm the day of the coronation."

"And so the king was never crowned," said Born. "Well, that should make your message go down easier, my lord."

Chutt didn't answer. King Ryons died in the fire that had consumed the palace, he'd heard. But later he'd heard that the boy king had escaped to Lintum Forest and was there now, someday to return to Obann. Or else he had gone east to fight the Thunder King: that was what the First Prester's vicar had said. Who knew? Because he himself was a liar, he'd dismissed Prester Jod's reputation for integrity.

But why, he wondered, did Jod stand so solid for the king? It could only be, thought Chutt, because he aimed at seizing power for himself that rightly belonged to the Oligarchy. By all accounts First Prester Orth was little better than an idiot, which left Jod as the real power in Obann—power that he would not want to share. At least, that was how Lord Chutt saw it.

"No Temple, no palace, and no First Prester," Born said. "It makes me wonder what we're getting into. It may be harder than we think to put things back the way they used to be."

"The gold we carry tells me otherwise!" said Chutt.

"I thought Ilfil would have come back to us by now," Born said. "He couldn't have run into any kind of trouble—but where is he?"

That was a question that had haunted Chutt all day. He couldn't believe the Wallekki would have gone very far, looking for an army out of Lintum Forest. Surely the gold would have drawn him back by now.

"You don't suppose they were scared off by that crazy story about the Thunder King being here, do you?" Born said. "I would've thought that was too tall a tale even for the Wallekki. But maybe they did believe it. Maybe they did!" He looked up at Chutt as if he thought it just possible that Chutt believed it, too. "If they did," he added, "they won't be coming back, gold or no gold. They'll be a hundred miles away by now."

"There's no accounting for Heathen superstition," Chutt said. "If Ilfil's not with us when we enter the city, there'll be no need to account for him at all."

While Chutt marched and Ysbott schemed, and King Ryons' men buried the Zamzu, the settlers at Carbonek in the heart of Lintum Forest wrestled with the message they'd been given.

Jandra knew nothing of the words that God had spoken through her mouth. The next morning she played with Fnaa, giggling breathlessly as he danced just out of her reach. Jack and Ellayne sat with Abgayle, watching.

"She's the only one here who doesn't know," Abgayle said. "I'd like to keep it that way, at least for a while."

It was Ellayne who'd written down the words of Jandra's prophecy. It made her feel as if she were back in King Ozias' cellar, beneath the cellar of the second Temple in Old Obann, with the sacred writings that had been lost for centuries. Who was she, to be entrusted with such things? And yet she'd done them. She and Jack and Martis brought the Lost Scrolls back to light, words that God Himself had spoken to Ozias. Why had God chosen two children and an assassin to do that? Ellayne didn't understand.

"You don't have much to say this morning," Jack said.

"Oh, shut up," she answered. She didn't feel like chit-chat.

"What I mean," said Jack, "is—well, look at her. She's just a little kid. Who would ever believe God spoke through her?" But he was thinking, "And who would ever believe God picked us to climb Bell Mountain and ring Ozias' bell?"

"We all believe," said Abgayle. "We heard it with our own ears."

"Then Jandra's bound to hear about it, sooner or later," Jack said. He went on: "It's funny, isn't it? The old prophets in the Scriptures—they were all great men. You can't imagine meeting one of them. The one who had the bearskin cloak, kings were afraid of him." He meant Sychas the Mighty, the terror of the wicked kings of old. "Meeting one of those prophets would be like meeting a giant. You'd be too scared to say a word! But Jandra? A little girl?"

"You've met King Ryons," Abgayle said. "He's just a boy like you and Fnaa. All the prophets were boys or girls, once. It's not all thrones and scepters. I think people must care about such things more than God does. 'My weakness is stronger than your strength, and my foolishness is wiser than your wisdom.'"

"I didn't know you knew the Scriptures, Abgayle," Ellayne said.

"It's one of those verses that Obst quotes all the time,"

said Abgayle. "And I've learned how to read a little. Fnaa's been teaching me. He's taught his mother, too. So now we can read from Obst's big book."

"Then you must know this verse, too, from Prophet Ika," Ellayne said. "I raise up the lowly, and I cast down the proud; to babes I give wisdom, and withhold it from the sages." She nudged Jack. "You don't have to be a great man to be a prophet. Some of the prophets in the Old Books, we don't even know their names."

Jandra caught Fnaa, and they sat down with the others.

"Someone ought to write down all of Jandra's prophecies and make a book of them," Ellayne thought. And she wondered if she ought to do it herself.

CHAPTER 27

How Chutt Entered the City

It didn't take Dotter a day to overcome his fear of Ysbott. Instead of pursuing Chutt, the Wallekki were sacrificing their best tents to make a pavilion for the Thunder King and a canopy for Dotter's cart. The delay troubled them, Dotter noted: they were all thinking about losing the gold. It would be locked up in Obann and they would be locked out.

It was all because Ysbott was afraid to appear before the city, Dotter thought. "They'd laugh at him in that scarlet gown. They'd laugh themselves sick!" And meanwhile, "He wouldn't last a day, among these Wallekki, without me." He wouldn't want to be in Ysbott's shoes when they saw through him. And Dotter thought it likely that Ilfil, for one, hadn't been fooled for a minute. But for how long would the chieftain keep his doubts to himself? When he had a chance to speak with Ysbott privately, Dotter brought it up.

"We'll have to win him over; we have no choice," he said. "If he denounces you, we're both dead men."

Ysbott grumbled. It was hot inside the mask. He didn't like the scarlet gown anymore, now that he had to wear it all the time. Having told the Wallekki he'd adopted mortal guise, he didn't need to explain why a god should have to eat and drink; but he didn't want them to see his face, either, so he'd consumed hardly anything since joining them and now he was hungry. He had no idea how a god ought to behave, but he was certain he should avoid behaving like an ordinary man.

"I think we'd be better off without Ilfil," he said. "I don't trust him."

"We need him to direct this army—unless you know how to do it," Dotter said. "I think he would be grateful if you named him your mardar. Then he'd be in on it with us, and less likely to turn against you."

Ysbott glared through the mask's eyeholes. Dotter knew too many things that he didn't know, and it chafed him to be dependent on the fellow.

"What's a mardar?" he snarled.

"It's a kind of exalted servant, or favorite, of the Thunder King. Every Heathen army has one. There's some kind of hocus-pocus involved, but I doubt Ilfil knows any more about that than we do. They say the Thunder King can see through the eyes of his mardars, and hear through their ears, and speak through their mouths."

"And how are we to manage that?" But then, Ysbott thought, maybe the mask could manage it. Trust in the mask, he thought: it has power. "All right, we'll do it," Ysbott said. "We'll do it tonight, and use one of the spare horses as a sacrifice. We'll make a great show of it—with blood." He was sure that such a thing would have to be done with blood. "Go tell Ilfil he's about to become a mardar."

"I think mardars have to shave off their hair and beard and paint their faces," Dotter said.

"Let Ilfil paint his face with horse's blood," said Ysbott.

So there was a ceremony that night, and Ysbott stood on the cart so all the men could see him. And the horse was killed, and the newly shaved Ilfil dipped his hands in blood and smeared it on his face.

"You are the first of my new mardars in Obann," said Ysbott, with Dotter translating. "I give you power over these men to rule them in my name. My thoughts shall be your thoughts, and your words shall be my words, and any man who disobeys you shall die. But you shall obey only me. Now swear to it."

"I swear as my people swear," said Ilfil. "When I speak, my lord, it shall be as if you spoke. And if I break faith with you, may this oath kill me."

Only Dotter and Ysbott saw the fleeting grin that Ilfil gave them through his mask of blood.

"He knows!" thought Dotter. "He knows, but he's throwing in with us." And Dotter was content.

As for Ysbott, he only thought the mask had again proved its power, and he looked forward to greater demonstrations of it in the future.

The next day Chutt marched into the city with the gold, and thousands of people lined the streets to cheer and marvel at it. So many wagons and each weighed down with gold! Even this great city had never seen the like of it.

Roshay Bault, with Prester Jod and Preceptor Constan, watched from the roof of the seminary. The students and scholars had all dashed outside for the parade. Constan knew better than to try to hold them back.

"There's not an ounce of all that gold," the baron said, "but was bled and extorted and robbed from conquered nations. Blood money, every bit of it! No good will come from bringing it here."

"Lord Chutt owns two great warehouses by the river," Constan said. "I suppose that's where he'll store it, under heavy guard."

Captain Born's men marched proudly, the sun glinting off their spear-points, helmets shining. They'd spent much of the previous night cleaning and polishing their gear. Lord Chutt rode before them, erect in the saddle, one fist cocked against his hip and head held high. He entered the city in triumph, although he'd never fought a battle, never beaten Obann's enemies. That was a nicety that seemed to be lost on the people of the city, but it galled the baron to think of it.

"Look at him!" he said. "You'd think he'd won a famous victory, when all he did was dig up a ruin." A few curses rumbled from his lips, until he remembered that Prester Jod stood next to him, and then with a great effort he abated his language.

"This is a shameful day for Obann," the prester said, "but God calls on each of us to do our best."

Martis watched from the street, just another face in the crowd. He was looking out for Gallgoid, and sighed with relief when he finally saw him, alive and unhurt, striding easily behind Chutt's horse. Lord Reesh's favorite poisoner, King Ryons' chief of spies, smiled absently, as if he enjoyed a private joke. Martis hoped to meet with him soon.

CHAPTER 28

The Ancient Law of Obann

Chutt called an assembly that very night, rejecting Gallgoid's advice to put it off.

"My lord, we first have to make sure of your votes," Gallgoid said. He had not yet had a chance to communicate with Prester Jod.

"I won't be asking for a vote tonight," Chutt said. "I just want to show them all that I'm in charge—that I'm still one of the High Council. There must be no doubt about that."

"At least wait for your Wallekki to return, so you can let them into the city, my lord. If General Hennen decides to use force against us, you'll need them."

"I won't wait, Gallgoid. They might not come back to us at all. They may be fleeing from their imaginary Thunder King."

The Great Hall of the Oligarchs, located in the palace, was no more, so the meeting was held in the guild hall of the wool merchants—a poor substitute, thought Chutt, but the best this wounded city had to offer. It did, at least, have beautiful wood paneling, several centuries old. He invited only the heads of wealthy families, former oligarchs, and presters. Of necessity Jod and Hennen had to be invited, too. Even this select audience filled the hall to its capacity.

As the sole survivor of the ruling council, Chutt shared

the dais with Jod, who was entitled to it as the First Prester's representative. As the general commanding the forces of the city, Hennen demanded a place, too, and Chutt had to grant it.

"No hard feelings—eh, General?" he said, as Hennen took his seat: for Chutt had recently held him prisoner in Market City.

"Oh, none at all," said Hennen, but didn't mean it.

No sooner was the meeting called to order when Roshay Bault rose up to speak. No one had told Chutt that the baron was present, and it came as an unwelcome surprise.

"I speak for the king—for Ryons, the descendant of Ozias!" said the baron. He had a powerful voice, and knew how to use it. He made the hall ring with his words. And he had no need to introduce himself; they all knew who he was. "No doubt you're all here to learn what Lord Chutt plans to do with all the gold he's brought.

"But do any of you know where that gold came from? It was dug out of the ruins of the Thunder King's hall at the Golden Pass. I was there. My men began the work, but Chutt came up with two thousand Wallekki and took the gold by threat of force."

"Only so I could bring it here," said Chutt, "as you well know! No man of yours, Baron, was hurt in any way. You left the Golden Pass in peace, and here you are to prove it. I have done nothing but what the law allows. I've done wrong to no man. You cannot say I have!"

"But you would wrong the king!" Roshay said. "While you were skulking in the north, and the Heathen host was breaking down the gates and pouring into this city, it was King Ryons, and a great beast that was a miracle of God, that smashed the enemy and saved our city. And even now, as if saving the city were not enough, our king has crossed the mountains to destroy the Thunder King.

"And you, Lord Chutt, in his absence, would rob him of his throne. In God's name, is there no gratitude in Obann? Are we grown so despicable, so base, as to turn against the king who saved us? Shame, shame, shame!"

He would have said more, but by now the murmur of the audience had swelled into a roar and drowned him out. Chutt pounded his gavel to no avail. At last he beckoned to Captain Born.

"Remove this disorderly man," he said, "and keep him confined until he comes to his senses."

"He's already said too much!" Born grumbled.

It took half a dozen men to overpower Roshay and wrestle him out of the hall. The unexpected show of force silenced the assembled citizens: all except for Hennen, who objected.

"Who are you, my lord, to arrest the Baron of the Eastern Marches? Order his release at once!"

"I am the president of this assembly, sir, and I will have order!" Chutt answered. "Besides which, I am a member of the High Council of the Oligarchy and, by the laws of Obann, the duly constituted authority.

"For centuries the High Council has governed Obann. Our authority is just and lawful. And when, and by whom, was that authority repealed? And what new law was lawfully enacted to replace it?

"No, my fellow citizens—there is no law in Obann but the ancient law, that has until the present time enabled us to live in peace with one another and enjoy prosperity. It's the law you were all born under, and your fathers, and your fathers' fathers. War, to be sure had disrupted our country and brought about confusion. But one thing the war has not done has been to set aside the law."

The hall was quiet now—quiet enough for Prester Jod to clear his throat and say, quietly, yet loud enough for everyone to hear: "My Lord Chutt, I believe you are in error."

Chutt stared at him. "What error, Prester?" he said. "Against what law do I transgress?

"Haven't I brought treasure to the city? Gold, for the rebuilding of the Temple! For making beautiful again all that's been ruined and ravaged by the war. Gold! And enough of it to restore our country to the way it was before the war. Tell me, Prester! Where do I err, in proposing to rebuild the Temple?"

There was a good deal of whispering and nodding over this, but Jod went on as if he were talking with a guest in his parlor, and all held their peace so they could hear him.

"You err in saying you're for the ancient law, Lord Chutt. The Oligarchy was our own invention, instituted some three hundred years ago to meet the needs of the time—which, well enough, it did. Even so, that time came to an end when the Heathen broke our city's gates and slew all the ruling oligarchs but you.

"Before the Oligarchy, we had centuries of disorder and confusion. Why? Because God thoroughly destroyed the Empire of Obann and all its works.

"We may well say the institution of the kingship is an ancient law." Jod raised his voice, but just a little. "Under

God, kings were anointed to rule in Obann for a thousand years—because the Tribes of the Law, having conquered a great city and made it their own, would have a king. But when they betrayed their last anointed king, Ozias, and took his throne from him, by God's will the kingship departed from Obann—until the present day.

"There is another law more ancient than the kingship, Lord Chutt. It is the Law of God, given by divine ordinance to the Children of Geb when first they set foot in this land, when as yet it had no name. It is this law that has never been repealed, although sinful men have often turned away from it to follow the devices of their own unrighteous hearts.

"It is this law, God's law, that remains in force today, as written in the Holy Scriptures. Not a word of it has changed. It has not been set aside."

He paused. Not so much as a whisper challenged him.

"It is God's law, Lord Chutt, that you would break," Jod said. "You would set it aside in favor of the Oligarchy, which is a mere tradition of men.

"You will not prosper in this, and your plans will come to nothing. For God has restored to us the kingship, awarding it to the seed of King Ozias—as promised in the Scriptures, and confirmed to us by signs and wonders, which we have all seen with our own eyes and which cannot be debated. Did not the Lord speak to Ozias through Batha the Seer? 'I have reserved the throne to you and to your seed; it shall be yours forever.' That is the law, Lord Chutt.

"As for the rebuilding of the Temple, God has chosen for us a new kind of Temple, not made by human hands, but consisting of His word and His people—a Temple that cannot be destroyed, as was the old one in our city. Again, this was promised to us in the Scriptures. In God's own word, as delivered to the Prophet Ika: 'I will write my law upon their hearts; and they shall be my people, and I shall be their God. And no more shall they say, the Temple of the Lord, the Temple of the Lord: for my throne is in the heavens, and the earth is my footstool.' That is the law, Lord Chutt, the Word of God. And you do greatly err."

Silence reigned in the hall, but not for long.

"Captain Born," said Chutt, "conduct the First Prester's vicar to a safe place and hold him there until I come to see him. And General Hennen, too."

Jod made no resistance. Hennen would have drawn his sword, but at a look from Jod, he didn't. Born's men were armed and ready to use force. The assembled citizens had brought no weapons with them. Both men were escorted out of the hall. No one had expected it, and no one knew what to do.

"I shall rebuild the Temple and restore the Oligarchy," Chutt told the assembly. "Search the laws yourselves, and you'll see I have the right. All will be as it was before. No man's blood is on my hands, nor shall be, if I can help it."

"I have underestimated him!" thought Gallgoid. Dread clutched at his heart. He never dreamed Lord Chutt would act so quickly. He wasn't used to being wrong about such things, and it unnerved him. But when the assembly was dismissed, and he rejoined Chutt at Chutt's own house, well-guarded by Born's spearmen, his face was beaming.

"Congratulations, my lord!" he said. "In one bold stroke you have cut off all your opposition—and without a drop of bloodshed. Now I'm sure the votes will go your way."

"Thanks, Gallgoid. I had a bad moment when Roshay Bault stood up to speak. But in truth, he made it obvious to me what I had to do."

"I only fear what Hennen's troops might do, my lord."

"Bah! A nice bonus in gold will settle them down at once," Chutt said. "And the people will be overjoyed to have their Temple back. They'll soon forget Jod and all his Scriptures."

"Be it so, my lord," said Gallgoid. His mind raced, trying to cobble together a plan, but outwardly he showed no sign of it.

CHAPTER 29

How Orth Preached to the Fazzan

When he took Kara Karram for his own, the Thunder King dispossessed the people and gave their lands to the Zamzu, all around the northeastern shore of Lake Urmio. Now Ryons' army encountered Zamzu towns and villages—but no fighting.

"The people are gone," Looth reported. "My scouts, they go into Zamzu houses. No one there, except for one old woman."

They'd found her in a village planted by the lake, hiding in a shed where fish were dried. Looth had her brought before the king and his chiefs. She was bigger than any of the Attakotts, but several of them had to help her along because she had an infirmity and could barely walk. Her face was seamed with wrinkles, under a mop of thin white hair. She spoke no Tribe-talk, but Obst could understand all languages. Still, it took some time and patient prodding before she would speak at all.

"She's frightened," he said. "She thinks we're going to kill her."

"I thought the Zamzu filed their teeth," Uduqu said.

"Only the warriors—not the women," Ghur Manyan said.

"Tell her we won't hurt her," said Gurun.

Obst found it hard to make her believe that. "She thinks we're lying," he explained. "All the nations hate the Zamzu, she says."

"With good reason," Shaffur interrupted.

"My lords, we have to be more gentle," said Obst. "She's only a crippled old woman who can't hurt anyone. She was left behind because she can't walk and she had no one to help her."

Piece by piece, he extracted her story. All the fighting men had been called to Kara Karram, where the mardars were massing an army. That left the villages defenseless, so the women and children packed stores of food and fled inland to the Zamzu homeland, east of Kara Karram. They believed the king of Obann would slay them all if they remained. "They believe it's our intention to exterminate the Zamzu."

"The world would be a better place without them," said Tiliqua the Griff.

Gurun, like Obst, had the gift of tongues. Now she used it.

"We will not hurt you at all," she said, smiling at the old woman. "We will feed you and care for you, and you shall ride in one of our carts. For we come here at the bidding of God, the father of all nations—even the father of the Zamzu, although your people do not know Him. We come to make an end of the Thunder King and restore freedom to all the peoples of the East. My name is Gurun, and I speak the truth. Won't you tell us your name, mother?"

The old woman stared at her, and then tears began to flow from her dark eyes.

"Long, long has it been since anybody called me 'mother'!" she said. "I have born two fine, strong sons. Both of them have died in battle. I had a daughter, but she died, too. My name is Zallakh, and I have no one in the world." Gurun translated for her.

"Shall we pity these man-eaters?" said Ghur Manyan. "Ask her how many of the Dahai she fed on when the Thunder King first conquered us!"

Shaffur frowned at him. "Peace!" he said. "We don't make war on wretched old women, not even if they're Zamzu. But I think we ought to ask her what happened to those Zamzu who died before we could meet them in battle. Maybe she knows."

But she didn't know; she couldn't tell them anything about it. All the warriors in her village had gone to Kara Karram a month ago and had not returned, nor sent any word. "All the men are there," she added. "They're waiting for you."

"She needs rest," said Gurun. "Come with me, Zallakh. I will give you food and water. Looth, bid your men be gentle with her." And the Attakotts helped her toward the wagons.

"Well, now we know what to expect when we come to Kara Karram," Shaffur said, "the whole force of the Zamzu—and them holding the high ground to boot."

"It'll be a glorious fight," said Chagadai. "A fight to be remembered for a long, long time!"

Martis met with Gallgoid the morning after the assembly, in the cellar of a tavern owned by one of Gallgoid's agents.

"The baron, the prester, and the general have not been harmed—not yet," Gallgoid told him. "Chutt has them locked up in rooms in his own house, under guard. I must admit he took me by surprise, arresting them so suddenly."

"I'm under orders from the baron to return to Ninneburky and deliver the tidings to his wife," Martis said, "but I find it hard to leave the baron in such jeopardy. I doubt the baroness would want me to."

"I'll send a messenger, if you like. You may be able to help the baron, if you stay."

"The whole city is already talking about it, Gallgoid. The people don't know what to make of it. They're stunned."

Gallgoid tugged a barrel out of a corner and sat on it. "They want their Temple back," he said, "but I think it was a misstep to arrest Jod. The people are quite fond of him. Lord Chutt has made trouble for himself."

"What about Hennen's troops?" Martis said.

"Too early to tell. For the time being, they're confused."

"Do you know of any way to get the prisoners out of Chutt's house?"

"Oh, I think I can do that," Gallgoid said. "But if I act too soon, they'll only be taken again—or else there will be fighting in this city. I'm reluctant to start a civil war."

"You like complications, don't you?"

"And you like the straightforward approach—a dagger in the back."

The two men glared at one another. They used to be rivals for Lord Reesh's esteem: the assassin and the poisoner.

Gallgoid chuckled, breaking the tension. "The past is past, Martis. We're both the king's men now, and must take care not to fall back into any of the old habits that our former master encouraged in us. I don't think Prester Jod would like it."

"I'm supposed to be guarding Roshay Bault's children," Martis said. "I vowed a vow to do that. But they'd take it hard if I let anything happen to their father."

"Chutt would have to be desperate to offer violence to any of his unwilling guests," Gallgoid said. "I'm sure the baron is quite safe for now. I'll find a way to advise him to keep a cool head. Chutt, you see, wishes to do everything under color of the law. To do murder would upset his plans."

"He's surprised you once already," Martis said.

Gallgoid's smile faded. "But he won't again," he said. "I promise you that."

Now that Dotter's cart had a canopy over it, and curtains that could be drawn shut, Ysbott could eat and rest out of sight of the Wallekki. It would not be good for him, he judged, if these men saw too much of him, mortal guise notwithstanding.

Only Dotter was to have access to him at such times. But when Dotter crawled into the forbidden precinct that morning to bring him a Wallekki ration of jerked beef and a skin of water, Ilfil crawled in after him and saw Ysbott without the mask. Ysbott nearly choked.

"Don't gape at me like that!" the chieftain said. "You've put a spell on my men, and I've helped you do it. But don't think you've deceived me, too."

Ysbott sputtered, but Ilfil cut him off.

"I don't know how you got the mask," he said, "and I wouldn't touch it for all the gold in all Chutt's wagons. What it will do to you, in the end, I'd rather not see. But as things stand right now, we're all in this together—three partners in the boldest crime I ever heard of. And by all the starry host of heaven, I intend to profit by it."

"I'm finished!" thought Ysbott, but he fought down the panic and his wits didn't entirely desert him. If the game he meant to play was lost, it was time to try another game. It would only insult Ilfil if he tried to keep pretending he really was the Thunder King. "How did you know?" he asked.

"Ah! I knew when I saw the ruins at the Golden Pass. Whoever was in that hall died!" Ilfil showed his teeth. "But to speak plainly, I knew the moment I laid eyes on you."

Now Dotter was alarmed. "How many others know?" he said.

"Maybe a few, who don't dare speak of it. I'll play the mardar for all I'm worth. I want my people to believe the Thunder King is with them." Ilfil cast a disrespectful look at Ysbott. "But tell me, man—and tell the truth. Who are you, and what mad folly brought you here? What were you hoping to do?"

Ysbott's smile, distorted by the scar that Wytt had given him, was not a pleasant sight.

"I wanted the gold, of course—the same as you," he said. And Dotter put in, "It's best we understand each other."

"We'll get the gold," said Ilfil. "Chutt owes me much! If he thinks he can keep me locked out of his city and send me away without my share of the gold, he'll soon learn otherwise."

Without Ilfil as his mardar, the Wallekki would surely rise up and kill him. Ysbott had no doubt of that. He'd given them too good a scare. But he only said, "Do you have a plan?"

"Not yet. But I will, by the time we get to Obann City."

The last thing Ysbott wanted to do, ever, was to go to Obann.

"We'll plan together," he said, because he was on this path now and there was no escaping it. The mask had decided it. And the mask would see him through.

The Fazzan were in revolt against King Thunder, and there was fighting all along the Green Snake River.

The whole Birch clan turned out to hear Orth preach. No man of Obann had ever been there before, and they were curious about him. For the time being, they'd driven out the small garrison of Zamzu that had held them down, and they killed the mardars. They knew the Zamzu would come back soon, and in greater numbers; but for a little while, they would have peace.

Orth stood atop an overturned boat with his back to the river, whose waters shimmered silvery in the light of the moon. The Fazzan were a populous nation, much more so than the Abnaks. Orth looked over a sea of men in wolf's-head caps, women, and children. Around him on either side stood Abnak warriors, well-fed and warmly welcomed by their hosts. Beside him stood Weshesh the chief, who would translate Orth's Tribe-talk into the Fazzan language when there was need.

"I have never in my life seen such a gathering to hear God's word," Orth began. "I know it makes Him glad to see His Fazzan children so eager to know Him. For He is not the God of Obann only, or the Abnaks, but of all the peoples on the earth."

He told them how God created the heavens and the earth, and filled the world with life of every kind, creating man last and giving him dominion over all things under heaven, to be His children and His stewards.

"You may ask why you haven't known this," he said. "Well, long ago, all men did know it. But as they multiplied, and spread out over the earth, most of God's people turned away from Him and forgot Him—although he was never, at any time, very far away from you.

"But the Lord is patient with His children; and because He is eternal, and bound by no constraints of time, He waited for you to come back to Him. Here in the world, age after age goes by, countless lifetimes of mortal men. It is not so with God. As He told one of His servants, a prophet, 'With me there is no beginning and no end. I am with your fathers' fathers, and with your children's children, and with you. A thousand years is but an hour, in my sight, and an hour is a thousand years.'

"In all the years of your ignorance, He has not forgotten you, not even for a day. Go, search among the gods of all the nations, and your own gods, and see if you can find, anywhere, a god who cares for you because He loves you. Has any of those other gods ever said, 'I love you'? Has any god, among all the gods of all the nations, ever said it is his desire to be loved by you?

"But the true God, of whom I speak, does love you, and even now has turned to you, so that you and all the other peoples of the earth shall know Him—and become His people once again, as you were at the beginning of the world. For the true God has remembered you, and He will save you."

The Fazzan stood entranced. They had never heard

such things before. Their gods were idols, things of wood and stone, powerless to help or to hurt; and yet for long generations had they made offerings to those gods who were not gods, and honored them. Then the Thunder King came and took their gods away and put himself in their place, so that they had a false god who devoured them.

"Poor, simple people!" thought Orth: the children of long years of ignorance. But tonight they listened, for God had willed it so. Orth knew many learned men in Obann, scholars, presters, and reciters, who had God's word at their very fingertips and yet had lost the power to be moved by it. The thought humbled him: he used to be one of them.

"Think nothing of me!" he cried to the Fazzan. "If the Lord had not disposed your hearts to seek Him, you would not hear me. We can only call on Him because He first called us.

"The Lord has made you ready to receive His word. He has purified you through affliction—not as slaves to be punished, but as sons and daughters whom He loves. He will free you from the Thunder King and from all false gods and idols, and He will give you back the land that He gave you long ago, to enjoy it in peace."

A few of the listeners began to weep, and then more and more. But soon their crying gave way to cheers, and that gave way to singing. Their voices filled the valley and echoed from its walls.

"What are they singing?" Orth asked.

"It's an old, old song," said Weshesh, "the oldest song we know. It's a song of love for the valley and the river, and tells how our fathers came to this land and loved it, after ages of wandering the earth."

"Does it say who gave them this country?"

Weshesh smiled. "The gods," he answered. "But they're changing it even as they sing—'gods' no more, but only 'God.' The one God."

CHAPTER 30

How the Thunder King Came to Obann

The message from Martis was a week old by the time the baroness received it. Gallgoid's swiftest rider had delivered it to Ninneburky.

Roshay, along with Prester Jod and General Hennen, was a prisoner. As yet they had not been harmed. Somehow Gallgoid would protect them.

Vannett sat in her parlor with the letter in her hand. A week! What else had happened since Martis signed it? Was her husband even still alive?

"Baroness, what's wrong?"

Enith, the girl who lived next door, stood in the entrance to the parlor. Her aunt was the baron's cook, her grandmother Vannett's housekeeper. Enith played with Jack and Ellayne and usually joined them in the afternoon for their readings in the Book. With Ellayne and Jack in Lintum Forest, Enith was company for the baroness, and much appreciated. But today Vannett hadn't heard her come in, hadn't heard her words of greeting. "How long have I sat here staring at this letter?" she wondered.

"It's the baron, Enith," she said. "He has run into trouble in Obann. This letter is from Martis."

"My lady, what will you do?"

"What I must." Vannett sighed. "What the baron expects me to do: muster the militia and put them on the alert, and pass the news on to the king's men in Lintum Forest. Enith, be a good girl, find Captain Kadmel and bring him to me right away. Later we can read together. That will be a comfort to me."

Enith ran off to find the militia captain, and Vannett sank a little deeper into her padded couch.

It took another week to get the news to Lintum Forest, to Ryons' chiefs at Carbonek. So Ellayne and Jack learned their father was a prisoner in the city, but their mother wanted the children to remain in Lintum Forest.

"Know that the militia under my husband's authority are assembling here at Ninneburky," Vannett wrote to the chieftains, "but the baron left orders that they are not to fight unless attacked. Martis assures me the baron will come to no harm and says we must be patient. Please pray for us."

While the chiefs prayed and debated, the children went off a little ways to fume.

"I knew this would happen!" Ellayne said, balling her fists. "Why did they let Chutt do it? Why didn't somebody stop him?"

"And who knows what else has happened," Jack said, "since Martis sent the message?" Ellayne glared at him for saying it. But Fnaa said, "If only we knew! And they've taken Prester Jod, too. That's bad."

It took so long to get news from Obann, and there was no news of King Ryons, either. "We don't know anything!"

Ellayne cried. "And there's no way we can find out, either."

Wytt had been squatting beside her, contentedly munching on a beetle, and listening. Now he stood up, thrust his sharp stick into the ground, and launched into a stream of chirps and chatters.

"What's he saying?" asked Fnaa. But Wytt was going on so fast, the question couldn't be answered. Finally he showed his teeth and hissed.

"He's mad!" Jack said. "He doesn't think any of us has done anything right. And he wants to help the baron." Jack shook his head. "That's daft. As if we could do anything that Martis and Gallgoid couldn't do! Everything would be over by the time we could get there, anyhow. And I think the baron, if he were here, would tie us to trees before he let us go."

"He would," Ellayne agreed, "but I'd get loose and go anyway."

Martis reported to Preceptor Constan, who so far had been left alone to continue his work of copying and distributing the Scriptures.

"The people want Prester Jod. They're not pleased that he's been arrested," Martis said.

"So my students tell me," Constan said.

"The clergy are divided down the middle. Gallgoid says Chutt would set Jod free today, if he'd promise not to oppose the restoration of the Oligarchy and the rebuilding of the Temple. But of course he won't."

"He'll never make that promise," Constan said.

"As for the troops," said Martis, "there have been some

scuffles in the barracks, but no one seems ready to take up arms. Maybe half of the officers are still loyal to Hennen, Chutt's offer of a bonus notwithstanding. We'll know better, after tonight."

Chutt had called another meeting of the former oligarchs, the leading clergy, and the heads of Obann's richest families. So far he'd been using the time to enlist support.

"He grows impatient," Gallgoid said, when Martis met with him that morning. "I don't like to touch off civil strife, but I've advised him to go ahead and ask for a vote. That's what he really wants to do, and his ambition, I think, will get the better of him. The city isn't ready for this vote, but I have advised him that it is."

"Why haven't you rescued the prisoners yet?" Martis said.

"That must come a little later," said Gallgoid. "Roshay Bault is steaming over it, but I think he understands."

Martis relayed the conversation to Constan, who absorbed it without a comment. Martis had heard about the slow and careful workings of the older man's mind, but found it hard to accept. Sometimes, he thought, it was like talking to a boulder.

And then a student burst into Constan's office without knocking at the door.

"Wallekki!" he panted. "There are Wallekki at the gate—and they say the Thunder King himself is with them."

When Lord Chutt received this news, he was meeting with an elderly man who was the Temple librarian under Lord Reesh. Prester Otvar, his name was, and Chutt was already thinking of him as a new First Prester to replace Lord Orth.

"This is all rubbish," Otvar said, "Orth and Jod and all this about a Temple not made with human hands—bah!

"Do you know what I had in my library, Lord Chutt? Books and documents going back five centuries, and some even more, much more: all catalogued and accounted for, everything in order. All gone up in smoke! Treasures of wisdom. A lot of it was one of a kind, and so is lost forever. Priceless! But do you know what my library was, Lord Chutt? It was the Temple's memory! And a Temple without a memory is hardly a Temple at all, any more than a man who has no memory."

"But now we have the gold to replace whatever we can," said Chutt, trying to soothe him. "I know that any new Temple we build on the site of the old can never be the same as the Temple that you knew and loved. But it will be as great and glorious as gold and scholarship can make it! I promise you: it'll be a worthy successor to the old. And it, too, will have a library, created and established under your direction."

Prester Otvar frowned. It was his habitual facial expression.

"Not if Jod has his way!" he grumbled.

"Well, I'm hoping that the clergy of Obann will see wisdom, and not let him have his way," Chutt said. "I think we'll have the votes tonight to set all things in motion—"

Gallgoid rapped on the door and let himself in.

"My lord, Chief Ilfil has returned. He demands entrance to the city. When the guards saw him coming, they shut the gates." He hesitated, then added, "Ilfil says they have the

Thunder King with them. You'd better go and speak to him, my lord."

That duty properly belonged to Hennen as the city's general and to Jod as the First Prester's vicar. It pleased Gallgoid to see Chutt at a loss for words. Whatever decision Chutt might make, Gallgoid thought, would very likely be a wrong one. This tree, he hoped, might fall without anyone setting axe to it.

"I think you ought to come now, my lord." Don't give him time to think it through.

Chutt muttered a curse and rose from behind his desk.

"Come with me, Gallgoid," he said. "I'll need your counsel."

"You'll need mine, too," Otvar said. Chutt didn't want the old librarian's advice, but had no tactful way to refuse it.

Gallgoid suppressed a smile.

Ilfil hadn't hurried to Obann. They'd needed time to make a plan.

"You can't let the city see you in that getup," Dotter advised Ysbott. "Don't you know that's a woman's evening gown? They'll laugh themselves sick before they kill you."

It was mortifying. Living all his life in Lintum Forest, Ysbott didn't know a lady's fine dress when he saw it. They'd laugh at him, all right. For a moment he saw himself, with dreadful clarity, as an ignorant yokel, someone for everyone to laugh at. It was good for Ysbott that that moment passed quickly.

Dotter's solution was to discard the dress and fit him out in a Wallekki chief's regalia. That was better, certainly.

But the closer they drew to Obann, the more fragile grew Ysbott's confidence. It galled him to realize that he was very much Ilfil's prisoner, and at his mercy.

Nothing would content Ilfil but to gain entrance to the city, where the gold was. "At least half of it's rightfully mine," he said, "and I mean to have it. Chutt has also promised me a generalship, and I mean to have that, too.

"But I know what to do, now, and you can leave it to me. The Thunder King has come to Obann to make peace. He has forgiven the plunder of his gold. Half of it he will donate to Obann for the rebuilding of the Temple. The rest he will grant to his loyal servants—me and my men. That's the plan."

"I wonder what the real Thunder King will think of it," said Dotter.

Ilfil scowled at him. "What else can we do!" he said. "We can't go home again, not ever. So we must try to live as comfortably as we can, here in Obann. Chutt will need our swords, so he'll protect us. If need be, we'll fight for him."

"And what about me!" Ysbott snapped. "How can the Thunder King make his home in Obann?"

"We'll never let them see you without the mask, or by the light of day," Ilfil said. "No man of Obann will be allowed to speak with you. And when all is settled down, you'll lay the mask aside and become one of many strangers in the city; and I will say King Thunder has quit his mortal guise and returned to his place at Kara Karram, traveling as a spirit on the wind."

"The mask is mine," said Ysbott.

"You can take it with you when you leave, and good riddance to it," Ilfil said. "I don't want it! I wouldn't touch it with the tips of my fingers. Let its curse fall entirely on you, and not on me."

"I fear no curse," said Ysbott. But of course that was a lie. And the next day, they were at the gates of Obann with Ysbott hiding in the covered cart.

CHAPTER 31

A Parley at the Gate

Of all these events in Obann, Ryons and his chiefs were ignorant. They marched along the shore of Lake Urmio like climbers fearful of an avalanche.

"There must be tens of thousands of warriors the enemy can throw at us," Shaffur muttered. "Where are they?"

"Waiting for us, like the old woman said—waiting at Kara Karram," Uduqu answered.

They marched past one Zamzu village after another, all of them deserted. In another three days, said Looth, they would stand before Kara Karram. The Attakotts had already seen it from a distance.

"We don't go close enough for their scouts to see us," Looth said. "And what can we tell that you don't know already? It's a big, strong place on top of a high, steep cliff."

But the march had to be halted when there was a disturbance among the Zephites. Jiharr quelled it himself, with his fists.

"I'm ashamed!" he told the other chiefs. "Some of my people are losing their nerve. Who ever heard of warriors of the Zeph afraid to meet an enemy! But what they're afraid of is the Thunder King and magic: the kind of magic that burns all life off a whole island."

"Those who wish to turn back, can turn back. It won't

make much difference," Uduqu said.

"I think it would do much good," Jiharr said, "if the king himself would speak to them. Queen Gurun, too, if she is willing."

"I'll tell you what I'm afraid of," spoke up Ghur Manyan. "Many years ago, when the Thunder King came out of the East and took Kara Karram, he had an ancient sword that his god of war had given him. It made him invincible in battle. Long has it been since anyone has seen that sword! But if he still has it—" Ghur shook his head. "Well, that's my fear."

"My king," said Obst, "will you speak to Jiharr's people?"

"And what will I say?" thought Ryons.

"Give them some of your sass, Your Majesty!" Uduqu said. "Like you used to sass the Abnak chiefs when you were still a slave."

"I'll speak to them," Ryons said. What else could he do?

"I, too," added Gurun.

Jiharr assembled the Zeph around the king. The rest of the army assembled themselves around the Zeph. Ryons' mouth went dry. Up close, the Zeph warriors in their horned headdresses looked like bulls about to stampede. Gurun held the king's hand. He licked his lips and tried to do his best.

"You Zephites," he said, "who joined us of your own free will: you're still free men, and if you don't wish to go on to Kara Karram, no one here will force you.

"I wouldn't go myself—no, I wouldn't!—only God wills it, and it was God who made me king. I didn't want to be a king, but it's better than being a slave. And I've seen God do things, He's done things for me, that make it impossible for me to turn against Him. I'd rather be back where I belong, on the other side of the mountains—but here I am. It's where

God wants me to be."

Ryons took a deep breath, then continued.

"Now there's something that you ought to know, and I hope you'll believe me when I tell you.

"There is no Thunder King!" he said. "The first Thunder King got old and died a long time ago, and ever since, his mardars have been pretending that he never died, and never will. Everyone has believed them because they do it so cleverly."

He told them how the Thunder King went up to the Golden Pass and built a hall, intending, when the snows of winter melted, to lead a new invasion of Obann, and how the Thunder King, with many of his mardars, perished in an avalanche.

"That we learned from someone who was there," Ryons said, "the only man who got out alive before the place was buried. He overheard the mardars as they made their plans, and this is what he heard.

"There is no Thunder King. It's only a man in a golden mask. That's all it's been for many years. The Thunder King who went to the Golden Pass is dead. If there's another by now at Kara Karram, it's just another man. And God has sent us here to finish it."

He ran out of words, but then Gurun spoke.

"It's all true, what the king has told you," she said. "My fathers and my uncles and my elder brothers—for so I think of you, because you have treated me as if I were your own near kin, for all that I'm a stranger from a country far away—we are all of us the servants of the Lord our God, who is the father of us all. He hasn't sent us here to die so that His enemies might triumph! If I ever believed that, I never would have made this journey.

"But what does it matter what I believe? Whether He gives us victory or chooses to let us die in His service, our God is well able to deliver us. I would rather be in His hands, here and now, than safe at home in my own bed. For I know that there is nothing too hard for the Lord, and I have put my trust in Him. I will go to Kara Karram because God wills it."

Jiharr turned to his warriors. "I speak as a man who would have died, yet lives," he said. "Now you have heard your king and queen. Will you turn back, while a boy and a girl go on?"

"No!" shouted all the Zeph. And "No!" roared the Dahai in the ranks behind them.

The army resumed its marching, singing "His mercy endureth forever." Uduqu looked up at the cliffs. "They'll come tumbling down on us if we sing much louder," he thought, and then sang louder.

But Angel the hawk flew over Kara Karram no more. There was much she could have told, had any human being the ability to understand her. Now when she flew, she flew high but not far. Chagadai noticed the change in her habits.

"I've had hawks all my life," he said, "but I don't know what's gotten into this one."

Cavall stuck close to Ryons. Normally it was his way to trot off on little excursions of his own, to investigate an odd scent or an unusual sound; but he didn't do that anymore, since they'd passed through the first of the deserted villages. Ryons didn't think to question the change in Cavall's behavior. It was a comfort to have the big dog always at his side.

Two thousand Wallekki horsemen, with Ilfil at their head, were waiting at Obann's East Gate.

Chutt didn't recognize Ilfil at first. He called down from the wall, "Where is Chief Ilfil? I would speak with him."

"Don't you know me, my lord?"

Chutt stared. The chieftain had shaved off his beard and most of his hair, and the lower half of his face was painted black.

"What is this, Ilfil? What does it mean?"

"It means I am a mardar in the service of the Thunder King, the lord of all the East," Ilfil answered. "In his name—and in the name of our own sworn partnership, my lord—I call on you to give us entry to this city.

"For my master has come to Obann to make peace with Obann's people: to end the war by restoring their Temple. It's his gold that we brought down from the mountain. It belongs to him by right! But he will make a gift of it, so that your Temple might rise again in glory, and there shall be peace between him and the people of Obann."

Ilfil spoke loudly, and in Obannese, so that all the crowd gathered on the wall could hear and understand.

Chutt thought quickly. There was no way that two thousand Heathen horsemen, with no siege equipment, could force their way into the city. Even with the defenses as yet in a poor state of repair, it would take many times their number to break in. So there was no threat here, he thought.

"Clever of him, though," he mused, "to make a show of giving away something that he doesn't have!" And what was this about the Thunder King? Chutt saw no Thunder King.

"You tell me that your master has come," Chutt said,

"but where is he? Let him show himself."

"All in due time, Lord Chutt. First let us into the city, for we come in peace."

"What's he playing at?" Chutt wondered. But he said, "It's not my decision to make, my friend.

"Tonight we will vote to reconstitute the High Council of the Oligarchy, and then the council will have to decide whether to let you in. That's the law of Obann. I suggest you move yourselves a little distance from our gate, set up a temporary camp, and wait for these necessary things to be done. I cannot open the gate to you on my own authority."

"My master has no wish to overturn the laws of Obann." Ilfil raised his voice even louder. "But know, all of you, that the Thunder King, the lord of all the East, has offered you peace, friendship, and a gift of gold! But if you would rather go back to war, just say so."

Hundreds of people lined the wall above the gate. Most of them had seen the vast armies that the Thunder King had once sent against Obann and had no desire to see such things again.

The old Temple librarian, Prester Otvar, spoke up.

"Where is our king—King Ryons?" he demanded. And Chutt marveled at Ilfil's answer.

"I regret to tell you that your king is dead! With great rashness he invaded the dominions of my master. He came looking for a battle, and he found one. Not one man of all his following shall ever return to Obann. King Ryons is dead."

All the people murmured, and then cries and wailing and loud exclamations broke out among them. Chutt ignored that. Ilfil's nerve took his breath away. It had to be a lie, he thought: "He can't possibly know whether the king is dead or alive!" But it was obvious the people believed what he'd said and were dismayed. Chutt held up his hands for silence, and got it after a long delay.

"King Ryons' death is grievous news to us who loved him and, cause for lamentation," he said. "It's even more needful, now, for you to give us time to set our country's affairs in order and to deliberate wisely on your master's offer.

"Tonight we choose a new council. Tomorrow, I hope, we'll have an answer for you. But we can do nothing until you move back from the gate."

"My master understands your difficulties," said Ilfil, "and deems your hesitation reasonable. Peace is worth waiting for! We will pull back for now and speak with you tomorrow.

"But remember this, you people of Obann. King Thunder offers peace! Do not choose war."

Gallgoid watched the Wallekki turn and slowly ride back into the east. They would not go far, he thought.

Like Chutt, he was sure Ilfil had lied about King Ryons' death. But it was the kind of lie that people would believe. Gallgoid had no doubt the vote that night would go Chutt's way. Having lost their king, the people would be anxious to have a ruling council back in power.

And he would have to act swiftly, this very night. His arrangements were not yet entirely complete, but there was no help for it.

"Well, Gallgoid?" Chutt said.

"You spoke very well, my lord—exactly as I would have advised you. But for the time being, you must devote all your energies to tonight's assembly. We must have a High Council, with you as governor-general."

"I won't have General Hennen on the council," said Chutt. "I want another general. And I suppose the First Prester's place on the council can only be held by Jod. There's no time to mobilize the presters to choose somebody else."

"If Jod believes the king is dead, he'll have but little reason to oppose you any further," Gallgoid said. Jod would have to be told, before the afternoon was out, that the king's death was a lie. That would be difficult to manage, but Gallgoid would see to it himself. "Just be sure you have the votes, my lord," he said.

"I'm sure," said Chutt. "I've already counted them, and I'll make sure again. I think Chief Ilfil's lie has helped me! But how can he say the Thunder King is here? I don't understand that at all."

"One thing at a time, my lord—one thing at a time. After you're confirmed as governor-general, then we'll see about the Thunder King."

"I can't imagine what Ilfil thinks he can accomplish by getting into the city!" Chutt said. "The man's not a fool, so why is he acting like one?"

"First things first, my lord," said Gallgoid. "Besides, you may yet make good use of Ilfil and his men. But first get your votes."

CHAPTER 32

How Gallgoid's Plans Prospered

Helki took the children aside, Jack, Ellayne, and Fnaa.

"There's a lot that I don't understand about people. It comes of living alone for most of my life," he said. "But even I can guess what you're thinking.

"You want to dash off to the city and try to help the baron. Trout saw you, Fnaa, stowing provisions in your bag. He hasn't told your mother, but he told me."

Fnaa blushed. Ellayne gave him a look that made him blush some more.

"By the time you got there," Helki said, "whatever's going to happen will have happened. I don't reckon Martis and Gallgoid will just stand by and let it happen."

Wytt jumped out of Ellayne's arms and chattered angrily at Helki. The man just grinned.

"No need to translate that!" he said. "But even he can't get to Obann in time to do any good. If I were to lead our whole army to the city, they could easily keep us out. So I reckon we'd all just better stay here and do our duty—which is to hold King Ryons' throne for him, here in Lintum Forest. I think we'll have excitement enough right here, before Lord

Chutt is finished."

"It's my father whom they've got locked up!" Ellayne cried. "How can we all just stay here and do nothing?"

"The last time you ran off by yourselves, the Griffs grabbed you and almost took you to the Thunder King."

Jack nodded. They were only saved, that time, because God struck the Griffs' mardar, Chillith, and took away his sight. Still, "It doesn't seem right, just staying here," he said.

"When God says stand and wait, you stand and wait," said Helki. "It's just as hard on me as it is on you. What I wouldn't give to be on my own again!

"But something tells me we're going to have a lot more to do than just sit here at Carbonek and keep the king's throne for him. It might be harder to do that than you think. We can't have him coming back from wherever he is, only to find Lintum Forest lost to him."

"Do you think he will come back?" Fnaa said.

"I never doubt it for a moment."

Helki made them promise not to run off to Obann—a promise Ellayne only gave because she knew it was exactly what her father would demand of her.

"And my promise," Helki said, "is this: to track you down, if you run off. You know I can do it! Don't put me to the trouble."

Wytt made no promise at all. It wasn't in his nature. Helki winked at him and went back to the castle.

"What do you suppose Helki thinks is going to happen here?" Jack said. "War?"

Wytt went into a torrent of assorted vocalizations, brandishing his stick for emphasis.

"What's all that about?" Fnaa said.

"Birds," said Ellayne—softly, because it mystified her. "He says the birds know something is going to happen, but they won't tell him what it is."

"Whatever it is," Jack said, "staying here and waiting for it is going to be harder than climbing Bell Mountain."

Gallgoid got to Jod before Chutt did, and warned him.

"Do everything you can to complicate the discussions today," the spy said, "but always stop short of provoking Chutt to lose his temper. Don't commit yourself. We don't want him to put you back under arrest. But hold his attention, and use up as much time as you can."

"And what will you be doing?" asked the prester.

Gallgoid smiled and said, "You'll see."

Roshay Bault remained confined in a room in Chutt's house that was nicer than his own room at home—and he and Vannet had the finest house in Ninneburky. The baron's prison was a guest room on the second floor, with a bed as soft as sleep itself, an antique wardrobe of polished oak aged almost black, and a window that once would have offered a fine view of the Palace. A polite, liveried servant who never spoke brought him three good meals a day, and from time to time, Lord Chutt looked in on him.

"The day you agree to swear loyalty to the Oligarchy," Chutt said, every time, "is the day you'll be allowed to leave." To which Roshay could not find it in himself to respond politely.

"You're the most pigheaded man I've ever met!" said

Chutt. "But I won't let you provoke me, and no one will be able to say you've been ill-treated here." But the door was kept locked, and one of Born's men guarded it.

Roshay found it all hard to take calmly. By the time word of his imprisonment reached Lintum Forest, he'd suffered two weeks of confinement. He would have gladly broken down the door with his fist and taken his chances with the guard outside, if not for the stout, grey-haired maid who came every other day to change his bedding and provide him with clean clothes. She brought notes from Gallgoid, which, after reading, he tore into little pieces and hid under the mattress.

Today, an hour after Ilfil's parley at the gate, he received the message he'd been waiting for. All it said was, "Tonight you leave this place. Be ready." But that was enough.

And in another room, a few doors down the hall, General Hennen received the same message.

Radiating out from the Temple and the Palace, Obann had a network of underground passages, some of them leading all the way out beyond the city walls. Few knew they existed.

Gallgoid knew. He'd used them on many errands for Lord Reesh and had devoted much time and effort to mapping them. Some were centuries old, others much newer. The newest of them all gave entrance to Lord Chutt's cellar. Since Chutt's return to the city, Gallgoid had set a crew to digging it, branching off a preexisting tunnel from the Palace. With a few more strokes of their picks, his men would be in Chutt's cellar.

The rest he would have to leave to the housemaid, Elbeth, and a young maid next door who flirted with the guards and gave them little treats, snacks and such, when they would let her in to visit her auntie. These were two of Gallgoid's people. He'd supplied them with the things they would need to carry out his plan.

Others of his people made sure the whole city knew about the meeting scheduled for that night. By the time he arrived at the wool merchants' guild hall that evening, the size and temper of the crowd outside the hall told Gallgoid that his agents had succeeded in their mission. Born and his biggest men had to clear a path to the door.

"This won't do!" Chutt said. "Send back for more men. We'll need them to keep order here."

"No Wallekki in our city!" yelled someone in the crowd.

"No Thunder King!" cried someone else. Yes, thought Gallgoid, Chutt would need more men tonight, and he'd have to pull them from guard duty at his house.

Many in the crowd cheered when they saw Prester Jod closely escorted by half a dozen mail-clad soldiers. They hustled Jod into the hall as quickly as they could, while others used the hafts of their spears to push back the crowd.

"How did this turn into such a cusset mess!" Chutt growled. "Are we to have a riot on our hands?"

As they went through the door, someone shouted, "Long live the king!"

"They're upset because of the Wallekki, my lord," said Gallgoid. "I advise you to be very patient with Prester Jod tonight. If you can win his support, the city is yours."

The hall was packed. Chutt took his seat at the great table on the dais, with Jod at his right hand. To his left sat

Born, the only officer they could find willing to act in Hennen's place. Born would be the new General of Obann before the night was out, if Chutt had his way.

Their task tonight would be to vote in the restoration of the Oligarchy and then fill three more seats on the High Council—those charged with overseeing revenues, commerce, and the administration of justice. If that could be accomplished, the new High Council would authorize the rebuilding of the Temple; and if they cleared that hurdle, they would discuss the peace offer of the Thunder King, tendered to them by Ilfil the Wallekki.

"We need to keep them here at least till midnight," Gallgoid thought. That would be Jod's part to play. And then Chutt would get a surprise when he came home.

A dozen hard raps of Chutt's gavel brought the meeting to order.

"First I wish to thank Prester Jod, sitting in for the First Prester, Lord Orth, whose whereabouts are unknown at this time," Chutt said, "and also Captain Born, an able and experienced soldier, sitting in for Hennen, who is indisposed.

"And let us first observe a moment of silence for King Ryons, who has fallen in battle somewhere in the East."

That rumor had already spread throughout the city, so Chutt's words took no one by surprise. The thought of it dampened the audience's spirit. There was no one to take Ryons' place as king, so they would need the Oligarchy.

"May I ask, Lord Chutt, how you came to receive those tidings?" said Jod.

"It was reported today by those Wallekki who spoke with us at the gate, Vicar."

"But how do we know it's true?"

The crowd rumbled. Chutt banged his gavel.

"Certainly those Wallekki believe it to be true," he said. "They have no reason to lie about it. What possessed His Majesty to invade the East with such a tiny army, who can say? It seems very unlikely he could survive such a rash enterprise."

With great tact that sorely tried Chutt's patience, but didn't break it, Jod managed to drag out the discussion for the better part of an hour. But Chutt had been shrewd enough to anticipate that and prepare his temper for it.

"Whether the king is dead or alive," he said at last, "we cannot leave our country without a governing authority. King Ryons was too young to have an heir. It must therefore fall to the Oligarchy to take up the reins of government. If the king does return to us someday, we are free to consider some other arrangement. But until then, Obann needs the Oligarchy. There are three of us here to vote on it, and I vote yea."

"Yea," said Captain Born.

"On the condition that King Ryons shall be our king again when he returns, and that we pledge ourselves to accept him as such without debate—for God Himself has given him the throne—I will vote yea," said Jod. "But only on that condition."

"I will accept the condition," Chutt said. "And I," said Born. They were lying, Gallgoid thought, and surely Jod knew it. They would assassinate the king if he ever showed his face again. But for the time being Ryons was still king in name if not in fact.

It took more than another hour to promote Born to general and formally elect him to the council. Chutt's argument was that he knew and trusted Born, had seen him skillfully exercise his duties, and that Hennen, made a general by the king's advisers, had never served on any council authorized by law. Again Jod argued gently, doggedly, against it. And again he proposed a condition: "That the king, when he returns, shall choose his general, and that we bind ourselves to abide by his decision without debate or demur." In the end, Chutt and Born agreed to that.

Many former oligarchs, rich men used to power, had proposed themselves for the other three seats on the council. Chutt had already chosen the ones he wanted.

But Gallgoid had advised him, "My lord, you must not appear a tyrant. Let Jod have his way with one of the three seats. If he favors a dissenter, what does it matter? The council will be under your control, four votes to two. But this way you'll appear reasonable and upright."

So, after much wrangling, there were three more councilors. By then it was nearly midnight.

Fully dressed and wide awake, Roshay Bault heard a key turn in the lock. Elbeth the maid opened the door. Behind her, in the hall, stood General Hennen.

"Time to go, sir," she said.

Roshay and Hennen shook hands.

"Where are the guards?" the baron asked.

"Drugged," said the general, "and sleeping soundly."

"Please, sirs, be quick about it—and try not to make much noise," Elbeth said. "Come with me."

Roshay took a closer look at her. He'd hardly noticed her at all when she'd come in to change his bedding. As she led them down the stairs, here and there you'd see a guard snoozing in a corner. "She did this!" he thought. This plain, stout, nobody of a woman—Roshay marveled at her courage.

She led them down to the cellar. A single lantern showed a hole in the brick wall, a hole big enough to be a doorway. Three men stood in the shadows. Martis was waiting there with them.

"Well-met, Baron!" he said. "This is Gallgoid's work, and I salute him. Sir, it's back to Ninneburky for you and me—where we can do some good. General Hennen, sir, Gallgoid and I have selected an excellent hiding place for you here in the city. Chutt will never find you. But soon you'll be needed; Gallgoid will explain it all to you tomorrow. Come—these men must block up this hole before Chutt comes home tonight."

Roshay turned to Elbeth. "Come with us to Ninneburky. You'll be safe there."

"Thank you, my lord, but my place is here. I'll go back upstairs now and drug myself, and they'll find me sound asleep in the kitchen, knowing no more about it than the others." She curtseyed roughly and hurried up the stairs.

Roshay and Hennen followed Martis into the tunnel, where one of Gallgoid's men waited to conduct the general to his hideaway.

"That woman is a hero," Roshay said.

"Someday I'll be able to reward her for her courage, God willing," Hennen said. "When the king returns."

CHAPTER 33

The Giant in the Lake

Unable to understand the report by Looth's scouts, Cavall raced ahead of the army, barking excitedly, to the next deserted Zamzu settlement.

This was on the shore of Lake Urmio, right on the water. But it wasn't much of a village anymore.

Broken boats littered the beach. Most of the houses were broken, too: roofs crushed in, walls thrown down, gouges in the earth.

Over it all lay a scent that Cavall had never encountered before, fresh and powerful, thick and heavy, as if the whole village had been dipped in something. Cavall couldn't make out what it was, but there was danger in it. Here something had come out of the water and destroyed the village; its scent clung to the wreckage. It reminded Cavall of the odor of a snake, but it was no snake that had done this.

A few minutes later, Shaffur's riders found him in the midst of it, barking out a warning to them. They dismounted and stood wondering at the sight. Cavall barked at them for all he was worth: this was no place for men to be. But they only waited for the rest of the army to catch up.

Cavall gave up on them, ran back to Ryons and barked at him. He was not a dog who would give way to being frantic, but he was getting frustrated. Only Baby seemed to have some shred of understanding. The giant bird had caught the scent, lowered his head, and hissed—the closest he could come to growling.

Angel took wing and flew in circles over the army.

"Cavall, what's the matter?" Ryons cried. Just as the scouts had reported, the village was deserted and destroyed. There was nothing to be seen that should upset a dog.

"He does not like this place," said Gurun. "If he could speak, we would hear something that would surprise us."

The whole army halted. Ryons saw Obst walk in among the ruins, shaking his head. The chiefs gathered around their king.

"Lake Urmio is dangerous," said Ghur Manyan. "Sometimes boats go out to fish and don't return. No one knows what happens to them."

"We should take a closer look," Chagadai said.

Ryons and Gurun dismounted and went to join Obst. Baby dug his claws into the ground and refused to take a step. Perkin couldn't budge him. Cavall stuck close to Ryons. He lowered his ears, and all the hair along his spine stood stiffly erect.

Looth trotted up to the king.

"As I told you," he said, "there's no sign of any of the people. But there's a bad smell in the air."

Ryons sniffed, but detected nothing. The Attakotts' senses, he supposed, must be keener than his own.

"I don't think the Zamzu would wreck their village before they abandoned it," Chagadai said. "There's been no storm, no earthquake. No trace of fire, either, that I can see.

It's a mystery."

Hawk and Xhama were forming their Hosa into battle lines. Shaffur took the hint and did the same with his Wallekki.

"What could it be, Obst?" Gurun asked, as they joined their teacher. "Do you think the Thunder King has done this?"

"I think this place was already abandoned before this was done to it," Obst said. "But who would take the trouble to break up empty houses?"

Cavall growled—a fighting growl, deep and deadly.

Then they all heard a splash, as if a huge stone had been hurled into the water.

Up from a patch of violent water, maybe twenty yards from shore, rose a long black head as big as a boat—for a moment Ryons thought it was a boat. A set of terrible jaws dropped open, displaying rows of white teeth like swords, all of it raised up on a long, thick neck. It had huge dark eyes that glittered in the sun. Cavall barked crazily, and many of the horses screamed. Some in their panic threw their riders.

Instantly the Hosa clashed their spears against their shields—boom-boom-boom, like rolling thunder—and roared their battle-cry. But before anyone else could react, the enormous head sank back beneath the water, and the surface of the lake was calm again before the horses were. Cavall sighed deeply and sat down.

For a moment all was silent, until all the men exclaimed at once. But Obst stood as though he'd been turned to stone.

"Pull back behind the Hosa!" Chagadai cried. "Everyone, go back! Come, come, Father—and you, my queen. It's not safe here."

The Wallekki struggled with their horses and finally brought them under control. The army backed up to the foot of the towering red cliffs, ready to defend itself, with Ryons and Gurun at its center, surrounded by the Ghols. Looth's men nocked their poisoned arrows to their bowstrings.

But the beast in the lake didn't show itself again.

"Well, that was something I'll remember!" Uduqu said. He leaned on his giant sword and mopped his brow.

"Obst, what was it?" Ryons cried.

Obst startled a little, as if awakened suddenly from sleep.

"Be at peace, all of you," he said. "We're in no danger now.

"But don't ask me what that was. I'm thinking of the Commentaries, which tell us how God's wrath against Obann, in the Day of Fire, came up also out of the sea."

"There are great whales in the sea," said Gurun, "but my people hunt them. That was no whale."

"Whatever it was, it was too much for my young friend here!" said Perkin, clinging to Baby's leash with both hands. But now the giant bird was at peace and had begun to groom his ruffled feathers with his beak.

"I can give no name to it," Obst said, "but you saw the beast made no move to harm us. Maybe the Hosa scared it off. But I think the creature was a sign from God. He is still protecting us."

"Maybe so," Looth said, returning an arrow to his quiver. "We hope so. Tomorrow we will all see Kara Karram."

"And then it will be over," Ryons thought. "All over."

Angel flew back down and settled on his shoulder.

CHAPTER 34

The New Governor-General

Ysbott cowered in his covered wagon the whole time Ilfil parleyed at the gate. One peek through the canopy was enough for him.

The city walls towered like mountains, and the sight of them wrung his guts with ice-cold fingers. How could human beings ever have created anything like that? Ysbott had never truly understood what a great and mighty city Obann was. It was like something built by the giants that were in the fairy tales his mother told him long ago. He'd believed those stories then, and they used to give him bad dreams, but he'd forgotten them until now. Were they really only men who lived behind those walls, or giants?

He clutched the golden mask to his breast, stroking the cold smoothness of it until his heart beat normally again. He was back in possession of himself when Dotter joined him.

"They won't let us in until tomorrow, if they let us in at all," Dotter said. "Ilfil has agreed to pull back a mile and wait."

"What are we going to do if they won't let us in?" Ysbott said, and secretly hoped they wouldn't let him in, not ever. But he wouldn't show his fear to Dotter. "Has Ilfil got a plan for that?"

"He thinks Chutt will make sure they let us in. It'd be bad for Chutt if Ilfil started telling all those people on the walls about the promises Chutt made to us. Ilfil could turn Obann against him, and Chutt knows it."

There were city-folk who would be petrified at the thought of entering Lintum Forest. Ysbott was a forest-dweller who feared to enter the city, now that he'd actually seen it. "That place could swallow us up without a burp!" he thought. "But I'll be all right, once I put the mask back on."

There was always the mask. It had power, and it was his.

Past midnight the new High Council wrangled with the question of letting the Thunder King into the city.

"There's nothing to be afraid of," Chutt said, over and over again. "What can two thousand Wallekki do to us, inside our own walls? As for this Thunder King of theirs, what have we to fear from him? Whatever else he may be, he's only a mortal man like all of us—and, in all probability, a mere imposter."

"But they say he's a god," said Lord Calagorn, formerly head of the wool merchants' guild, now the oligarch in charge of revenues: for they had elected Chutt governor-general.

"But we don't say so!" Chutt snapped at him. "I don't believe for a moment that this person is the Thunder King. Vicar, please speak up! Is the Thunder King a god, or just a man with ridiculous pretensions?"

"Blasphemous pretensions, I would say," Jod answered. "Of course he is no god. I agree that he's surely an imposter. But there is such a thing as spiritual wickedness, and we should not bring it into our city."

"Whatever we bring in," Chutt said, "we can quickly snuff it out if it becomes a threat. Or would you rather those Wallekki rode all over the countryside, looting and burning? Let them come into the city, where we can control them."

In the end Chutt had his way, four votes to two, as Gallgoid had predicted.

Chutt adjourned the meeting. Everyone was weary. The question of the Temple could be taken up tomorrow. As for the Wallekki, Born promised to have all the troops ready to suppress them at the first sign of trouble. "Horsemen aren't much good in the city," he said.

"You'll have to kill Ilfil," Chutt said. "That'll take the wind out of their sails."

"It'll be a pleasure," said the new General of Obann.

Most of the crowd outside the hall had dispersed by then. The remainder cheered Prester Jod and rejoiced when they saw him come out without an armed guard around him. When he headed toward his own house, they followed to make sure he reached it unmolested, and several dozen men remained in the street to protect him. But Chutt had gotten what he wanted from the prester and made no attempt to return him to captivity.

The new governor-general was in a good mood. "You must stop and have a sip of wine with me, Gallgoid, before you go to bed. We have much to celebrate."

"Thank you, my lord. I don't mind if I do."

"Once work begins on the new Temple, and the people can see it, they'll forget they ever had a king," Chutt said. "He was only a boy, after all, and a foreigner to boot—and he didn't spend much time here, did he?"

He rambled on and on, as men do when they are exceedingly tired but too happy to go to sleep. But then he saw there was no sentry at his door.

"General Born, this won't do!" he said. "Where's the guard?"

"He'll get some lashes when I find him," Born said.

They found him just inside the door, propped up in a chair in a corner of the hall. He didn't wake when they came clattering in. Born slapped him in the face, but that only made him grunt.

"There's mischief in this!" Born said. He yanked the guard from the chair and shook him. Even this produced only some mumbles. The man couldn't keep his eyes open. When Born threw him against the wall, his head made a loud bump on the paneling and he slid to the floor, senseless.

Chutt and Born, with Gallgoid following at a slower pace, raced from room to room, Born bellowing men's names, but every man they found was sleeping. Even the maid, Elbeth, they found slumped across a table in the kitchen. Shaking her did no good.

"My lord, they've all been drugged," said Gallgoid. "This is no natural sleep."

"The prisoners!" Chutt cried. He and Born charged up the stairs.

Roshay Bault and General Hennen were gone.

Chutt lost control of himself—the first time Gallgoid had ever seen that happen. The new governor-general cursed and pounded his fists against the walls. "Good!" thought Gallgoid. With some difficulty, he and Born conducted Chutt back to the kitchen. After repeated dousing with cold water, they finally roused the maid.

"What happened here, woman!" Born shook her.

"Speak!" roared Chutt.

"My lord, my lord!" said Elbeth. Her eyes rolled, unable to focus on any object in the room, but at least she didn't slip back into a stupor. "My lord, a man came and told us you were now the governor-general of Obann and gave me a drink of mead. And that's all I know! And even that, I'm not sure of. I think I may have dreamed it."

One by one, they roused the half-dozen guards left in the house, along with the butler and the footman. None of them remembered a man offering them mead. None of them remembered anything.

Roshay had a fine horse from Prester Jod's own stables, a steed with a glossy black coat, one of the team that drew Jod's carriage. Martis rode his own wiry little Wallekki horse, Dulayl, who once had taken him a long way up Bell Mountain.

"We ought to go as far as we can before we rest," Martis said. They'd come out of Obann near the North Gate to make a long detour around Ilfil's camp. "They might send some of those Wallekki after us."

"I hate to leave this city, and Prester Jod, in Chutt's dirty hands," said Roshay.

"Well, after tonight's business, I have a great deal more respect for Gallgoid," Martis said. "He may yet upset all Chutt's plans. But the thing for us to do is to return to Ninneburky. You may yet have a war to fight, Baron—holding the Eastern Marches for the king."

"I admit that I've been longing for my family," Roshay

said. He spurred the horse into a trot. "For all the luxuries of Chutt's house," he said, "freedom under the stars is better."

CHAPTER 35

How They Came to Kara Karram

During the night, clouds jostled each other into the sky above Lake Urmio, and in the morning it rained.

Obst walked among the mounted chieftains. They all had their eyes on the brooding red cliffs, waiting for their first sight of the fortress of Kara Karram. The name meant "Black Cliffs" in the language of the people whom the Thunder King had expelled from their country, said Ghur Manyan. "But the cliffs are red," thought Ryons.

Just before noon, they saw it.

A mighty fortress to begin with, the Thunder King had added to it over the years. It perched close to the very edge of the cliffs, but you couldn't see all of it from this far down below.

They saw crenellated battlements of black stone, defensive works that seemed to stretch into some unknowable distance. At regular intervals rose tall watchtowers. Everyone peered up at those intently, trying to see faces in the narrow windows. But no watchers showed themselves.

"Nevertheless," said Shaffur, shading his eyes from the rain, "I think we can be sure they watch our every move.

Why they haven't attacked us yet is more than I can understand. We're between the water and the cliffs with no room to maneuver. They could come at us from two directions and crush us in the middle." But the Attakotts were skirmished far out on both flanks, and so far had sent back no tidings of the enemy.

Ryons looked up at the long, long battlements and tried to count the towers. "But that's only the part that we can see," he thought. "What about the parts we can't see?" Imagining great gates, behind which lurked hosts of Zamzu ready to spring out at them when his people least expected it, he shuddered. "And there must be archers in those towers."

Obst called out to Ghur Manyan. "Where is the Thunder King's New Temple? I can't see it! I thought it was built right next to the fortress."

"It's set farther back from the cliff," Ghur said. "We won't be able to see it from down here."

Not one of the chiefs could look up at Kara Karram without realizing the sheer impossibility of taking it by force. The cliffs were soft. You could climb them if you chopped out handholds. But they were forbiddingly high, and even if attackers could get to the top without being decimated by archers, what then?

"Let us make camp here, my king," said Xhama. "My Red Regiment is valiant, but we can't fight the rain and the enemy at once. Maybe when the sun comes out again, we'll see a better way to the top."

"We'll have to go up some distance from here," added Jiharr, the Zephite, "and then come at the fort on level ground. Only a madman would try to start a battle here."

The chiefs agreed. And so, with Kara Karram glowering down on them from high above, as if it were more a part of the sky than of the earth, they made their camp and waited for fair weather.

As the king and his army halted under Kara Karram, Ilfil's Wallekki entered the city of Obann.

Sullen citizens watched from their rooftops and from upper-story windows. Born had given orders that no civilians were to watch from the street. Instead, the street on both sides was lined by silent spearmen, ready to attack the Wallekki at the first sign of trouble. "When they see you," Born said, "I want them to understand that they have no power in this city. Intimidate them with your eyes!"

Chutt had provided for Ilfil, until more satisfactory arrangements could be made, to encamp his men on Government Plaza, between the ruins of the Temple and the ruins of the Palace. What they would think when they saw those ruins, Chutt didn't care. "As long as a watch is kept on them, and they're not allowed to run around loose in the city, there's nothing they dare try to do to us," he told the other councilors.

Ilfil met with the High Council and promised peace; but the real conversation took place in Chutt's own parlor, with Born and Gallgoid to advise him and Ilfil there alone. Chutt's house was like nothing the Wallekki chief had ever seen before.

"My lord, you live deliciously!" he said, as he went around touching the carved and padded furniture. Chutt let him satisfy his sense of marvel until he was willing to be seated.

"So where is this Thunder King of yours, my friend?" Chutt said.

"My master and my god has adopted mortal guise, and it is irksome to him," Ilfil said. "By day he rests, because it greatly taxes a mortal body to house the spirit of a god. You'll see him either this night or the next, depending on his pleasure."

Chutt leaned back on his couch and softly laughed. "Ilfil, Ilfil!" he said. "You don't expect me to believe any of that malarkey, do you? And if you yourself believe it, you're not the man I take you for."

"I am King Thunder's mardar now."

"And I'm now the governor-general of Obann—but that doesn't mean that either of us has taken leave of common sense and grown credulous. And what's all this about donating to Obann half the gold of the Golden Pass, when I already have all of it in my possession?"

"That gold was to be divided between us," Ilfil said.

"And it will be, if you follow my advice." Chutt leaned forward, lowered his voice. "Where can you go from here, my friend? You can't go back across the mountains with another Thunder King. You'll all be killed. But you could remain in Obann as the commander of my personal bodyguard and enjoy life as a very rich man.

"I have enemies in Obann, and plenty of them. I'll need men around me I can trust. Captain Born is now the General of Obann, but it will take time for him to win the loyalty of all the troops. It would ease my mind to have a bodyguard who is an outsider to this city's politics."

"A mardar is greater than a bodyguard," said Ilfil.

Chutt laughed again. "A mardar of what?" he said. "Two

thousand Wallekki who can never go back home again! And even if I gave you all the gold, my friend, where could you spend it and what could you buy? But here in the city, and nowhere else, you can buy anything your heart desires. All you and I have to do is keep to our original agreement, and we'll both be rich and happy men."

Gallgoid listened attentively. "I must never underestimate this man again," he thought. But already he was pondering what counsel he could give to Chutt that would seem good to him, but in the end destroy him.

The first thing Prester Jod did with his freedom was to order Constan to flee to Durmurot—along with all his scholars and students and copyists, and the work itself. "I'd order you to take the whole seminary building with you, too, if I thought it could be done."

"It will interrupt the work, to move to Durmurot," the preceptor objected.

"It is a command," said Jod. "Bring with you everyone you need to do the work and everyone who wants to come with you. God's word must be removed from Obann before a new Temple can be built to lock it up again."

And so, as Ilfil marched into the city through the East Gate, the Word of God, in scrolls and parchments, and in books, the whole contents of the seminary's library, departed through the West Gate. It made a train of twenty carts, paid for out of Jod's pocket and carefully, expertly packed to shield the precious cargo from the weather. The whole town was watching the Wallekki; few came to see off this procession. Only a small handful of seminary personnel chose to stay behind. Things might have been different had Jod first sought the opinion of the other presters who were in the city, but he'd had no time for that.

Constan sat silently in the lead cart. No one could get him to speak. His thoughts picked a slow and thorough way into the future, and his students knew better than to distract him.

Jod couldn't be there. As the First Prester's representative on the High Council, he had to meet Ilfil. He and Constan had said their farewells the night before.

"Don't be surprised if I join you in Durmurot before this year is out," Jod said. "For I fear the city of Obann is lost to us—even as the prophets hanged by Judge Tombo said it would be. First the Temple itself, then the Palace. The city is going piece by piece."

"Our work will go on in the west," said Constan. "It will be as God wills it."

Dotter was losing his nerve.

"Sooner or later they'll do away with us," he said to Ysbott. "Now that we're in this city, we'll never get out alive."

Ysbott had his own fears to keep him company, but Dotter's words grated on him.

"There will always be a Thunder King!" he said. "That's what those fools don't understand."

"But what will you say to the High Council when you meet them? Are you ready for that?"

No, not quite ready, but Ilfil had spent some time preparing him, and Ysbott had spent most of his time thinking about it. And he was wise enough to understand that if he ever let his fear show, before the councilors of Obann or anybody else, his whole enterprise was finished. If the council didn't kill him, Ilfil would. So now Ysbott found boldness in the same place a cornered rat finds it.

"What do I care for any council of Obann!" he snarled. "What are they? But I tell you there will always be a Thunder King."

"That's what the people of this city used to say about their Temple," Dotter answered. "Have you seen it? Nothing but a great mountain of trash! A thousand years old it was, or so they say. But now they'll have to build a new one."

Ysbott shoved him backward, almost right through the wagon's canopy.

"Get out!" he said. "Go snivel somewhere else, where I won't have to hear you." He whipped his knife from its sheath. "Go, before you get a taste of this!"

Far, far away from Obann, too far away for any of its rumblings to reach him, Orth preached the message of the Scriptures to the Fazzan. He preached every night on the bank of the Green Snake River, to greater and greater multitudes, some of whom had journeyed many miles to hear him. By day he taught, sitting on a fish barrel, often with many children gathered round him. His Abnaks held themselves ready to take the lead in any fighting, but as yet no enemy had dared to venture this far up the river. By all accounts they were slowly pulling back. The Fazzan greatly outnumbered them, and now attacked them fearlessly, every chance they got. Most of the mardars in the country had been killed.

The night King Ryons camped below Kara Karram, Orth preached as usual. But this time he was interrupted with a question.

An old man, white-haired and lean, made his way to the front rank of the crowd. He walked with a cane, and the people respectfully made room for him: an old man with a warrior's cap had honor among the Fazzan. He put the cap on the tip of his cane and held it up so Orth would see it.

"Hear me! Hear me!" he cried.

"I hear you, my father," Orth said. He had learned that this was the polite form of address among the Fazzan. "All of you, please listen. Sir, let me have your words."

"I've come from the far end of the river," the old man said, "and it's taken me all this time to get here." His dialect was hard for Orth to understand, but Chief Weshesh translated it for him quickly. "I came because I heard you were teaching everyone about the God of Obann, so that He might be our God, too. But you are not the first to speak of this.

"In my part of the country, we have heard that the Thunder King has built a great stone house for Obann's God, to honor Him. How can it be so, that Obann's God would be against him? The New Temple, we have heard, is to be a place for every nation in the world to come and pay homage to this God, and also to the Thunder King.

"So, man of Obann, what of this New Temple? Is it not God's house? Why would God help us against the great king who has built a Temple to Him? What sense does that make? If you know, please explain it to me."

But Orth did know how to answer, and after Weshesh quieted the people, Orth spoke.

"My father, look around you," he said. "Look up at the stars in heaven, which are more in number than any man can tell. Behold the river, and try to count the moonbeams shimmering upon its waters. And consider the earth beneath your feet.

"And then look around at all these people. They are but the tiniest fraction of all the people on the earth. Look well!

"For I tell you truly, my brothers and sisters, that this sky above, this earth below, and all the waters everywhere—these are the Temple of the Lord. And even they, in all their vastness, can't contain Him. But God created all of this to house and feed His people. All people everywhere, too, are the Temple of the Lord. A temple created not by human hands but by the Lord, for His good pleasure! All this, and also all the things you cannot see, because they are not in the world—all of this is the true Temple of the Lord. And the Thunder King's New Temple, which he boasts of, and which he built for his own glory and not the Lord's, is nothing but a snare to catch the simpleminded."

Orth heard not even a breath among the people: nothing but the ripple of the waters and a soft wind rustling the nearby trees.

The old man lowered his cane and put his wolf's-head cap back on. He smiled up at Orth.

"Man of God, I've heard you," he said, "and I know a noble and great-souled answer when I hear one!" He looked at the people around him and spoke to them. "This man, I say, has told the truth! And his God has fought for us already. I will serve this God from now on. Let this good man from Obann teach me how."

CHAPTER 36

The Council and the Thunder King

The rain continued into the night at Kara Karram, but the city of Obann enjoyed a clear and starry night.

The new High Council was to have an audience with the Thunder King. It was to be a secret. The audience would be held in the middle of Government Plaza, in the camp of the Wallekki. Born's troops would be posted around the perimeter to keep the people away. "We can't keep them from knowing something's happening," Born said, "but we can keep them from seeing or hearing anything."

Ilfil spent some hours with Ysbott in the covered wagon, instructing him.

"Your life—and probably mine, too—depends on your saying the right things to those councilors," the chieftain said. "Remember that you are a god, albeit one in mortal guise. Don't bandy words with them! Don't answer questions. That's not how a god behaves."

"Do you know how a god behaves?" sneered Ysbott.

"No more than you. But if you let them see through you, you'll put us all in danger."

Ysbott had never in his life given much thought to gods

of any kind. He'd never been inside a chamber house, never prayed a prayer. If he had an immortal soul, that was more than he knew. That he might be punished in the next world for crimes he'd committed in this one was a notion that had never crossed his mind.

"They won't see through the mask," he said.

"If they do," said Ilfil, "the first spear through your heart will be mine."

The six councilors stood in a row before the wagon. Surrounding them stood Wallekki with torches alight. Behind Chutt stood Gallgoid. Chutt wanted him there. Gallgoid had never seen the Thunder King, but Lord Reesh had, and had told his servant all about it.

The councilors waited for what seemed a long time, amid two thousand Wallekki who kept the strictest silence. "Whatever he may be," thought Gallgoid, "these men believe in him." Their fear was like cold air pouring off an enormous block of ice. And if you couldn't feel it, you had only to look at their faces.

Ilfil, with half his face painted black, stood beside the wagon with a short spear in his hand. At last Dotter crept out from the canopy and whispered in his ear. Ilfil raised his spear and uttered a wild, quavering cry that made some of his warriors flinch.

"He comes, he comes!" he wailed. "All honor to the Thunder King, the god, the lord of all the East! God of war and god of peace!"

Out stepped Ysbott, to stand on the driver's seat.

Torchlight flickered redly off the golden mask. "That's

it, just as Lord Reesh described it—no imitation," Gallgoid thought. But where was the robe of shifting colors that Reesh had spoken of so many times? This man was clad in the full regalia of a Wallekki chieftain, with gold bracelets clanking up and down his arms. But even so, the mask was genuine: Gallgoid had no doubt of that. Someone had retrieved it from the ruins of the golden hall.

And Chutt thought, the moment he first saw it, that the mask was the most beautiful and desirable object he'd seen in all his life. It fairly stopped his heart. It would have pleased him to stand there all night, just looking at it.

As for the Thunder King himself, Lord Chutt hardly noticed him. "It could be anyone!" he thought. "It's just a man; he doesn't matter. The mask is what's important." It came to him that the mask itself, and not the man who wore it, was the Thunder King. And the mask was real.

The Thunder King spoke—in Obannese.

"Lords of Obann! We have been at war too long. To make peace, I will do you good instead of evil.

"You have brought my gold into your city. My gold! Your city. But what is gold to me? All the gold of the East is mine. I gather it as a man might gather pebbles from a brook.

"For peace and friendship between us, I give you my gold! For peace and friendship between Obann's God and me, I give you gold to build your Temple. To bring glory back to Obann!

"Befriend my people who are here among you, reward them well, and let all be as it was before the war.

"I have spoken. I give you peace."

He turned and went back into the wagon.

Ysbott felt as if there were iron bands tightening around his chest. His own voice amazed him: it would carry all the way to Lintum Forest.

He trembled head to toe, and once inside his wagon, nearly fainted. But he'd said what Ilfil had taught him to say, and said it because he could think of nothing else. He half-expected the councilors and Ilfil to barge in after him and stab him to death on the spot. But they didn't, and he gasped gulps of air until he could breathe normally again. The mask made it hard, but he didn't dare take it off.

"I have to get out of this city!" he thought. They could have their cusset gold; he still had seven sheets of it cached on the mountain, if he could ever get back to claim it.

He almost jumped out of his skin when Dotter crept in to join him.

"Splendid!" whispered the former slave dealer. "What a performance! I half-believed in you myself!"

Those words, Ysbott thought, were the most surprising words he'd ever heard.

Five of the councilors clapped loudly, but Prester Jod stood like a granite statue.

"Better than anything we dared to hope!" Lord Calagorn said.

Ilfil strode up to them. "Now, my lords," he said, "you have seen with your own eyes and heard with your own ears. You'd be mad not to accept the peace my master offers you.

He's not always so generous!"

"We accept his peace," said Chutt, "and we accept his friendship, too. By all that's glorious, we rejoice in it! Eh, Gallgoid?"

"There's no doubt, my lord, that our eyes have seen the Thunder King tonight," Gallgoid said. But he was thinking, "Avaricious fool! Now he wants the mask, wants it for himself. There'll be yet another new Thunder King, before this game is over." The thought of Chutt as Thunder King, ruling in Obann, forced a grin to Gallgoid's lips. Chutt seemed not to notice it.

"This is blasphemy and great folly," Jod said.

Chutt slapped him on the shoulder. "You'll feel better about it, Vicar, when you see the new Temple going up."

"The Thunder King has already built his own New Temple at Kara Karram," said Jod.

"Well, what of it? Two Temples are better than one. Besides, his New Temple is so far away, it might as well be on the moon. We'll have our own Temple here in Obann, and that's as it should be."

Jod didn't answer. Gallgoid studied the prester's face, trying to read his thoughts. He supposed Jod would have to be protected: that Jod would not give in to Chutt, never give his blessing to any plan to rebuild the Temple. It would be better, Gallgoid thought, if Jod were back in Durmurot. But he would never leave Obann unless the First Prester returned.

By tomorrow morning Gallgoid's agents would be busy, and all hope gone of keeping this night's business a secret. All Obann would know that the High Council had met face-to-face with Obann's enemy and were now his friends.

Gallgoid had the rest of the night to shape the story to his needs.

Jod couldn't sleep when he got home, so he sat at his desk and wrote a letter to Constan.

"This will have overtaken you before you come to Durmurot, but under no circumstances should you turn back to Obann. I command you to make all good speed to Durmurot.

"The new High Council has joined hands with the Thunder King—or rather with a man who is passing himself off as such. He wears the golden mask of the Thunder King. How he came by it, I know not.

"I fear Chutt will convince all Obann that this truly is the Thunder King. Why? I am unable to say, but I fear the consequences.

"Pray for the safe return of King Ryons, and for me: Jod."

He sealed the letter shut with wax, gave it the impression of his signet ring, summoned his trustiest servant out of sleep, and told him to take the best horse from the stables and set out at once to deliver this message.

For the rest of the night, until sleep finally came to him, Jod prayed.

CHAPTER 37

The Fall of Kara Karram

In a drizzling rain that made everything look grey and cheerless, King Ryons' army marched past Kara Karram. It seemed to stare down at them, as if it had a mind to pounce. Passing below it, they looked for a safe way up the cliffs. They might be attacked at any moment, but they weren't.

"I don't know what they're waiting for," Chief Shaffur growled. "Surely they don't expect us to try crawling up those cliffs!"

"We can't get up," said Chagadai, "but they can't get down. Somewhere along this road, they're waiting for us."

They marched half the day, until they were well out of sight of the fortress. Then the chiefs halted because it made no sense to go too far. As the men ate, and set up what shelter they could, the chieftains sat in council.

"Do these cliffs go on forever?" Shaffur said.

"Not forever, but certainly for some miles yet," Ghur Manyan said.

"We can climb them when it stops raining," said Xhama, "but there is no way up for the horses."

"We can't go on without the horses!" Shaffur said.

At last they decided that when the rain stopped ("If it ever does!" Shaffur said), the Attakotts should climb the cliff and see whatever they could see. If there was no enemy waiting for them, then the Hosa and the Zeph should go up, too, while the horsemen would go on to find their own way.

"I don't like splitting our force," said Tiliqua the Griff. But there was nothing else they could do.

"In another five or ten miles, I think, you should find a way up for the horses," Ghur said. "Now you have seen what a good site this is for a fortress. It cannot be attacked from the west."

Ryons stroked Angel's feathers. The hawk wouldn't fly, but at least she was eating normally again. "Come to think of it," Ryons said to Gurun, "I haven't seen any birds at all today up there. Not even crows."

"The crows always know when there will be a battle," Gurun said. "Maybe there will be no battle."

It rained all afternoon and into the night. Except for scouts and sentries, the army slept.

Shingis, chief of the Blays who were Gurun's own bodyguard, remained awake. He tried to pray silently, as Gurun had taught him, but he had no confidence that God would hear him. The gods of the Blays, which the Thunder King had taken away from them, were wooden idols: posts driven into the ground with carved and painted faces. To pray to them, the villagers had first to blow raucous-sounding horns and clash tin pots together. Only then would the gods listen to the shaman. Each village had its own tutelary idol.

"And what good did they ever do us?" Shingis asked himself. All the same, he would have felt more secure praying to the real God with horns and clashing pots.

Somewhere up in the fortress, perhaps lying piled up in a dungeon, were the Blays' own village gods—unless the Thunder King had already used them up for firewood.

"Poor little gods!" thought Shingis. It would be good, he thought, to weep for them.

But he was distracted when Cavall suddenly jerked to his feet from his place beside the sleeping king—stood up and wagged his tail as if he wished to cast it off his body, whimpering delightedly.

What had made him do that? But before he could get up to investigate, Shingis felt a delicious wave of sleep wash over him. He lay down and closed his eyes with the conviction that God had heard him, after all.

Cavall had seen the man before. It seemed like a long time ago, but Cavall knew him instantly. He could have leaped for joy. He would have barked, but his heart was so full, he could only find the breath to whine.

The man nodded to Cavall, put a warning finger to his own lips, and patted his head and stroked his ears.

Ryons slept fitfully, and his dog's first whimper woke him.

For a moment he thought he was dreaming. But there stood Cavall, wide awake and rapturously happy.

Ryons looked up and recognized the man who was standing over him—an old man with a shiny bald head and a snow-white beard, and eyes that twinkled as if each one had a living star inside it. He wore an old set of farmer's overalls.

Cavall settled down on his belly, quiet now, tail still wagging furiously, pink tongue lolling, with a dog's toothy grin.

"Well met, King Ryons," said the man. "So you've got here at last. Well done!"

Ryons had met him twice before: first, to point him on the way to Obann, and again, to lead him out of the palace by night and set him on his way back to Lintum Forest. And he had seen him also at the gates of Obann City.

"Please, sir—who are you?" the boy whispered. How had the man gotten past the scouts and sentries?

"A servant of God, my boy—like you," he answered. Around them the rain continued to drizzle down, and everyone slept but Ryons and Cavall. "Rise up, King Ryons. We have a small journey to perform."

Ryons shed his blankets and got to his feet. "Where will we go?" he asked.

"To Kara Karram," said the old man. "You are to see it for yourself: for no man of this army will be permitted to set foot there, or to lay a finger on its stones. It isn't safe."

Ryons turned and looked back in the direction of the fortress. He couldn't see it, of course; but over the cliffs where Kara Karram overlooked the lake, the dark night was faintly discolored with a dull red glow. Was the fortress burning?

Gurun woke suddenly.

"Make no noise, Gurun, but rise up and come with me."

Although the night was so dark, she clearly saw the man who spoke—young, handsome, and clad in the sealskin boots and brightly colored woolen tunic of a Fogo Islander. This was her filgya, the spirit that had first guided her to Obann and given her the power to understand and speak its language—and after that, many other languages.

Ryons was up already.

"Gurun shall come with us," the old man told Ryons, "but no one else." He turned to Cavall. "My friend, you're to stay here and keep watch. Kara Karram is no place for a good dog like you." And Cavall nodded as if he understood the words. Ryons was sure he did.

This was the second time, he recalled, that he and Gurun had both seen God's servant. But Gurun had seen him in another form, a man of Fogo Island. Ryons was young enough to accept that as the way it was. In what form, he wondered, did Cavall see him?

"Come now," said the messenger, "and don't look back."

They followed him through and out of the slumbering camp. The men who stood on guard seemed not to notice them at all.

Gurun fought a strong compulsion to look back over her shoulder. If she had, she would have seen herself and Ryons sleeping soundly with Cavall sitting up between them. And she would not have been able to go on. But she obeyed God's servant, and didn't look.

They should have been terrified to go to Kara Karram, Ryons thought; and yet he felt no fear at all, just now. An emissary of the Thunder King once told him that the tyrant would put out his eyes and confine him in a dungeon until he died. The fear of that now left him.

The messenger led them back the way they'd come, along the lake. No one felt like talking. The rain fell all around them, but they felt neither wet nor cold. It had taken the army half a day to come this far, but it seemed to Ryons that the three of them on foot made much better time. Or maybe, he wondered, God somehow made this night longer than an ordinary night. He would have to ask Obst if that were possible. He had a feeling that it was.

The dull red glow sat over the fortress on the cliff. When he looked up, Ryons could see the battlements silhouetted against it.

"This way," said the old man.

He turned and began to plod up the face of the cliff. Ryons and Gurun followed. It should have been a grueling climb, Gurun thought, and yet it wasn't. Her breath came easily. The cliff seemed to be made of some kind of hard-packed sand, possibly mixed with clay. Gurun noticed that the filgya and Ryons, ahead of her, left no footprints in it.

"We are in the spirit," she thought, "as were some of the prophets of old. That's why we can do this."

They came to the top of the cliff. Before them towered the walls of Kara Karram, taller and darker than even the great walls of Obann.

A mighty gate yawned open. Around it lay scattered the dead bodies of men, Zamzu by the look of them. Gurun saw them clearly under the red light.

"What happened to them?" Ryons asked.

"Come and see," said the messenger. "You may speak. There's no one to hear us."

They entered Kara Karram through the open gate.

The walls were made of great stones, seamlessly fitted together. The fortress was a city of the dead, no one left alive in it.

"It seems to me that there ought to be many more people here," Gurun said. "Have most of them deserted it?"

"Those who could," said the messenger.

He showed them throne rooms, halls, and kitchens. It was all emptiness and desolation. Here and there lay bodies, face-down, face-up. He took them up to see the battlements, and they marveled at the strength and vastness of the defenses. There were machines up there, untended, for hurling stones and fireballs.

South of the fortress—it was hard to gauge the distance—squatted another dark mass, set back farther from the cliff.

"Is that the New Temple?" Ryons asked.

"It is," the old man said. "It's not quite finished, and never will be. We won't be visiting it. But come, there's more to see."

He brought them into a hall packed with idols from every country in the East, the conquered gods that were no gods, carried off by the Thunder King's mardars. A few of them, carved exquisitely in marble, diorite, or sandstone, had some pretense of beauty; others were but monsters. But most were rude—some stones, or stocks of wood, with sightless holes for eyes and silent mouths.

"Men made these with their own hands, then worshipped them as gods," said the messenger. "See the folly of it."

"You shall make no image and bow down to it," Gurun

quoted from the law given to the Children of Geb, the first of the Tribes of the Law in ancient times.

"Now I will show you another kind of work wrought by men's hands," said the messenger.

He led them down a long stone stair to some place deep in the bowels of the cliff. It should have been dark enough to blind an owl, but a feeble red light haunted it. Down, down they trod, until at last they came into a cavernous hall bathed with a light the color of watered blood.

A few dead men lay on the stone floor. Filling most of the space, Ryons and Gurun saw what looked like an enormous iron furnace. It had many windows that revealed a fiery interior, and a profusion of handles and levers.

The whole chamber vibrated. You could feel it through the soles of your feet.

"Your friend Martis was right to fear that the enemy dug deep into the rubble of the past to acquire the power of the ancient world," the old man said. "With the power confined in this chamber, he incinerated all life on a populous island. With this power he intended to incinerate your army, O King. To destroy you with a greater army would not have satisfied him. He wished to strike terror into all the world and bring it to its knees before him."

Ryons remembered the burnt island, and shuddered.

"But this power was greater than his, too great to be confined," said the messenger, "and with it the enemy destroyed himself. As in the Day of Fire, so today. For it pleases the Lord our God to turn evil against itself and to let pride devour pride.

"Every living thing in Kara Karram has been fatally poisoned by this power. In the morning, if a man shall look for this place, he will not be able to find it.

"Now you have seen what the Lord your God has shown you, and you shall report it as you saw it, so that all the world may know." He turned to them, and his grave face broke into a soft smile. "Come—it's time you returned to your place."

When they arrived back at the camp, God's servant said, "You will sleep now, children, for a little while. When you wake, you'll remember everything you've seen tonight.

"You will awaken just before the dawn, and when you do, King Ryons, you must rouse your men and bid them all look north. What they see will betoken the destruction of Kara Karram.

"Forbid any man of yours to go there! The very earth on which it stands is poisoned, and shall be for very many years. Anyone who sets foot there will die.

"You will not be able to march back the way you came. The whole cliff will fall in on itself and block the way. Your army will have to march a southern route, around the lakes, to return to Obann—a long march, but I think you'll march in peace. For you have done as God commanded, and your Lord is pleased with you—the seed of King Ozias and a wise and valiant girl."

Gurun felt tears in her eyes. How could that be, when they were in the spirit?

The servant led them through the camp. Sentries kept watch, but didn't see them.

Cavall was still awake. He stood up and wagged his tail. The old man petted him while Ryons and Gurun lay back down in their places. The rain had stopped.

"Sir, will we ever see you again?" Ryons asked.

The old man smiled down at them, eyes twinkling.

"Who knows?" he said. "There's much hard work awaiting you at home, and some of it will be dangerous. But remember, King and Queen of Obann: God is never very far from you, and you are always in His thoughts."

They fell asleep before they saw him go. Cavall watched, longingly. But what he saw, he couldn't tell.

They woke together, and suddenly, in the tail end of night. Faint stars shone overhead in a sky now clear of clouds.

"We have to get everybody up," said Ryons. As the servant had promised, he remembered everything he'd seen.

"Wake up, wake up!" he cried. "Captains, rouse the camp!"

"Awake! Awake!" cried Gurun.

Hands clutched at weapons. Sentries sounded the alarm. Expecting an attack, chiefs and warriors woke up quickly. Commands rang out, equipment rattled harshly. Horses neighed; Cavall barked.

It took some minutes to sort out the confusion. Ryons' chiefs obeyed him, not pausing to ask for explanations. When all were on their feet, or on horseback, Ryons and Gurun climbed onto a wagon so that all the men could see them.

"Look north," cried Ryons, "back to Kara Karram. All of you, look—and wait—and see!"

Puzzled, and not a little afraid, the men turned. The few

minutes that they had to wait seemed very long.

Over the place of Kara Karram, several miles to the north, a flash of white light, whiter than day, stunned them into silence. It lit up everything, like lightning.

A moment later, a deep rumble as of distant thunder smote their ears.

Then it was dark again, and still.

"Kara Karram has fallen!" Gurun cried. "The whole cliff has fallen down—that's what you have heard!"

"What is all this?" said Shaffur. He didn't have to raise his voice for everyone to hear him.

"It was the end of Kara Karram," Ryons answered. "Hear me, all of you, and I'll tell you more."

The army, all of them, pressed closer to the wagon, and Ryons and Gurun told them everything they'd seen. As they spoke, the sky turned pale and then rosy as the sun began to rise.

Silently they wondered at it. Could such a thing be true? But as the sun peeked over the eastern edge of the world, they knew in their hearts that it was true, and rejoiced.

"It seems we've accomplished our mission," Uduqu said. "So I guess we can all go home."

CHAPTER 38

Lord Chutt's Peace Treaty

The morning after Kara Karram fell, Roshay Bault and Martis came home to Ninneburky. No word having been sent ahead, the baroness gasped when she opened the front door to her husband.

"But how—? Did Lord Chutt let you go?" she cried.

Roshay grinned. "Gallgoid contrived my escape. I'm sure Chutt wasn't pleased!"

Vannett laughed and threw herself into his arms. Nor did she forget to say, "Welcome home, Martis!"

"Where are the children?" Roshay asked.

"Safe in Lintum Forest with Helki! But I suppose we can have them back, now you're here."

"Maybe not yet. We'll have to talk about that."

"After we get some food and beer into the two of you," Vannett said.

Lord Chutt had his morning tea with Gallgoid, just the two of them in Chutt's parlor, with the door closed.

"You never told me that Lord Reesh escaped the burning of the Temple and that you accompanied him to the Golden Pass. Why did you never tell me that you'd been there before?" Chutt was feeling suspicious.

"My lord, I've told you now—when I might have easily kept it to myself, and no one the wiser," Gallgoid said. "I only try to give you the best advice I can. In my judgment, based on Lord Reesh's description of it, what we saw last night was no counterfeit but truly the mask of the Thunder King, recovered somehow from the golden hall."

"And to think we missed it!" Chutt gnashed his teeth. "To think that if we'd only dug a little deeper, we would have found it!"

"Unless it had already been removed before your people arrived there."

"And the man behind the mask—who can he be?" Chutt said.

"Lord Reesh saw the Thunder King unmasked. He was amazed at how young he seemed to be." Gallgoid had not told Chutt what he'd learned while at the hall: that there was no Thunder King, but only a succession of men who wore the mask. "Let Chutt's imagination have its way with him," he thought. "It'll tell him wilder tales than any I can invent."

"Ilfil thinks this person truly is the Thunder King," said Chutt, "that he climbed out of the wreckage of the hall and came down the mountain for his gold. At least that's what Ilfil says! What do you think of that?"

Gallgoid shrugged. "It's more than I know." He doubted Ilfil believed in this Thunder King.

"Whoever it is," Chutt said, "he has the mask and Ilfil has him. What does Ilfil plan to do with him? I wish I knew!"

Ilfil left a cordon of armed men around the Thunder King's wagon. Mask or not, thought Gallgoid, the man seemed to be Ilfil's prisoner.

Chutt rose from his chair. "It's time to go," he said.

Today at noon the High Council would formally proclaim the rebuilding of the Temple and the league of friendship with the Thunder King. Prester Jod was expected to vote "no."

"Let him vote as he pleases—it will be five to one in favor of the Temple," Chutt said. "And in this I know the people will be with us."

"Certainly, my lord," said Gallgoid; and he thought, "But that could change."

The council met on the front porch of the guild hall, with as many of the people gathered before them as could squeeze into the street. Chutt made a speech announcing the good news, the end of the war and the rebuilding of the Temple, to be paid for entirely with the gold donated by the Thunder King.

He finished on a high note. "And so our country enters a new era of prosperity and peace. Many of you will work on the construction of the Temple and be well paid for your labor. Even then, there'll be plenty of money left to repair the city gates and build a new house for the government. Obann will not be put back to the way it was before the war. It will be greater and more beautiful, and richer, than it ever was!"

The crowd cheered. Gallgoid's agents would not try to dampen their enthusiasm—not today. Later, he thought, something would be done.

One by one, the councilors voted for the Temple and the treaty, until it was Jod's turn.

"My lords, what is this?" he said. "In God's name you propose to make a treaty with an enemy who has sent armies into our land to ravage it—worse, an enemy who has declared himself a god. Would you make a league with blasphemy?

"Furthermore, you seek to authorize the building of a Temple without the approval of the First Prester, who has renounced any Temple made with human hands. If you think God will bless this enterprise of yours, you are mistaken. I implore you to change your votes."

The crowd cheered that, too—a testimony to Jod's popularity among the people. But when the cheering died down, Chutt showed himself equal to the challenge.

"Vicar, I'm glad you mentioned that," he said. "True, Lord Orth is our First Prester, chief of all the clergy of Obann. But where is he? What has become of him? Will we ever see him again? Is he even still alive?"

"You know where he is, Lord Chutt—preaching God among the Heathen, east of the mountains. He has won many converts among the Abnaks and is now visiting the Fazzan. He is engaged in holy work and laying the foundation for a peace more lasting, and firmer, than any that you have imagined."

"For which we all applaud him!" said Chutt. "But in the meantime there is no First Prester in Obann. It may be years before Lord Orth returns—if ever.

"And then, why should we call him back from his work among the Heathen? He can't do that work from here, nor can he do his work for Obann from the Abnak country. I say we would all be better served if the clergy were to name a new First Prester. It's the only sensible thing to do."

"The clergy has not considered such a thing," Jod said.

"Then I urge the clergy to consider it, and soon! We cannot be without a First Prester in Obann."

Shrewdly put, thought Gallgoid. He knew that Chutt had already sounded out several of the leading presters and found them receptive to his plan. Not a few of them hoped themselves to become the next First Prester.

"The First Prester may only be replaced in case of death or incapacity," Jod said.

"If he can't be here, then he might as well be dead or incapacitated," Chutt answered. "A conclave should be held as soon as possible to decide this matter."

Jod had no choice. He had no authority to overrule the mass of the clergy.

The crowd grumbled. The people hadn't expected this and knew not what to make of it.

"For the time being," Chutt said, "we'll leave that business to the clergy. And for the time being—and hopefully for all time—the vote is five to one to accept the peace and build the Temple. Today is the day our city begins to rise again."

A day's march brought the army to the end of the cliffs, which gave way to rolling, grassy hills as far as the eye could see.

To Ryons' surprise, as soon as he finished feeding her, Angel flapped her wings and took off, circling high overhead until she was just a dark speck in the cloudless sky. After a few circles she took off into the northwest, back the way they'd come. Ryons whistled her back, but to no avail.

In a matter of minutes she approached the place where once she'd encountered a barrier, where the great nest of humans had stood above the lake.

The barrier was gone. The air was fresh and clear. A few crows flew there, below her, looking as if they were trying to get up their courage to land. They didn't notice her.

And everything was changed. There was no fortress anymore. There was no cliff: only a great gouge cut out of the cliff and a slope of rubble extending into the blue water. It was as if the earth had torn itself open for Kara Karram, which had collapsed under its own weight. A man would not have been able to tell there had ever been a castle there.

The other building, the Thunder King's New Temple, perched black and desolate on the brink of the crater that had not been there earlier. Angel saw no sign of life in it.

What goes through the mind of a hawk? There was no one she could tell, not even Cavall. Only Wytt might have understood her.

But although she had no use of words, Angel felt an exhilarating sense of triumph and rejoiced in flying over the place without being made ill by something in the air. There had been some nameless danger here, and now it was no more. That much she knew as well as any human being could have known it.

She flew back to the army, whistled to her king, and landed on his outstretched forearm.

"That's a happy bird, if ever I saw one," said Chagadai.

"She has been to Kara Karram and seen its ruin," Gurun said. "And I think she knows we are going home again."

She realized with a start, as soon as she had said it, that this was the first time that "home," when she thought of it, did not mean Fogo Island.

"So be it, O Lord," she prayed silently. "So be it."

CHAPTER 39

A House for the Thunder King

Ysbott did not like being Ilfil's puppet, who would live only for as long as the chieftain found him useful.

He remembered how he'd first become the leader of an outlaw band in Lintum Forest. He certainly hadn't done it by hiding in a wagon and tamely appearing and withdrawing on command.

"Am I the Thunder King, or am I not?" he asked the mask. And the mask seemed to answer, "You have asked the wrong question. Are you Ysbott the Snake or Ilfil's slave?"

Ysbott grinned—because the action that sprang instantly into his mind was so bold, so desperate, that it would only mean one of two things. Either he was so distraught over his predicament that he'd lost his mind, or else the mask had shown him what to do.

But it was not so different from a thing he'd done before, when he was young, and a mere underling to Alf Poison, whom all men feared. If he could do it then, surely he could do it now. The mask had shown him the way. He donned his robes and called for Dotter.

"Bid Ilfil and all the warriors to gather round the wagon—now," he said. "I want to speak to them."

"Now? In the middle of the day?"

"Yes, now! Go!"

Something in his face made Dotter obey. As he adjusted the mask, Ysbott heard Dotter outside, calling the men to assemble. Ysbott climbed out from under the canopy before Ilfil could come in to stop him, and stood on the driver's seat.

Ilfil came up with a face like thunder, pushing his way through the men until he stood before the wagon.

"What's this, my lord!" he demanded.

"Turn and face the men, my mardar," Ysbott said. "Silence, all of you!"

Ilfil turned, at a loss to do anything for the moment, but obey. Dotter stood beside him, trembling with confusion.

"Am I not the Thunder King?" Ysbott cried. "Am I not entitled to sacrifices?

"You've brought me to this great city, and yet here I am, shut up in a covered wagon. Why have I not been given a palace in this city? Why have I not been presented with a sacrifice?"

Without another word, he stooped down suddenly, seized Ilfil from behind, and with a skill born of much practice, cut his throat.

It stunned the men. Ilfil fell down dead. Ysbott rose to display the bloody knife.

"There's my sacrifice!" he said. Dotter, nearly fainting, translated. "And now for my palace! You men, who are my men now—not Ilfil's, but mine, my own—take me to the High Council of Obann! Now, with no delay."

He came down from the wagon, still flourishing the knife. "Choose men to guard me," he hissed to Dotter, "and the rest are to follow. Right now!"

Dotter picked some men, cried out Ysbott's order. The Wallekki obeyed like dumb beasts. Soon they were marching out of the plaza, up the widest street they could choose.

A handful of Born's guards confronted him. Ysbott barked at them.

"Take us to Lord Chutt! Do it, or die where you stand!"

They couldn't oppose the whole mass of the Wallekki. No one wanted a battle in the city, and they weren't ready for a fight. A corporal said, "Follow me," and two of his men ran off to report to their officers. Ysbott let them go.

It took only minutes to march to Chutt's house, but the governor-general was already waiting for them on his steps, with a line of armored guards in front of him.

"My lord," he said, "we are at peace! Where's Chief Ilfil?"

"Dead," said Ysbott, "I claimed him as a sacrifice." He felt as if a wind were rushing through his head. He couldn't feel his own feet on the cobbles. "We are indeed at peace, Lord Chutt," he said, "but it's time you did right by me. I demand a house, and servants, befitting my greatness. A fine house!"

Chutt smiled as if he were greatly relieved.

"If it's a fine house you want, O King," he said, "then it's a fine house you'll have. Bid your men rest, O King. And come into my house with me, as my guest, while we find a house for you. It shall be done with all speed."

"My guards and my slave shall come in with me," Ysbott said. As he had once done to Alf Poison, so he'd done to Ilfil the chief. But he was not about to give Chutt a chance to do the same to him.

Now that he was governor-general, Lord Chutt's favor

was well worth having. He had no difficulty at all in finding a rich man willing to part with his townhouse. He would be paid in gold, and Chutt would be obliged to him. Chutt sent out his servants to make inquiries, and before the day was done, they had a fine house for the Thunder King.

Chutt had King Thunder in his parlor for several hours. It was too bad the golden mask hid his face. One look at that face, Chutt believed, would tell him much. Even so, the man didn't know how to sit comfortably in a deep, well-padded chair, and he was as tense, all over, as a bowstring.

"But what an extraordinary man!" thought Chutt. "How did he ever get the mask, when I had two thousand men who couldn't find it? And I thought Ilfil was the kind of man who could survive the Day of Fire—and yet this fellow's killed him. And it seems he's convinced the Wallekki to believe in him." What Chutt could not yet decide was whether this extraordinary man would be, to him, an asset or a liability. "What am I to do," he wondered, "with the Thunder King?"

Ysbott was glad this great lord couldn't see his face. He'd never imagined anyone could live like this. A painting in a gilded frame hung on the wall above an alabaster mantelpiece: a scene of mounted huntsmen cornering a wild boar. Ysbott had never seen a painting before and half-suspected it was something magical. Had the figures in it once been living men and animals, now shrunken, frozen, and strangely imprisoned by some witchcraft? Was Lord Chutt a sorcerer?

"You'll enjoy your stay in Obann, O King," Chutt said. "Unfortunately, you're not seeing our city at its best. I wish we could have shown you the glory of the Temple and the grandeur of the palace. But someday, thanks to your generosity, Obann will be glorious again. I hope you'll be able to see it then."

With the courage he'd mustered to murder Ilfil ebbing away, Ysbott hardly trusted himself to speak at all. But he had to say something; he couldn't let Chutt see he was afraid.

"Maybe someday you'll be able to visit my cities in the East," he said.

"It would be a pleasure."

Lord Chutt wished to serve him cakes and wine, but Ysbott declined. To eat and drink, he would have to take off the mask.

"If you don't mind my suggesting it, O King," said Chutt, "you may be more comfortable if you remove your mask. It must be rather heavy."

Ysbott only stared at him through the eyeholes, and Chutt hurriedly apologized. "Forgive me, Sire. I meant no offense."

"I will dine in my own house," Ysbott said, "with only my slave to serve me." Dotter had been sent off to the kitchen, and the Wallekki guards stood outside the parlor's doors. What Born would have said about that arrangement, Chutt didn't know.

After what seemed an interminable time, Lord Chutt's butler returned with the news that a house had been selected for the Thunder King, and the former owner with his family was moving out.

"I'll go there now," said Ysbott, "and my own people will stand guard over it." He didn't thank Chutt for his hospitality. "Whoever he is," thought Chutt, "he's mighty sure of himself." But it was only fear that motivated Ysbott, and it was fear that hid behind the golden mask.

It was hard to get away from Chutt, but Gallgoid managed to visit secretly with Prester Jod at his home, arriving at midnight. Jod had ordered all his servants to bed and answered the door himself. "We can be safely private in my study," the First Prester's vicar said.

By now he knew that the Thunder King had killed his mardar with his own hands and occupied a great house that had until today belonged to a former oligarch from Caryllick.

"God has yet more wrath to pour upon this city," Jod said. "So the prophets warned us—the prophets that Judge Tombo hanged."

Gallgoid could not answer that. As one of Lord Reesh's confidential servants, he had helped to arrange the hangings. Reesh had given his consent to them, but it was presented to the people as all Judge Tombo's doing.

"I cannot prevent the calling of a conclave," Jod said. "There are good men who stand with the First Prester, but much of the clergy desire the rebuilding of the Temple and a return to the old ways. As soon as more of the presters can be gathered here, a conclave will be held—with what result, I don't have to tell you."

"It's a good thing you sent Constan to Durmurot with all the scrolls," Gallgoid said. "But if there's a new First Prester and he overturns Lord Orth's policy, what will you do?"

Jod spread his hands helplessly. "I will continue to have the Scriptures copied and distributed throughout Obann, because I believe God wills it," he said. "What else can I do? It was the Lord's will that the Temple be destroyed and that His word and His people, everywhere, should be His Temple.

And if I continue on my course, the new First Prester will try to stop it and there will be a schism. It will split the clergy, and it will lead to war—such a war whose kind has never been known in Obann in our history. A war of religion."

"Obann versus Durmurot," mused Gallgoid, "and Lintum Forest and the Eastern Marches, too—if King Ryons ever returns."

"For which I pray daily!" Jod said.

"It may not be wise to call Lord Orth home again," Gallgoid said. "I fear Chutt will assassinate him."

"Lord Orth does the work to which the Lord has called him," said Jod. "And we must do ours."

CHAPTER 40

How the Birds Departed from Lintum Forest

Lord Orth received good news from the upper reaches of the Green Snake River.

"They've lost heart, they're leaving—the Thunder King's Zamzu and Wallekki," Chief Weshesh reported. "They've killed their mardars, they've burned down their own forts, and they're leaving. Obann's God has beaten them."

"He is God of the Fazzan, too, my brother," Orth said.

Summer was over. All along the river, green leaves were turning brown and yellow, red and gold.

"We can be back home before the first frost, Preacher," the Abnaks said. "We've been here a long time without any fighting. The enemy never came this far down the river."

So Orth assembled the people for a service of thanksgiving, and the Fazzan held a great feast. He spoke to them beside the river, reminding them of the great things God had done to free them from the Thunder King. News of the fall of Kara Karram had not yet reached their country.

"This winter," Orth preached, "you'll have rest from your labors and respite from your enemies. As for me, I must return to the Abnaks and see what news may have come to me from my own country of Obann. If God permits, I'll come back to you again in the spring.

"If your enemies return, know surely that the Lord shall fight for you again and give you victory. Only be firm in your trust and of a good courage: for the Lord who created you loves you and will not forget you. Trust in Him and lift up prayers to Him, as you have learned to do, and He will write your names on the palms of His hands. He will never fail you nor forsake you, but see that you never turn away from Him."

"Never! Never!" roared the multitude.

Later, as Orth prepared himself for sleep, Weshesh asked him, "Do you think the enemy will come again?"

Orth pondered the question for some long time before he answered, "No, I don't. I think your war is over.

"But it will take years before your people truly know God and become His people. Many years! You have much to learn. The war is over, but our work has just begun."

"And you'll come back to us, my lord?"

Orth smiled at him. "Yes—and with God's Scriptures in my hand."

No one knew how long it would take to march around Lake Urmio. Now they missed the boats they'd left behind.

Much of the land around the lake had been given to the Zamzu, but they were gone and had not yet begun to return. Maybe they never would.

"This land won't stay uninhabited for long," said Ghur Manyan. "These are rich waters, even if they are a little dangerous." He turned to Obst. "Or do you think, Teacher, that now that God has destroyed the Thunder King, He will take away the dragons that dwell in the lake?" That was the only name he could think of, dragon, for the great beasts in Lake Urmio. "No one ever saw them until a few years ago."

Obst paused to think. He looked at Baby, tamely following Perkin who'd raised him from a chick. Like the dragons in the lake, the monster birds of the plains were only one of many kinds of strange creatures that had only lately appeared in the world. Where they'd come from, only the Lord knew.

"I believe the world has changed," Obst said, "that God has sent these creatures into it as a sign of His sovereign lordship over His creation. I think some of them were here in ancient times, and now they're here again—as a reminder."

Ryons had reined in his horse so he could hear what Obst had to say. He himself had seen the greatest beast of them all—not just seen it, but clung to its back as it crossed the great river to rescue the city of Obann from King Thunder's hordes. The beast went away after that, and no one ever saw it again.

"And if we needed any more reminders," Uduqu spoke up, "we need only look at you, old man! Did you know that a few of the hairs on your head have turned black since we left Kara Karram? I've been watching closely."

It should have made Obst happy to hear that his white hair was reverting—slowly, a strand at a time—to its original dark color, Uduqu thought. "You go all moody every time I mention it," he added, "but you ought to rejoice. It can only mean that God is strengthening you for whatever's left for you to do. I wish He'd do the same to my legs."

"I don't feel any younger!" Obst said.

Gurun laughed at him. "Obst! You march all day on foot, mile after mile, and you are as tireless as the best of the horses. Surely All-Father is with you."

Obst for a moment looked as if he would have liked to snap at her, but it passed quickly.

"All I want, for now, is to get back home to Lintum Forest," he said, "and we can't do that if we just stand here talking all day long. Come—see if your horses can keep up with me!"

Word came to Lintum Forest of Roshay Bault's safe return to Ninneburky. But the baron commanded Jack and Ellayne to stay in the forest until he sent for them.

No one west of the mountains had heard yet that Kara Karram was no more. No one in Lintum Forest had yet heard that there was a new High Council in Obann and that the Thunder King was in the city as its guest.

"We have to be ready for anything," Helki said, "and that doesn't make me happy!"

Jack and Ellayne were happy to continue staying at the new cabin that the settlers had built for Fnaa, his mother, and Trout. They spent their days with Fnaa, exploring the ruins of the castle and playing in the woods.

Wytt spent most of his time in the treetops, observing the birds that had flown in from some place far away in the East. The native birds fought with them for roosting places and were too upset for Wytt to get much sense out of them. The humans down below were oblivious to the turmoil overhead. Even Helki hardly seemed to notice it. Wytt was disappointed in him.

The morning after the message came from Ninneburky, the birds from the East gathered in the topmost branches. This time they ignored Wytt as he climbed closer and closer to them. They were all clustered together: for the first time, Wytt could see how very many of them had come to Lintum Forest. The treetops bent under their weight. They made a racket. Helki stood alone on the forest floor, staring up at the commotion, but Wytt had no time for him today.

The birds assembled, great and small, into a flock of several different kinds of birds in different colors, black and brown, yellow and green, all squawking, cawing, peeping. Before this, they always flew away if Wytt got too close, but today they didn't seem to see him. He decided not to get too close. They kept it up all morning, and then, as if on command, they all took off at once with a buffeting of wings. Straight up they flew, but not too high, and then wheeled, all their different kinds together, and flew off as one flock into the East.

Wytt watched until they were out of sight, even out of his keen sight. He'd never seen anything like it. Not a single one of them turned back.

He hustled headlong to the ground and leaped to land at Helki's feet. He brandished his stick and shrieked, but couldn't make Helki understand him. But he made so much noise that Jack and Ellayne came running.

"What's he so stirred up about?" Helki asked.

"Stranger birds have gone! They go back home, far away, all at once! Their place is safe again."

Unable to slow him down, Ellayne translated.

"He's been at me for days, trying to tell me something," Helki said. "There have been some strange birds here, kinds of birds that don't belong in Lintum Forest. I'm afraid I didn't pay as much attention to it as I should have."

"Something has happened, far away in the East," Jack said, "something bad that made those birds come here in the first place, and now something else that's made them go back. What was it, Wytt? Do you know?"

Stupid humans, Wytt thought. "Birds know—we don't!" he growled. "Some great thing they know. Maybe someday we can find out." He glared at Helki. "Why didn't you listen to birds? Maybe you forgot how to listen. Maybe you become like a little pink baby that knows nothing."

Helki laughed when Ellayne translated that.

"Whatever those birds know, it must be good news," he said. "And I know the news that I'd most like to hear—that the Thunder King is done for and our own King Ryons is coming home!"

"That would be the best news of all," said Ellayne.

As for Ysbott the Snake, now ensconced in a rich man's house in Obann, with a fine supper in his belly, a soft bed under him, and a stout oaken door between him and a dangerous world, with his own Wallekki warriors guarding it—his fear had washed away, leaving him just this side of soothing sleep. His mind began to work again; he was able to make plans. Was he not the Thunder King, friend and ally of the greatest men in Obann?

There were scalps to be had in Ninneburky and in Lintum Forest, and Ysbott meant to have them—Helki the Rod, who'd driven him out of his home, Baron Roshay Bault and his accursed daughter who'd nearly burned out his eyes with her accursed witchcraft.

"Sacrifices to the Thunder King!" he crooned to himself, fondling the mask. "There will be many sacrifices to the Thunder King—but those are the scalps that will dangle from my belt."

Follow the Entire Adventure with the First Seven Books in this Exciting Series!

You won't want to miss a single moment of this thrilling adventure, so be sure to get *Bell Mountain, The Cellar Beneath the Cellar, The Thunder King, The Last Banquet, The Fugitive Prince, The Palace,* and *The Glass Bridge* to complete your collection. These engaging stories are a great way to discover powerful insights about the Kingdom of God through page-turning fantasy fiction.

Ordering is Easy! Just visit ChalcedonStore.com